W9-CHY-575

Jackpot Justice

Jackpot Justice

Marilyn Wooley

Thomas Dunne Books
St. Martin's Minotaur

New York

THOMAS DUNNE BOOKS.
An imprint of St. Martin's Press.

 For information, address St. Martin's Press, 175 Fifth Avenue, New York, N.Y. 10010

Design by Heidi N.R. Eriksen

ISBN 0-312-25455-5

First Edition: April 2000

10 9 8 7 6 5 4 3 2 1

Many thanks to my husband for keeping me fed,
my mother for her tireless research,
Jessica and David for their support,
Luci for reading,
and finally to Ruth for being ruthless.

It comes as a great shock around the age of five, six, or seven to discover that the flag to which you have pledged allegiance, along with everybody else, has not pledged allegiance to you. It comes as a great shock to see Gary Cooper killing off the Indians and, although you are rooting for Gary Cooper, that the Indians are you.

James Baldwin, speech at Cambridge University, February 17, 1965

One

Anerd Woods, king of used auto parts, gagged on the stench of rotten cabbage and spoiled meat. A high-pitched *beep—beep—beep* jolted his eyes open.

The groan of a heavy machine made the ground tremble. Its steel blade grumbled unevenly, scraped across putrefying refuse, and sent a flood of soured milk cartons and shit-filled disposable diapers onto Anerd's naked torso. He couldn't find his legs, but he could feel his balls crushed in the vise of his fleshy thighs. That was the least of his problems.

"Hey! Hey! I'm down here. Stop!" His words drowned in the *beep—beep—beep*ing. The foul stench blistered his lungs.

The bulldozer groaned into forward gear and the blade came down again, propelling another avalanche of decay onto Anerd. This time it oozed up to his neck wattles and over his plump right arm.

"Hey! Hey!" His voice rose another octave in panic. He thrashed against the garbage but it pulled him down like quicksand.

Beep—beep—beep. The scrape of the blade. Anerd raised a flawlessly manicured pudgy left hand against the approaching bulldozer and waved frantically. The boulder-sized diamond on his gold pinky ring sent a laser beam of light across the dump. He screamed and gagged on spittles of blood. His brain squirmed with the certainty of his fate, and without thinking he uttered unfamiliar words:

"Forgive me, God."

A muddy cloud smothered the autumn sun. He shrieked until the dregs of household waste knocked his overpriced dentures down his throat.

Had Anerd's plea for God's mercy been heard under different circumstances it might have been considered fulsome. He didn't ask for forgiveness for his sins, which he minimized, but for surrendering his auto parts empire to his wife, Mavis, round-shouldered from carrying the weight of the world, and for forsaking his daughter, Sally. The small part of Anerd's mind that remained rational as the garbage cascaded over him recalled that Sally was the reason he lay at the bottom of the dump.

The day before, Sally had brought two of her skinhead boyfriends and an Indian into Anerd's recycled auto parts shop. He preferred the term *recycled* to *used* because he felt it sounded more sophisticated and citified to simple rural folk. Sally's friends inquired about a carburetor for a '67 Chevy station wagon, which Anerd didn't have in stock, but thought he could filch from his competitors—one more small step in helping them go out of business. He informed the boys that he could receive the carburetor by UPS next week for a small additional charge of $25.

The boys and the Indian and Sally left the store in a battered baby-shit yellow Toyota pickup with the "TO" and the "TA" painted out leaving the "YO" as a tailgate greeting. Anerd noticed that Sally climbed onto the Indian's lap in the three-person cab. He didn't like that Indian. He didn't like Indians much to begin with and this one had looked a little too clean, which meant he must be uppity.

Anerd went about his business until closing, at which time he counted his cash, stuffed it into an envelope, and placed it in the breast pocket of his Levi's Western jeans jacket. He drove home in his brand-new Ford Explorer to find the house empty. This didn't concern him much as his wife, Mavis, tended to annoy him and he relished the rare nights she found someone else to torment. Mavis was a professional victim and made sure everyone knew it.

Anerd threw a beef burrito into the microwave and popped the tab on a Coors. He moved to the front window to close the curtains and noticed a strange sight. In the dim light from the waning moon he could see that the Indian who had come to his shop earlier in the day was standing motionless in the front yard. He was holding a pair of gloves, which he dropped on the ground when Anerd's face appeared at the window. The Indian kept standing there in the dark, black eyes staring into the house at Anerd, not moving a muscle, and looking like he belonged in front of a cigar store.

Anerd clutched the breast pocket of his jacket and headed toward the safe in the bedroom. Before he got there he heard the back door being kicked in. He ran for the bedroom but didn't make it halfway down the hall before a hand yanked him up by his collar.

Anerd struggled to keep his balance, all the while keeping his hand over the envelope of money in his pocket. He was pushed forward and a thick musty blanket was thrown over him. Fists pounded his head, then something heavy smashed down on his back—a baseball bat? He felt his feet sliding out of his Tony Lama snakeskin boots. Time stretched into slow motion. Odd bits of reality struck him—the smell of burned burrito, the Coors burp earthy in his nose, the sour sting of bile in his throat. He struggled until the bat whacked his head and the next thing he knew he was up to his ears in garbage.

The spotter at the Cedar Gulch Sanitary Landfill was a twenty-two-year-old high school dropout named Billy whose primary pastimes were smoking pot and trying to screw virgins. He'd been partying the night before Anerd showed up in the dump and didn't get to work until well after seven-thirty in the morning, at which point Norm, the Caterpillar operator, had already started leveling the garbage left over from the previous day. Billy drove his minibike past the rows of yellow garbage trucks and parked as close to his watch position as possible. He set his helmet on the bike, squinted in the early-morning sun, pulled his shades out of the pocket of his leather jacket, spit on them, and rubbed them on his shirttail.

Billy was in the process of making himself comfortable on a webbed aluminum lawn chair when the glint from Anerd's diamond ring flashed across a smudge of dirt he'd missed on his glasses. At first he dismissed it as an aluminum can or a bottle, but something about the brightness of it made him look a second time. He saw the sparkle attached to Anerd's hand the moment before the Cat pushed a load right over it.

Not prone to reacting quickly, Billy walked to the radio and summoned the Cat operator.

"Norm, man. Better stop a sec. Something pretty weird down there."

Norm backed up the machine and climbed down. Billy motioned him down the garbage mountain and they met at the bottom.

"What's up?"

Billy led the Cat operator to the place he'd seen the glitter from Anerd's ring. He took a long moment to pull on a pair of canvas gloves and then kicked his army surplus boots at bursting soggy paper bags and disintegrating white plastic grocery store sacks until he hit something. It was Anerd's shoulder.

Norm, upon seeing a human body part lying under his handiwork, spun into action. He pulled frantically at the garbage until he freed Anerd's head.

He hollered at Billy. "Get the hell up to the office and call an ambulance right now!"

Bending over Anerd, he pulled open the man's flaccid jaw, and with great effort and trembling fingers yanked the dentures out of Anerd's throat. "Come on, you old fart. Don't give up."

He began mouth-to-mouth on Anerd's polluted maw and only vomited twice in the process.

Perhaps Anerd's plea for forgiveness helped, or maybe he was just damn lucky, but miraculously he revived. He coughed and sputtered and opened his eyes to a gray northern California autumn sky and a wide-eyed Caterpillar bulldozer operator. Although he had no teeth and he was still encased from the nipples down in garbage, he seemed to feel his words couldn't wait. He pulled his rescuer close and hoarsely gasped, "Uh inan id ih."

"What?" Norm wanted to tell the man to calm down, help was on the way, but the urgency of the man's voice gave him pause.

"Uh inan id ih." Anerd pulled at his rescuer's jacket and repeated himself, working his way up to as much of a scream as he could muster as though that would help transmit the message better.

Finally the Cat operator got it. "The Indian did it?"

Anerd nodded with his last ounce of energy and passed out.

Two

I headed home across the river by the way of the old two-lane bridge north of Cedar Gulch and watched the last stains of November rust fade from the summit of Mount Shasta. Cold air blew through the side window of the Volkswagen Beetle and slapped my face but didn't fend off my fantasies of a warm bed. The staccato thud of tires over speed bumps warned me that I'd drifted over the center line. I jerked the steering wheel, overcorrected enough to make my heart leap, and flashed on the image of myself testifying in a full body cast.

"Dr. Cassandra Ringwald, please raise your right eyelid to be sworn in," the court clerk would say.

My first forensic psychological evaluation was scheduled in the morning and the week of anticipatory sleepless nights was catching up to me. I squinted through a windshield filthy with dust and bug bodies. The road vanished in the glare of the first oncoming headlights in ten miles, and the cranky gears grated as I downshifted to get control around a curve.

I barely had time to swerve to avoid the motionless lump in the right lane. At first I thought someone had hit a bear but a closer look revealed a man lying supine. He was half the size of my car, and looked like a giant beer-bellied slug. I pulled a U-turn over the double yellow line, and stopped ten yards away to shine the headlights on him. The back of my neck tingled. I rolled up the window and pushed my thumb down on the driver's side lock, then stretched across the seat to do the same to the passenger side.

Maria Callas's voice floated sweet and clear through the cold autumn air. I ejected the tape and waited for either courage or brilliance to strike me. The headlights shot over the man into the moonless night. My knee jangled my keys and a moth fluttered into the light and spiraled to the ground.

The first sign of life was the man's plump and weathered hand, which flopped spasmodically next to his belly. I fumbled with the seat belt and yanked at the door handle a couple of times before I remembered to unlock it.

Before I could climb out of the car, a gang of three skinheads emerged noiselessly from the forest. They were uniformly dressed in white T-shirts and camouflage chinos tucked into black military boots. Sweat gleamed on their bare scalps and pale skin. They stomped over to the man with hatred etched in their faces.

I called out, "Help him," but they were on him faster than my words. They attacked fiercely and with calculation, like starving hyenas on a wounded water buffalo. Baseball bats cracked against pavement and bones, and brass-knuckled fists ripped cloth and flesh. Tissue and blood exploded into the air—a macabre fireworks display in the headlights.

My eyes froze on the carnage. My fists were as white as glue around the black plastic steering wheel. My head seemed to float, my body became leaden with fear. The mundane preoccupied me. I tried to wiggle my toes and wished I'd worn socks. I thought about turning on the heater but I couldn't move my hand.

The skinheads' boots pummeled the man's head and made hollow thudding sounds that came to me in slow motion. White swastikas glowed eerily from black leather heels, blurred with their kicks, and left pale green after-images streaked across my field of vision.

"Fucking war hoop."

"Get back to the reservation."

"Kick him in the balls."

"Scalp him."

"Got him good that time."

Spit and venom spewed from their angry mouths until the ringing in my ears drowned out shouts and thuds.

Fast and brutal, they were actors on a stage in a bitter spotlight of oppression. When it was over, the tallest among them turned and looked right at my eyes. He pointed at me and his mouth formed the words, "Shut up." Then he drew his middle finger across his throat, a melodrama that elicited an apprehensive giggle from me. His face appeared featureless in the glare of the headlights, except for a black Hitler mustache, a villainous goatee, and eyes that glowed ice blue.

They disappeared as quickly as they'd come, leaving blood pooled on the blacktop and the man limp and splattered with crimson. After an eternity, I jumped out of the car and ran to him, telling myself over and over that there was nothing I could have done.

It occurred to me later that I could have turned off the headlights.

I don't recall how the man came to be in my car. I do remember the goo that used to be his left eye and the smell of feces and blood coming from him. I rolled down my window and gulped in the frosty air to keep from fainting.

He hung on the edge of consciousness for the twenty-minute drive to the emergency room. He spoke his only words through shattered teeth. "Did they see you?"

Emergency room hassles, police reports, and waiting to see if the man was okay kept me at the hospital until midnight. By the time I got home my hands were so shaky, I had to use both of them to unlock the back door. I dumped my briefcase on the kitchen counter and poured a glass of wine, which I downed with one of my Great-aunt Liz's sleeping pills from the bottle in the cupboard. I staggered down the obstacle course of sideboards in the hall, left my slacks and blouse where they fell, tumbled into bed, and prayed not to dream or have too bad a hangover in the morning.

The alarm jolted me out of a solid five hours of sleep, more than I'd had all week. I boiled water for tea, took Aunt Liz's breakfast upstairs to her, then hung the jacket to my blue suit, in truth my only suit, in the stall while I showered. When most of the wrinkles were out, I used a blow dryer on the remaining dampness and put it on with one of my two good blouses. By the time I opened up the front door for business, two Trinity County Sheriff's deputies and my new client were standing on the front porch.

Three

I don't have to like every client who walks through my door but the instant I saw Homer Johnson I regretted signing on to be an expert for the defense. Tall enough to have to duck under the ironwork chandelier in my waiting room, he seemed underage to buy the cigarettes advertised by a cartoon dromedary tattooed on the back of a hand large enough to snap my neck. Other than the decoration, he looked the archetype of Native American manhood, gently sloped forehead, chiseled jaw, sculpted cheekbones, eyes the color of coal, ponytail fashionably wrapped in yellow and red yarn, hard brown body stretching the fabric of the orange jailhouse jumpsuit.

And new white Nike Airs adorned with black and red swastikas.

To say he walked through my door was inaccurate. Shuffled was more like it—the shackles around his ankles prevented anything more than that, and the handcuffs that pulled his huge wrists and muscular arms behind his back threw him slightly forward, giving him a posture of deference not reflected on his face. He dwarfed the two deputies who posted themselves at his sides and gripped his arms as though they expected him to make a run for it any moment. I invited them into my interview room.

"You're Ringwald?" asked the taller of the deputies, whose gold-colored name tag read Nash.

"Yes, I'm Dr. Cassandra Ringwald."

Unimpressed, Nash walked in and made great show of searching the room from top to bottom, checking the window latches and my desk. He picked up a letter opener with his thumb and forefinger held it aloft. "I'd keep this out of sight. Never can be too sure about those Indians." He dropped it into a drawer and walked back out to the waiting room. I followed.

He gave me a sour look before releasing one of his prisoner's hands and recuffing his arms in front of him. The cuff ratcheted unevenly as he struggled to close it over the thick wrist. The fat deputy, Endicott, stood seven feet away, with his plump fist around the butt of his Beretta. He braced his stubby legs into a stance as though he needed only a trifling excuse to fire his gun.

The prisoner straightened his shoulders, threw off the forced slump, and shook his head in petty rebellion. He stared past his guards as though they were desiccated mouse turds and shuffled disdainfully into the interview room. Nash sat in a Windsor chair in the waiting room; Endicott grabbed a small armless upholstered chair and swung his leg over the seat so his gut flattened into the chairback. His scruffy cowboy boots barely touched the floor.

"Was there snow over Buckhorn?" The mountain summit divided Shasta and Trinity Counties. Upon receiving no response I asked, "Would you like some coffee? This evaluation won't be finished until after lunch." Endicott shook his head no, picked up an *Architectural Digest* without looking at the cover, held it partially obscured by the back of the chair, and riffled absently through the pages. Deputy Nash leaned his chair back, pulled his off-white straw cowboy hat over his eyes, and rested his Vitalis-laden head against the wall.

I closed the door to the waiting area and motioned for the prisoner to sit in the brocade wing chair next to my testing table. I shuddered at the thought that this young man who flaunted a symbol of hate and intolerance was sitting in the house of my great-aunt, who in spite of having lost the love of her life to depression and despair was the most tolerant and forgiving person I ever knew. The distaste rose in my throat.

"Mr. Johnson . . ."

"Homer, call me Homer, ma'am, uh, Dr. Ringwald, ma'am." Behind the proud face, his eyes were pleading and he looked at me as though I were his last hope. "Thanks for getting me out of the Jackpot jail for this. It's pretty bad in there. Worse than . . ."

I glanced at the swastikas on his shoes. "I didn't get you out. Your attorney, Mr. Peck, managed to convince the judge that the Trinity County Jail in Jackpot didn't have adequate facilities for me to perform a psychological evaluation on you. He thought it would be too distracting and distressing. That's why the deputies brought you down to see me in Shasta County." I didn't tell him to call me Cassie as I do with other clients.

"Well, this is a real nice place." His eyes scanned the room.

I smiled politely and dug into my testing materials, pulling out pencils, booklets, and stopwatches, which I arranged on the table between us.

"You understand, Homer, that I am performing a psychological evaluation on you to be submitted to the Trinity County Superior Court. Whatever you tell me will not be confidential and may be reported to the judge and the district attorney."

"Yes, ma'am, Dr. Ringwald. My lawyer told me that. Mr. Peck."

"You're fortunate to have such an excellent attorney."

"My grandmother said it'd take most of my college money but the public defender didn't act like he wanted to get me off. And I didn't do it."

"I see. Well, I'm sure Mr. Peck will work very hard for you." I leaned over the trash basket to sharpen a pencil with a blue plastic sharpener.

Richard Peck was one reason I took this case. He puts his heart into his cases and I admire the fact he's not afraid to stick up for the underdog. What he saw in Homer wasn't clear to me.

The other reason I agreed to evaluate Homer Johnson was that I needed the money to complete the renovations on my Great-aunt Liz's house, which serves as both my home and my office. The forty-year-old cedar shakes were more of a sieve than a roof, and the south wall sagged from too many years under the northern California extremes of dry heat and rainstorms.

I scribbled Homer's name and the date at the top of a yellow legal pad. "You are here today to take personality and intelligence tests. But before we start with them, tell me a little about your life." I had to gain his trust to learn how he became embroiled in a conspiracy to kidnap and murder an old man for a few dollars in used auto parts.

His black eyes managed to look puzzled and vacant at the same time.

I prompted, "Where were you born?" I forced another smile and admonished myself to work a little harder to achieve the unconditional positive regard I'm supposed to have for my clients.

"Shasta County Hospital. Right here in Cedar Gulch."

His mouth remained open but no more words came out. I waited a moment and filled in the "o" on Homer with my pen. I nodded for him to continue. When he kept still, I asked, "Tell me about your family."

"I'm mostly Indian—uh—Native American Indian."

"Tell me about your parents." I scribbled on the notepad and nodded and smiled at him.

"My pa is half Ajumoui from Modoc County and half white. My ma was Wintu from Shasta County."

"Was?"

No response.

I sighed with impatience at Homer's meager answers and tried again, a little too sternly. "Is your mother no longer alive?"

He nodded and froze his eyes onto his right Nike. "She was killed four years ago when I was fifteen. In a drunk driving accident."

"Sorry. I didn't know." I fumbled through my notes to give myself time to think of the next question. This time my silence prompted him to talk.

"The guy in the other car was the drunk. And he got away with it." His voice was flat.

A knock on the door startled me and I jumped up to answer it. Deputy Nash handed me a large brown envelope. "Gal delivered this." He glared past me to Homer. "That boy there gives you any trouble at all, you just holler."

"He's fine," I answered, but when I looked back I saw that Homer's face tightened in anticipation on a confrontation with the deputy. I closed the door and watched him relax.

The envelope contained the report from Richard Peck's investigator. I had hoped to have time to review it thoroughly before the interview.

The report noted that Homer's deceased paternal grandfather made a fortune in Oklahoma oil before the family settled in Shasta County. Homer's trust fund allowed him to pay for the services of a top attorney and a psychological evaluation by an expert witness.

And from what I could tell he came from a good family,

a happy one until his mother was killed. He had a private education, designer clothes, a cellular phone, a new Ford truck.

"Why did you come home from Arizona?" I had to ask him twice.

"From Presidio? The prep school you mean?" He stretched and yawned. His shirtsleeve pulled up over his biceps and revealed an amateur tattoo of a red "A" encircled in black on his arm. "Sorry, I didn't get much sleep last night. They got me up at five."

"What made you decide to drop out of Presidio Boys' Ranch? Sounds like it was a good school."

"After my ma died, I didn't feel like doing anything. So I flunked my classes." His voice softened and cracked on the last syllable of the sentence.

"You must have felt sad about your mother's death."

His eyes clouded but he shrugged casually. "Nah, just wanted to come home. Too hot in Arizona. Besides, I'm Indian. Why do I need school?"

Cultural confusion I could understand but not the reason he had thrown his life away to associate with losers, bigots, and wannabe Nazis.

I decided to end the interview until I could peruse the rest of the report and talk to Richard Peck about what he wanted from me. "We'll start on the testing now, Homer. Can you name four men who have been presidents of the United States since 1950?"

"Yeh. Sure can. Nixon, except I didn't much like Kissinger. Not gonna count Kennedy because he was a pinko, Pope-loving fornicator, so then there's Reagan . . ."

Four

We broke for lunch at half past noon. Deputy Nash parked Homer in the most uncomfortable chair in the waiting room and stood guard while Deputy Endicott drove across the street to Igor's Burger Pit hamburger stand for some gut bomb burgers. I ate a plain yogurt and an apple at my desk while I scored Homer's intelligence test. He was no rocket scientist, but he was certainly smart enough to know better, and his knowledge of the natural world was exceptional. I called Richard Peck and told his secretary to page him while I ignored the belches of the men in my waiting room.

"Richard, your client is not exactly cooperating. I can't get much out of him. What else can you tell me?"

He groaned and answered with crisp diction. "He's been the same with me and my investigator, but here's what I know. Homer's buddies are Verlan Crumm and Anerd Wood's very own daughter, Sally. Verlan is a skinhead. Sally's beyond description. They were arrested on the same charges as Homer after Anerd was found in the dump. Verlan just happened to be driving Homer's truck with Sally in the passenger seat.

"In any case, Anerd's blaming it all on Homer, saying that he manipulated Sally and Verlan. Did Homer tell you any of his side of the story yet?"

"We haven't gotten that far. He and the deputies from Jackpot are still in a pissing contest."

"Well, when you get them calmed down, ask Homer why he dropped the gloves and didn't run away. He wouldn't tell me. And what I basically would like from you is an explanation of the reason he wanted to join a white supremacist group. I would like as sympathetic a picture of him as possible to the jury."

I bit my cheek before I said that belonging to the White People's Brigade might be an advantage to some people in Trinity County.

I hung up and read some more of the report. When Homer and the deputies were done with lunch, I was ready.

"Homer, tell me about the night you were arrested." I held the report in my left hand and my pen in my right. I shoved enough papers aside to make room on my desk for my notepad.

"What's to tell?"

"On the night Anerd Woods was assaulted, kidnapped, and left in the Jackpot dump, the police found you standing alone in his front yard with a pair of unused latex gloves at your feet. What were you doing there?"

Homer shrugged. "We'd been partying. I was loaded. What else do you want to know?"

"The report says you weren't under the influence."

Homer was silent.

"Why did you stay there? Why didn't you run away?"

Homer shrugged.

"Were Verlan and Sally at the party?" I tapped my pen on the desk.

Homer shrugged again. "I s'pose." He glanced to the window where a fly buzzed and banged against the glass. "Let it out. It wants to be outside."

I had an image of Homer leaping through the opened window and running down the street in shackled feet.

"Open it," he repeated.

I opened the window and guided the fly outside with my notepad. I closed the window and sat down. "Homer, my job here is to help you. I can't do that without your cooperation. Mr. Peck trusts me and you are going to have to as well or we will get nowhere. Do you have a problem talking with me for some reason?"

"Thanks," he said. "It needed to be free." Then silence again.

"Were Sally and Verlan at the party?" I nearly shouted it.

"Yeh, they were at the party. But none of this was her fault."

"Whose fault? Sally's?"

"That bum Verlan talked her into it. I don't want to get her into trouble."

"So you'll take the heat instead?"

Silence.

I was torn between hitting my head against the wall and slamming his into the door. I gritted my teeth and stared at the investigator's report while I told myself to be professional and not to take the swastikas on Homer's Nikes so personally.

"Anerd Woods told the police that on the night he was kidnapped you threatened him when he looked out the window at you. What do you have to say about that?"

"He's a bastard."

"Could you be more specific?"

He glared at me. "No."

"Tell me about the swastikas on your shoes."

Homer grinned. "Cool, huh?"

"Why do you have them?"

"They mean I belong to the White People's Brigade."

I raised an eyebrow but he didn't pick up on the cue. "Why do you want to belong to them?"

"I can meet cute chicks." He laughed and looked at me mischievously.

I didn't join him in his joviality. "Besides that."

"They know the score. About the righteous war."

I lifted my eyes from my notes and waited.

"Hey, if you're an outsider you don't understand. They take care of their own. They'll protect me. And they like me." He glared defensively.

I glanced back at the investigator's report and took a moment to read it. "What would your grandfather have thought of them, given that he was a Jew?"

Homer's eyes flashed blackness. "He wasn't any fucking Jewboy. Just because he made money doesn't mean he was Jewish." Spittle sprayed across the table.

I sat back, stunned at the intensity of his reaction. "The report here says he was Jewish."

"Well, you tell that fucking investigator that he better keep his mouth shut, and you better, too. Your job is to get me off so stick to the point. You don't need to be telling anyone lies to do it either. No jury in Jackpot will feel sorry for me if you tell them I'm a Jewboy." His eyes weren't pleading anymore.

I met his eyes and kept mine steady. "My job is not to get you off, Mr. Johnson. My job is to help in your defense. If you wanted a whore, I know a few but they'd cost more than me."

The slam of Homer's fist on the table didn't frighten me because I half expected it. "Are you a fucking kike bitch too? I don't want no fucking kike to get into my head—" The pounding at the door interrupted him.

I kept my eyes on his. "There's no need to try to intimidate me, Homer." I got up just as Deputy Nash opened the door. I blocked his view of Homer.

"We're doing fine. Just had to get some things straight." The deputy tried to look around me but I smiled and pushed the door shut. I'd had enough confrontation for one day.

So this was the man I was to help. My head spun as Homer vacillated between spitting venom and playing the wounded pup. The three hours I'd known him had given me more questions than answers. Why would a gang of racists who hated his heritage accept him? Was he twisted by grief over losing his mother at a young age and lured into hatred by his need to be accepted? Or was he sitting here behind his attitude, empty black eyes and shriveled raisin of a soul, looking at me, a white woman, hoping I would say the disadvantages of his race somehow mitigated the cruelty of his crime? Did he believe that my psychological evaluation would get him out of what he got himself into, and that the generous fee I was to be paid would make it easier to swallow the bile? If so, his hatred wouldn't change, he wouldn't learn tolerance, he'd continue to inflict blind cruelties in a thousand different ways.

How was I going to be objective in helping Homer, much less make sense of him to a jury?

"Okay, Mr. Johnson. You win. End of interview. I'll call your attorney and tell him my results. Have fun in the Jackpot jail."

"My family's getting the bail money. I'll be out in no time."

I ended the interview and refrained from saying good riddance. Then I called Richard Peck to say that I would interview his client again, but only if there was some cooperation.

Richard's voice was deep and calm in contrast to my agitation. "Homer can be difficult. I'll drop by at your convenience so we can review your interview and plot some strategy. I'd also like to give you some moral support."

I thought of my great-aunt sleeping upstairs. "I'll drop by your office tomorrow. I have other obligations this afternoon." I hung up and organized my notes until my headache nagged me to give it up for the day.

Five

My Great-aunt Elizabeth was snoring softly by the time I closed my office and walked up the squeaky staircase to her bedroom. Her door was ajar and I squeezed through the opening so as not to wake her.

Pale pink roses on the wallpaper faded into the early-evening sunlight, and lace patterns filtered through the curtains onto the needlepoint rug she had crafted decades before I was born. The dark wainscotting and moldings looked in need of a good oiling, and recent water stains on the ceiling reminded me about the leaky roof. The books in the walnut glass-front bookcase—among them Emily Post, several books on rose gardening, the Ringwald family Bible, and biographies of Catherine the Great, Mary Queen of Scots, Eleanor of Aquitaine, Hannah Dustin and a seemingly out-of-place copy of *Cadillac Desert*—were well worn with repeated readings.

Auntie Liz's long white hair fanned over the pink pillowcase like the spun glass she spread across the sideboard at Christmastime. She did a great deal of sleeping these days—the last heart surgery sapped her strength and she never really bounced back. Still, for eighty, she was mentally alert and fairly happy. Her bedside table held an open cloisonné pillbox with small white tablets in it, a carved leather-bound book with a fountain pen sticking from its pages, a brass and porcelain hurricane lamp, and a photo of my Great-uncle Chester as a young and handsome colonel dressed in his World War II army uniform. I ran my finger over the top of the picture frame to collect the dust and felt guilty for not doing a better cleaning job.

The room had a chill. Aunt Liz seemed to be losing her sensitivity to temperature as she aged. I was on my way to her sitting room to put another log on the fire when she stirred.

Her eyes opened wide, as clear and gray as I had always remembered. She smiled and rolled her eyes to her dead husband's photo. "He was a good looker back then before that awful war turned his beautiful blond hair white. But then men in uniform always are handsome."

"He was, Auntie Liz. I have some Earl Grey brewing."

"Your fellow gone?"

I stretched my neck to work out some of the tightness. "He's not exactly my fellow. More like a wannabe Nazi. Not the most enjoyable client I've ever had."

She looked at my face and wrinkled her brow, then reached out to pull my hand to the bed. "Now you'll do a good job because you always do. But don't get yourself into a tizzy over this character."

"I'm not in a tizzy. I just don't like having to work out of your home. I feel that I'm invading your privacy."

Her eyes sparkled. "You are invading my privacy but I wouldn't have it any other way. You coming to live with me has been the happiest time I've had in years."

"I just wonder if it's safe. Some of the people I get are a little scary."

"No scarier than some of the people who should be seeing you and aren't. Besides, what difference does it make? Everyone in three counties knows where we live."

I accepted the conceit and held her hand. "I don't want

anything to happen you. You're all I have for family now."

I thought about the violence of last night, and the trip to the emergency room with the victim of the skinheads. I figured what she didn't know wouldn't hurt her.

She entwined her fingers through mine. "When you get enough saved you can find another place for your office. Until then I like having you here during the day in case something happens and I need you." She looked into my face and her eyes became serious. "Have you thought any more about trying to find your sister?"

I shook my head no. My mother and my sister Viola were always in the back of my mind.

She reached gently for my arm. "It's been ten years. Viola would be almost seventeen. I think they would have forgiven you for leaving by now, if they ever blamed you at all."

I smiled half-heartedly. "I wonder if they stayed away from him."

"Your father was an angry man, Cassie. Don't allow his violence to make you bitter."

"Bitterness isn't the problem. Right now, starting a practice is my major concern."

She groaned. "You are too much business, young lady."

I helped the old dear sit up and propped a pillow behind her. "And you're entirely too good to me, Auntie Liz. I'll never be the lady you are."

"Nor the cook. Which reminds me. Maria called this morning and said she's working all night at the dispatch center again. Why don't we invite that cutie pie of a brother of hers over and I'll make some supper for the both of you?"

"Isn't he on duty tonight?"

She craned to peer out her window. "I can see his red truck in his driveway."

"Cooking is too much trouble," I objected. "Why don't I pick up a pizza? Tony likes junk food better than home cooking anyway."

She chuckled, and pulled open a drawer and found a small pad of paper and her reading glasses. "Now I'll tell you what to buy at the store, and we can make a wonderful little green bean casserole with some roast chicken." She put her glasses on the end of her nose and busied herself with the grocery list.

"Auntie Liz, you just sandbagged me." We both knew she could do barely more than make the trip downstairs and chop a few vegetables before exhaustion drove her back to bed.

She smiled, chewed the end of the pen in thought, then scribbled some more. "Now you know you love a good meal, dear."

"Auntie Liz. You're not listening. You and Maria are not going to light up a romance between me and Tony by using these little tactics."

"Yes, dear. Here's the list."

Nobody was paying attention to me today, so I gave up and went to the market.

Tony came over from next door at seven just as Auntie Liz instructed me for the tenth time how to baste the chicken. She sat in the platform rocker next to the woodstove, sipped her sherry, and encouraged him to massage the tangle of knots in my neck while I snapped the green beans. I yelped when he dug in a little too hard.

Liz motioned for him to sit at the huge mahogany Chippendale dining table that had been crammed into a corner of the kitchen after I had taken over the formal dining room to use as my interview room. The table's ball-and-claw feet scraped on the wood floor when Tony squeezed into the chair next to the wall.

"A glass of wine, dear boy?" she asked.

"Beer if you got it." He wore a real shirt, not the usual Grateful Dead tank top he sported off duty. It did little to conceal his hard body. I pulled a Coors from the fridge and shook it before tossing it to him. He flashed his dimples and his eyes, which looked green today, and set the unopened can on a bamboo coaster on the table.

"And how is your job at the police force?"

"Just fine, Auntie Liz. I hope to get that promotion to sergeant. Taking the test in July."

"How nice. Will they have a ceremony?"

"Nah. They're pretty informal."

"What a shame. I'd hoped to see you in your uniform." She turned to me and winked. "Don't you think the chicken is done, dear?"

I pulled it out of the oven and heard Tony tell her the next time he was invited to such a nice dinner he'd wear dress blues just for her. The table rumbled again when he pushed it away to get up. He steered Aunt Liz to the table and went to the fridge for a cold Coors. While Auntie Liz checked the configuration of the tableware, he slid the cold can up my back.

"Yikes." I turned to jab him in the ribs and he popped the tab, spraying me with beer. I lunged for him and he dodged me, sending the platter with the chicken skittering across the counter. It stopped an inch short of the edge. We straightened up and feigned innocence for Auntie Liz, who studiously rubbed at a smudge on a butter knife. She couldn't hide the smile on her face.

The remainder of dinner was conducted in polite overtones for Auntie Liz's benefit. We put her to bed and began to clean up.

I filled the basin with sudsy water. "I'll wash; you dry."

Tony reached around me to grab a dish towel from the oven handle.

We did the dishes in silence for a while before he asked, "What was the deal with the Trinity County Sheriff's vehicle outside your office this morning?"

"Psych eval on a wannabe Nazi. Kidnapping of a used auto parts dealer, but the district attorney wants to get him on attempted murder, too. The boy has an attitude on him, but I took the case to pay some bills and because Richard Peck asked me to."

"That puts you in a bad position, doesn't it? Suppose you can't help him and he has some nasty assholes for friends?"

"I guess I'll tell Richard whatever I come up with and he can use it or not. Unfortunately, the big bucks are in court fees, and if Richard doesn't use my report I won't get paid to be an expert witness."

"Then I guess you gotta do it. Richard hired you because he knows you'll keep your integrity. But those Trinity County folks do things their own way. Whatever you say might not make a big difference." He handed me the last dried dish. "Heard about your escapade last night with the guy who got beat up on the highway. I was off duty. Why didn't you come over?"

"It was late. I just wanted to go to bed. Besides, I thought you might have company and didn't want to interrupt." I didn't mention the cute brunette whose Mustang had been parked in front of his house. I figured it was none of my business, even if I was a bit jealous.

"You want to talk about it?"

Guilt for not doing something to stop the beating tugged at my gut and I busied myself arranging silverware in the drawer. "That's supposed to be my line."

Out of the corner of my eye I saw his shoulders slump a half-inch. "Okay. Just promise me that if any of those skin-heads bother you at all, you'll tell me right away."

"Thanks, bud, but I'm a white woman. They don't dare

defile my virtue. Anyway, I don't think they could see me behind the headlights."

"It's not funny, Cassie. Those idiots are pretty random, and they could have recognized your car. You need to watch out, especially considering that you're evaluating one of them."

"That's what doesn't make sense about this case. My client's an Indian. What's he doing with a white supremacist group?" I saw him to the door. "Say hi to Maria and thanks for entertaining my aunt."

"My pleasure. She's my second favorite next-door neighbor." He winked and was off over the low stone wall between our houses.

Six

"It's a pretty unusual request." Richard Peck stuck his index finger under his slightly lopsided wire-rimmed glasses and rubbed his eye. His attire was perfect. He wore a well-cut navy blue suit and tie that concealed his plumpness and complemented the beige and blue striped wallpaper in his office. The daytime temperature had dipped into the fifties, but he'd dressed the same during last August's heat wave.

"I have to know in my own mind exactly what Anerd Woods saw and what he thought of Homer." I pushed up the sleeves of my sweater and noticed Richard's eyes flit to my chest. By the time he looked back at my face, his neck was pink.

He grabbed a rubber band off his desktop and wound it through his fingers. It snapped suddenly and his leather chair creaked with his surprise. "I'll ask, but Anerd will probably not talk to you even if the judge gives you permission to interview him."

"I'd like to talk to Homer's co-conspirators too." I pulled my sleeves down again and hunched forward. "Your client's behavior hasn't made much sense so far and I need all the help I can get."

"Verlan Crumm and Sally Woods? Good luck. I'm not sure either has adequate command of the English language to carry on a decent conversation." He took a breath and looked me in the eye.

"I'm expecting a client," I said. "Call me when you find out."

"Lunch sometime?" he asked when I was three-quarters out the door.

"Sure. I'll look at my book to see when I'm free." My schedule wasn't all that busy but no sense advertising it.

Richard called back within two hours and left a message with Auntie Liz that not only had the Trinity County judge authorized me to interview Anerd, Mavis, Verlan, and Sally, he'd ordered it.

"My, Peck sounded like such a pleasant man. Is he single? How about inviting him for dinner?"

I rolled my eyes. "Auntie Liz, you need a hobby. How about organizing your memoirs or reading the encyclopedia to keep your mind busy? Besides," I told her, "Richard Peck is the type of man who would think he'd been thrown from his horse and drug through cholla cactus after a night with me."

I found the listing for Anerd Woods's auto parts store in the Cedar Gulch Yellow Pages. He answered the phone on the first ring. "Yo. Farts. Anerd."

I looked at the receiver. "Is this Woods's Auto Parts?"

"Yeh. Wood Farts. Anerd here."

"Hello. This is Dr. Ringwald and I'd like to speak with you if I may about what happened when you were kidnapped."

"Not much to say. Told it all to the cops." His words ran together and a bunch of consonants were missing, but I finally deciphered, "What the hell, come on down."

Anerd Woods's Recycled Auto Parts store was as big and gaudy as he was. I'd never seen so much neon in one place—

not even the casino in Reno where I worked after I left home at seventeen. Anerd had a neon fetish, chronic undifferentiated. Every inch of wall space was covered with glowing logos of brands of every possible auto part known to man. I wondered if Anerd's decorator had swallowed a few too many magic mushrooms. I kept my eyes on the floor to keep from having a seizure.

Anerd waddled up to me. His T-shirt stretched across his chest, and shouted in Day-Glo orange that he loved his Hooker Headers. His stomach hung like an apron, obscuring his belt. I wondered if it was neon, too.

"Howdy, miss." He had no teeth. His eyes were tiny, his pasty skin reflected yellow and blue from a Napa Auto Parts sign.

"Good afternoon, Mr. Woods. Thank you for seeing me on short notice."

"Can't say it's a pleasure." He picked his nose with a thick thumb. I stared at a flickering blue Kragen shooting star.

"Well, on second thought," he said, looking me up and down, "come on in." He winked and his entire pudgy face seemed to fold in on itself.

I followed him into his office, a veritable trash bin of contracts, tattered catalogues, grease-laden car innards, and of course the ubiquitous neon advertisements. A pink plastic radio with blackened cigarette burn scars all over the top buzzed a country-western yodel in sync with the flashes of neon. A photo of a matronly looking lady and a pudgy faced blond teenager posed in front of what appeared to be a junkyard leaned precariously against the unpainted drywall. His wife and daughter. I wondered if he ever actually looked at the picture. A Mason jar on the desk held a full set of dentures.

Anerd nodded toward the jar. "New set. Don't fit. What you wanna know?" Anerd's brain didn't do small talk.

"I came here to talk about what happened to you. The Trinity County judge gave me authorization."

"No need to bother me. It's in the police report."

"I'd like to know more about Homer Johnson's friendship with Verlan Crumm and your daughter, Sally."

"The Injun? He came in here with them looking to buy a fuel pump, but I knew there was something else up." He scratched the pleat underneath his belly and futilely hitched up his pants. The motion knocked a pile of John Birch Society magazines onto the floor.

"What made you think that?"

"That gal of mine, Sally. You met her?"

I shook my head.

"Let's just say Sally has peanut butter thighs. Especially for low-lifes."

" 'Peanut butter thighs'?"

Anerd grinned so wide I could see tonsils where his teeth should have been. "Yeah. Easy to spread."

I gasped, which Anerd took to mean I was laughing at his joke. He bent over double, slapped his knee, and howled at his daughter's expense.

While Anerd hacked and spit, I collected myself. When he could breathe again I asked, "How well did you know Homer?"

He wiped his eyes with the hem of his T-shirt. A Grand Auto parts sign on the wall became absolutely fascinating to me.

"Didn't know the asshole at all until that day. But I know his type. He's a shit stirrer. A wannabe badass. And pardon my humor but my gal Sally didn't have nothing to do with it and I wrote to the judge telling him so. I don't want her to take no blame for what happened. You can talk to her ma, too. She works at the courthouse over the hill in Jackpot. She'll tell you it was that Injun."

"What about Verlan Crumm?"

"That boy ain't smart enough to plan anything, if you ask me. Besides he comes from a good ol' boy family. Never gave me no trouble, and his daddy bought lots of parts from me over the years. He'd have no reason to do nothing like that."

"What reason would Homer have?"

"Well. Let's just say there's some bad blood."

"Between you and Homer? But I thought you didn't know him."

"Not him. I had the displeasure of knowing his family. Or sort of his family, that is."

"Who in his family?"

"Asshole by the name of Bruno. Bruno Mario Seronello."

"What relation is he to Homer?"

"His grandma's main squeeze. I say main because that old bat got around but she never would give none to me." He winked again.

Anerd sat between me and the door. I flashed on the image of being pinned beneath his bulk on the cold slimy floor, assaulted by the buzzing and flashing of the red and white Grand Auto parts sign and Anerd's incongruously well-manicured fingers.

I hunched over and tried to look like a schoolmarm. "Why would Bruno dislike you?"

"Let's just say we had bad blood about . . . business."

"Enough bad blood for him to send Homer to hurt you?"

"Can't trust them Injuns."

"Is Bruno an American Indian?"

"Might as well be. He's fucking one. That about settles it in my book."

My book was about settled, too, at least with Anerd, and I was getting a headache from the buzzing and flashing. One last question. "Do you know anything about a white pride militia group? One that Homer and Verlan and maybe Sally belonged to?"

Anerd's face went blank—a nonreaction to the reaction behind it. "Nothing you need to worry about."

"Have you heard about it?"

"Mostly a bunch of yokels making an excuse for target practice and running around in the woods when it's not hunting season. Not a big deal."

He stood up, the conversation over. "Now mind you, I'm gonna be real unhappy if you say Sally was in on this in your report."

I started to tell him I'd been threatened by bigger jerks than the likes of him, but smiled instead and said, "I may need to call on you again."

He opened the door for me to leave, his first act of gallantry since I arrived. I wasn't sure what I'd accomplished except to find out that Anerd was every bit the pig he resembled.

Seven

I just visited with your husband at his shop. I can get to Jackpot in an hour," I said to Mavis Woods from the pay phone at the gas station on the way out of Cedar Gulch. I told her about the judge's request that I interview her. She didn't sound overjoyed, but agreed to meet me after she got off work.

I called Aunt Liz while the pink-cheeked, flat-topped attendant obsessed over cleaning a pulverized bug off my windshield. I felt a twinge of guilt but I wanted to catch Mavis before I interviewed Homer again the next day. "I'll be home late, Auntie Liz. Don't wait up and there's leftovers in the fridge. Call Maria if you need anything."

"Don't worry, dear. She's already been here and brought me some tea. I'll just take a little nap and see you later." She made an effort to keep her voice strong but the telltale quiver gave her away. She'd had a rough day.

"I can go tomorrow instead."

"I'll not hear of it. You need to do a good job on this case. Remember we need the new roof before this break in the weather comes to an end and we get the next big storm."

Given that I was going to feel guilty whether I went or not, I decided to go. The gas station attendant squeezed a last drop into the tank and tilted the nozzle upward to avoid spilling the excess gas. Only a quarter cup or so fell onto the orange paint of my 1973 Volkswagen Beetle. The bug was temperamental and about as fast as frozen molasses but it got me through grad school so I never complain, at least within earshot of it.

The VW protested around the mountain switchbacks and nearly swooned at the prospect of attaining six thousand feet. I kept my foot to the floor and avoided the passing lanes until we reached Buckhorn Summit. The bug sighed with relief and picked up speed and raced logging trucks all the way into Jackpot.

The Trinity County courthouse is a three story, turn-of-the-century Italianate granite edifice that houses the county offices, the district attorney's office, and the sole courtroom.

I found a spot under a black oak and squeezed in back of a spotless red Ford pick-up with a king cab, chrome roll bar, Baja lights, and a temporary registration on the windshield, and in front of a weathered green Chevy truck with a pock-marked camper shell on the back. The pile of clothing and food cans stacked to the ceiling of the Chevy's cab indicated the owner was either going to make a generous contribution to Goodwill or that the camper was the main residence. I suspected the latter.

I locked the bug, and started across the street. The sky seemed especially blue at this altitude and gray-white clouds drifted lazily above the snow-capped mountaintops. I took a breath of air scented from pine trees and cedar logs burning in woodstoves.

"Dr. Ringwald?"

The voice came from the direction of the courthouse. A tall blond man in a well-cut suit bounded across the street and invaded my personal space. "I'm Max Valentine. We met a few months ago at Richard Peck's party."

As if I could forget. The new district attorney of Trinity County was well over six feet tall, with perfect teeth accentuated by an ever so slightly crooked smile. Dynamic yet charming, he was the heartthrob of practically every unmarried woman north of Sacramento. Auntie Liz would have donated her best Limoges bone china to the Sisters of Charity soup kitchen to get him to come to dinner. But I was half a foot too short and not interested enough in acrylic fingernails or politics to snag Maxwell Valentine.

"Are you up here to interview Homer Johnson? I thought the judge ordered him to go to your office in Cedar Gulch." He widened his eyes, inquisitive.

"He did. I'm here to talk to Mavis Woods."

"Oh, right. You'll want to talk to Sally Woods, too. I'm afraid you'll have to do it up here though. Mavis and Anerd somehow managed to claim financial hardship, so Laurence Troutman was appointed to defend her." He shook his head as if amazed at their poor judgment. "Well, let me know if I can help." He shook my hand warmly and hopped into his tricked-out red Ford pickup.

Mavis Woods was just closing up her desk in the courthouse law library when I walked into her office. I introduced myself and she looked at her delicate gold wristwatch.

"I have to get home and fix dinner." Her dark eyes were centered in a cloud of puffiness, deep lines, and red sclera. Any attractiveness of her youth had tarnished.

I wanted to say, You knew I was coming and don't tell me I drove over Buckhorn Summit in a consumptive Volkswagen for nothing, but instead I told her I appreciated her time and this shouldn't take long.

"Well, I can spare only a few minutes." She took a red silk scarf from a hook and wrapped it around her head, then pulled a beige canvas purse out of a desk drawer and held it in front of her with both hands.

"I hoped this would be more convenient for you than

having to come all the way down the mountain to my office on a workday."

Her eyes darkened for an instant then she forced a smile and suggested we go for coffee. We ended up in a sixties coffee shop about the size of the backseat of my car. Our waitress waved in the direction of a tiny booth with cracked red plastic seats and a peeling blue speckled Formica countertop. Mavis squeezed in, her brown knit matronly dress pulling at her modest bosom as it caught on a snag in the seat. The pea hen to Anerd's pea cockiness.

"Anerd gets cranky if dinner isn't on the table."

I knew from the sign on his shop he didn't close until six. It took me an hour to get to Jackpot from Cedar Gulch, so he'd never get home before seven. It was only five now, but okay, give her the benefit of the doubt that her husband had been through an ordeal and she wanted to keep him happy.

"I realize this may be difficult. I'd like to ask you about anything you may know about Homer Johnson and his relationship with Sally."

She lowered her eyes to reveal a crease of blue eye shadow on her eyelid. She pulled a paper napkin from the dispenser and folded it into fourths, creasing each fold with an thumbnail bitten to the nub. Thick blue veins made a road map across her hands. "I really don't know. I met him a few times and he seemed nice but . . ."

A bleached-blond waitress whose name tag read Beverly interrupted to take our order.

"Go on." I touched her hand to get her attention. "He seemed nice but . . ."

She sighed and patted at her stiffly waved graying brown hair. "I got the feeling he wasn't as honest as he could be."

"About anything in particular?"

"Well, no. But he told me some things that made me uncomfortable." The paper napkin ripped under the pressure of her thumb and she spirited it under the table. She reached for another and changed her mind. She dropped her hands onto her lap, then tucked them under her bottom as though to prevent them from inadvertently revealing her thoughts.

"Uncomfortable in what way?" I felt like a snake charmer swaying from side to side to maintain eye contact with her.

Beverly the waitress returned with our drinks. Mavis took great effort to make sure the cream and sugar were well mixed with the coffee in her cup. I poured a half glass of milk into my cup to disguise the bitter taste of the cheap tea bag.

"What did he say that made you uncomfortable?" She was about as easy to interrogate as Homer.

"He said that Anerd was mean to Sally and he didn't like it."

"Was he? Mean to Sally?"

"My husband may have his faults but he loves our daughter and I can't imagine him being anything but wonderful to her."

I could imagine it but I wasn't going to say anything. "What else did he say?"

"One day, I heard him and Verlan talking about how much money Anerd made at the shop." Her eyes darted back and forth from her coffee cup to me.

"Do you think Homer wanted to hurt Anerd?"

"I don't want to think that but it could be. Would you excuse me? I have to visit the ladies' room." She pulled herself out of the booth, smoothed her dress, and walked in her sensible canvas pumps to the back.

Beverly came over to offer a warm-up. She opened my water pot and poured lukewarm water into it. "She's such a saint."

I looked up and raised my eyebrows inquisitively. "Beg your pardon?"

"Mrs. Woods. She's the nicest woman. And she tolerates

that jerk." She turned quickly as Mavis came back to the table. "More decaf?"

"No thanks. We'll be leaving soon." Mavis sat down and hunched forward.

"Tell me about Sally. I want to interview her, too. How do you suggest I approach her?"

Mavis put the spoon in her cold coffee and stirred it, clanking the stainless steel on the thick white stoneware cup. "She's shy and insecure. She never had too many girlfriends and always seemed to like the boys better. Please be kind to her."

"Who is her attorney?" I asked knowing full well that the Trinity County Public Defender had been appointed.

"Laurence Troutman. We've known him for years. His wife, Connie, and I grew up together in Jackpot."

The waitress presented us with the check. I grabbed it and looked at Mavis to continue. She looked at her watch.

"I really have to excuse myself. Anerd will be home soon, and I need to fix his supper. You see, he gets so tired at work." She stood. "Maybe you can help my daughter."

She turned and left before I could say that wasn't my job.

I left and walked a half block to my car. The owner of the battered Chevy was dipping into a can of creamed corn and watched me from the cab as I drove away. The bug grunted over the summit and we headed home in the dark.

Eight

I drove down the alley in back of our house and was welcomed by the yellow warmth of the kitchen light. The staccato of gravel under the tires punctuated the crisp evening air and the glow from the gibbous moon scattered shadows of tree limbs across the clapboards of the cottage. I parked the bug under the tin-roofed carport, rolled up the window, and ran up the back stairs. I tripped as I always do on the back porch, and let myself into the kitchen.

Auntie Liz was not in the dining area and the silence indicated she had already gone to bed. She had left me a tossed salad and a note to eat all of it. I poured myself the last of a bottle of Pinot Gris and sat at the counter with an American Psychological Association Monitor propped against the green tile backsplash. When I finished my dinner and an article on the controversy over the pros and cons of gender change, I started upstairs to check on Auntie Liz.

I dodged the Chippendale sideboard that took up most of the width of the hall and gave the impression the walls were closing in. Now that the living room was the waiting room for my clients, and the dining room was my interview room, Aunt Liz's imposing antiques dominated the tiny rear rooms of the house.

The hall light was partially obscured by the seven-foot-long scrolled mirror hanging over the sideboard. I switched it on knowing the oddly shaped shadows would only contribute to the spooky atmosphere.

I switched on the lamp in my bedroom, went back to turn off the hall light, and ran back to my room. The steep and narrow staircase to Auntie Liz's bedroom clung precariously to a knotty pine alcove across from my room, which we euphemistically called the television room. I worried about her feeble body plummeting down the stairs, but she had insisted that she get a view of Mount Shasta from her bed and turned the upstairs half story into her bedroom and a separate sitting room.

Her snoring filtered down the stairs. I tiptoed up to check on her. A copy of a book on English gardens lay open on her lap. I gently picked it up and dog-eared the page, but before I could put it in the bookcase someone began banging on the front door. Aunt Liz snorted, the warning she would awaken and have trouble getting back to sleep. I ran to the stairs, skidded down to the first floor, and tore down the hall to the waiting room. Friends come to the side door, so I couldn't imagine who it could be and it was way too late in the season for trick-or-treaters.

I unhooked the latch to the filigree peephole and peeked through. Nothing. The tiny cast iron door creaked as I shut it. I yanked open the door with the intent of telling whoever it was to leave an old lady in peace.

No one was at the door, but something on the doorstep caught my eye. I bent down and picked up an American flag. Unfurled, it revealed a black swastika painted across the red, white, and blue.

My first inclination was to throw it in the trash. Instead, I wrapped it in a bag, and set it on the highest cupboard in the kitchen where Aunt Liz couldn't reach it.

I locked up and went to bed.

Nine

The phone in my office started ringing at seven in the morning. I listened from the kitchen as the machine recorded the first three messages, but on my way down the hall with Aunt Liz's breakfast I could hear Richard Peck's voice telling me to pick up, it was important.

I set the tea and toast on the sideboard and ran to my office. My bare feet went numb from the chilly hardwood floor, and I stubbed a cold toe on my desk. Electric icicles shot up my leg. I cursed at the desk as I picked up the phone.

"I'd like to speak with you about Homer. In person," Richard said.

"I'm not decent. Can I come over in an hour or so?"

"I'll be at your place in fifteen minutes."

"Make it thirty."

I ran upstairs and set Aunt Liz's breakfast on the gate-legged table. The sunrise through her sitting room window set the hall aglow in orange-pink and spilled onto the floor of her bedroom. I wasted a moment defrosting my toe in the warm sunlight, then went to her bedside.

She opened her eyes and blinked. "What time is it?"

"It's just after seven but we're having company, and I need to hurry."

"So early?" She rubbed her eyes and reached blindly for her glasses. I handed them to her then propped her up with pillows. I pulled the table closer and poured milk and hot tea into her cup. She sniffed with satisfaction. "Perfect. Earl Grey." I dabbed some strawberry-rhubarb jam on a piece of toast and plopped the plate on the bed next to her. The toast slid off the plate onto the coverlet, leaving a stain of red-pink.

"Cassie, dear, if you're in such a hurry, I'd rather do it myself. Have you eaten?"

I shook my head. "I can't right now."

She grabbed my arm with her talons and held on. I have no idea how an old lady could have such strength—I've met weaker arm wrestling champions—so I folded. She wasn't about to let go and motioned toward the toast with her eyes. With my free hand, I reached the toast, took a bite and chewed. I had to stuff the entire piece into my mouth before she released me.

I ran wordlessly downstairs, to the shower, grabbed my toothbrush on my way in and scrubbed bread crumbs out of my teeth while the conditioner was in my hair. My blue suit wasn't too bad. I pulled on panty hose, turning the runner to the back.

The knocker banged just as I reached for my pumps. I charged precariously down the hall and pulled open the door. The waiting room clock hadn't yet struck eight.

The person at the door was not Richard Peck. The person at my door was a very tall young man with blue eyes and a shaved head.

"May I help you?" I held on to the door handle and pulled up the back of my shoe where I'd smashed it down with my heel.

"That your orange bug in the back?" He smiled benignly.

"Yes. Why?"

"I was walking down the alley and noticed it had a flat."

He opened the screen door and put his foot on the doorstep. The legs of his camouflage pants were tucked into his green canvas combat boots. "I was wondering if you needed it fixed."

"Well I guess I do. I can call Triple A. Thanks for the information."

"No problem. You don't have to call anyone. I can fix it." His smile crinkled the left half of his face and he winked a blue eye at me.

The back of my neck went clammy with foreboding and I fluffed my damp hair to chase away the chill. "I wouldn't want to trouble you."

"I'll do it for free, ma'am." He smiled wider and revealed his need for dental care. He put his weight on the foot on the doorstep and leaned forward. The heel of his other foot lifted off the porch. Another half second and he'd be in my house.

I held up my hand, my palm an inch from his chest. "I'm sorry. I have an appointment and I can't deal with this right now. Thank you very much for your trouble. I'm sure I can get it fixed without taking any more of your time. But thanks. I mean it. Thank you so much. You've been most helpful."

He leaned back and widened his eyes at the force in my voice.

With an assertive smile, I closed the door.

I hobbled to my interview room window and watched him. He stood looking at the door for a minute, then walked backward off the porch, staring at the door until he was on the walkway. He ambled off, turning with every other step to look back at the door. His face was blank and slack.

Richard pulled up in his sky blue Mercedes and walked up the front pathway. I unlocked the door and let him in.

"Was the skinhead a friend or a client?" Richard wore his usual impeccable suit and polished wing tips. He looked at me intently.

"Neither. He wanted to fix my flat tire."

"Looks like a punk. He probably would have taken off with it. Or the entire car for that matter."

"Well, he's gone now. Let me call Triple A before we talk."

I called from the kitchen phone while making a pot of tea. I took the pot into the interview room and poured him a cup, and settled into my chair with mine.

He sipped it graciously, then set his cup carefully on a coaster on the side table and dabbed at a spilled drop with a tissue. He neatly folded the tissue into fourths and put it in his breast pocket. "I have some news I wanted to get to you right away."

"Shoot."

Richard pulled his briefcase onto his lap. "Homer was released on a two-hundred-fifty-thousand-dollar bail yesterday." He opened the case, dug into it, and removed a manila folder. "His grandmother, Winema Johnson, came up with the bond money."

"Good. So he can come to my office by himself for the rest of the evaluation?" The news was good, at least for Homer, but nothing Richard couldn't have told me over the phone.

"Yes. And I want to discuss my strategy for the trial. Jury selection starts next week and I'd like your report before that." His eyes slid over me as he handed me some papers. "I made some notes about points I'd like to address when I examine you. During the trial, of course."

"That's pushing it." I took the notes and huddled into my chair. "I still have a lot of work to do."

"I realize that. But don't make it too hard on yourself. I expect that much of the evidence will mitigate—if not disprove—Homer's participation in the kidnapping. What motive could he have? He has plenty of family money and barely knew Anerd. The difficulty is that Homer will have to become more verbal and participate in his defense." He smiled. "That's your job."

"Your client may be trying to protect someone. Anerd said there was bad blood between him and Homer's grandmother's boyfriend."

"That's a long stretch. All I basically need from you is an explanation of the reason Homer wanted to join a white supremacist group. My theory is that he's just a mixed-up kid who wouldn't have the personality type or motivation to plot a kidnapping."

"After I talk to Verlan and Sally, I'd like to talk to Homer's grandmother about him. She may have some information he's not giving us."

"You're putting a great deal of effort into this. Not that I don't appreciate it." He ran his fingers across his thinning hair.

"At this point I don't have much choice," I said, wondering about Richard's motivation for hiring me. "I have no clue why Homer hooked up with the White People's Brigade and I don't get the impression he's going to share it with me even to save his own butt."

"Doesn't that show even more how mixed-up he is?"

"Maybe. And maybe not. He could have another agenda altogether."

Ten

Richard and I finished our business around nine. He'd made noises about getting together sometime, and I nodded sure and looked at my appointment book. I had private pay clients at ten and eleven and nothing for the rest of the day. I told Richard thanks, maybe next week, saw him to the front door, and waved good-bye while I planned my schedule.

The sky was overcast and the heaviness of the clouds threatened to bring late-afternoon rain in the valley and snow in the mountains. I figured if I was going to interview Verlan, I should to do it this afternoon before the weather set in.

After I finished with my last client at quarter past noon, I went to the kitchen to warm up some soup for Auntie Liz. She had come downstairs to thank the tire repair man and then parked herself in the television room. I brought her a mug of cream of asparagus, her favorite, and some soda crackers.

"How about a bit of wine with my lunch?" She began to crumble up the crackers into her soup.

"Isn't it a little early?" I turned the volume down, and put the remote control on the side table next to her chair.

"It's good for my heart. Besides, at my age I should be

able to start at breakfast if I like." She macerated the crackers into a thick goop then turned up the volume to a decibel below what would shatter the aged windows.

I ran back to the kitchen and opened a bottle of Pinot Grigio, and poured a third of it into a plastic fast-food Darth Vader tumbler. I figured she'd be asleep before *Oprah*. By the time I got back to the TV room, she was deep into a soap opera and dribbling soup down her chin.

"I'm going to drive up to Jackpot this afternoon, Auntie Liz," I shouted. I held out a napkin to her. "I'll be back before dinner."

Auntie Liz didn't look up until the commercial came on, then she took the napkin and dabbed at her chin. She peeked through the lace curtain at the sky. "It's dangerous to drive in the mountains. The weather's coming in. Why don't you wait?"

"I'll never get this case done if I don't get busy. Call Maria. She'll fix dinner if I get home late." My ears were ringing with the sound of a woman singing with joy about her new overnight laxative. "Can you turn it down for a minute?"

"Have Tony take you. He can take you in the police car." She pushed the mute button, but didn't turn down her voice accordingly.

I rubbed my ear. "I don't think that will work, Auntie Liz. I'll be fine. Tell you what, I'll take a toothbrush and a change of undies in case I get stuck up there." I gave her a peck on the forehead. Before she could think up anything else, I charged out the kitchen door to my car.

The steel and concrete Trinity County Jail is up the street from the courthouse and behind the sheriff's office on the east side of the highway. It looks about as tasteful as everything else built in the sixties, hence its nickname Jackpit Jail. During the summer, oak and birch trees conceal some of its tackiness, but the last of the leaves had turned brown and fallen onto the asphalt, leaving tree skeletons framed against the naked metal and fake stone.

I drove to Jackpot and found a parking place in the jailhouse lot next to a silver Mercedes 450SL, which could only have belonged to an attorney. I grabbed my briefcase and went through the glass door. Inside, cracked yellow plastic chairs were hooked together in a row along the cold gray concrete wall. A snoring drunk curled up on one of the chairs and the air was thick with the smell of cheap wine and bile.

The deputy behind the cage was pudgy, bored, and hopelessly slow. His ID badge read Martin. I handed my driver's license to him, and said I was here to see Verlan Crumm. He licked something off his fingers and leaned as close to the cage window as his paunch would allow. In a lazy drawl he started to tell me about visiting hours. I dug through my briefcase and handed him the court order from the judge that stated that I could interview Verlan. Deputy Martin held the paper four inches from his face and looked at it for a long time, moving his lips as he read. He looked at my license, then at me, then back at the letter four or five times before he finally said he guessed it was okay and buzzed to let me in the door.

The Trinity County Jail apparently didn't have the funds to install a metal detector. The deputy led me to a dank and tiny interview room with pale green concrete walls and gray metal chairs that dated from before the *Miranda* case.

The door to the cell row clanked open and another deputy appeared with Verlan.

He swaggered into the room wearing white Nikes and a baggy orange jailhouse jumpsuit open to midchest. His eyes roved over every inch of me like a starving dog looking through a chain-link fence at a barbecue.

I stuck my hand across the dented gray metal table that

divided the tiny room. "Good afternoon. I'm Dr. Cassandra Ringwald."

He leaned on the table with his left hand and reached across it with his right one. His hand was hard with bone and sinew but barely larger than mine. When he straightened up I saw he was no more than an inch or so taller than I was. "A doc, huh? So how did I luck out?" His pale pointy tongue darted out from his skinny lips like an eel poking out its head from a hidy-hole. His breath was sour with jailhouse slop, and he winked at me in cryptic conspiracy.

I motioned for him to sit down. "Are you Verlan Crumm?"

"Verlan Ferrell Crumm. That's me. You must be the shrink lady." He sat down hard and leaned back, balancing the chair on two legs. He grinned at me and the harsh overhead light exaggerated his ugliness. His eyes were like tiny black beads embedded in bony sockets. His jaw was long and thin and his upper lip jutted out sharply over two large yellow protruding incisors that dwarfed the rest of his teeth. His nose was prominent and lumpy, and it twitched and sniffed in perpetual motion. Occasionally he reached up and rubbed it in the way a rat would wash its face. Put whiskers on him and I'd expect to see him foraging in a garbage dump.

"The judge has ordered me to interview you regarding the kidnapping of Anerd Woods."

"Ain't he saying it was Homer that did it?" He made an attempt to look innocent but didn't pull it off.

"That's what I heard, but since you were arrested too, I wanted to get your side of the story." I set my briefcase on the table, opened it, and took out a notepad.

"Oh." His chair wobbled precariously. He thrust his hips forward. "Well, my lawyer said not to talk to you anyway."

"I certainly do understand. Mr. Troutman wouldn't be doing his job if he told you otherwise."

"Then why're you here?"

"The judge wanted me to ask you about what happened. That's all. I'm trying to help Homer with his case. It can't hurt your defense."

He looked at me more bewildered than guarded. "Why don't I get me no foxy shrink to help with my case?"

"I'm sure Mr. Troutman will do whatever he feels necessary to help you in the best way he can."

"Wadda ya wanna know?"

"Tell me about Homer. How did you meet him?"

"At a party in high school. A beer bust—you know—a little weed, couple of 'shrooms, a lotta beer." He seemed disappointed when I didn't act shocked.

"You and Homer went to the same school?" I scribbled some notes.

"Nah. He went to some rich kids' place in Arizona. That is until his ma died in a drunk car accident. I hear she was a real boozer, like most Injuns."

"What made you want to be friends with him?"

Verlan shrugged. "Dunno."

"Why did he decide to become a skinhead?"

"Who said anything about skinheads?" He curled his lip into a smile.

"Homer said you introduced him to the White People's Brigade." Actually Homer hadn't said it but it was worth a try.

"Don't know nothing about it." He crossed his arms defensively, and tipped the chair against the wall.

The direct approach wasn't working so I tried another tack. "So you grew up in Trinity County?"

"Yeah. 'Bout thirty miles from here. By Trinity Lake."

"In the country?"

"Sweetheart, everything's in the country in Trinity County." He leaned closer, resting his elbows on the table.

"Your family still up there?"

"Yeh, my pa's a farmer." He winked.

In these parts, farmer is the code word for marijuana grower. "And your mother?"

"Pa ran her off when I was ten after he caught her with a fishing guide. Ain't seen her since." He sounded almost proud of it.

"That's too bad." I nodded at him for a moment, then asked, "How did you know Sally Woods?"

"Same high school. Her pa Anerd and my pa are hunting buddies."

"Then you and Sally met Homer around the same time?"

"Yeh, we all went to the same parties." He rubbed his rat face and picked at a tooth with his thumbnail.

"It's nice to hear that your families are so open-minded about you hanging with a Native American."

He laughed. "An Injun, you mean. Homer ain't so bad. And he does supply the beer most times." He winked again then pointed his finger at my chest and waved it up and down as if he was caressing me.

I tried not to flinch. "It must be difficult for your father to see you in this trouble."

"He's used to it. 'Bout the third time I been in here," he boasted. "Nothing much. One time for possession and another for disorderly conduct."

"Oh, really?" I leaned forward as if to hang on his every word.

He slid into cool mode. "Yeah, we was demonstrating our pride in Christian America. Pissed me off 'cuz it was on private property but some asshole complained 'bout the cross burning. Wasn't no big deal."

I clucked sympathetically. "I suppose they were worried it was a fire hazard."

He laughed and set me straight. "It was in the middle of winter. Nah, some Commie just wanted to make trouble and deny our free speech rights. But we got him later." He turned his head away and pressed his lips together. "Asshole sheriff thinks he's too good for some of us. Some of his deputies are on our side though."

"Well that's good." I kept my voice low to disguise the sarcasm in it. "So you and Sally and Homer became friends."

"You might say that. I heard that Homer was pretty stuck on himself, too, before his ma died. Then he got some sense—I guess things like that change ya."

"Why do you think it changed him?"

He leaned back. "He was pretty clueless before that. He was real close to his ma—a mama's boy from what I heard—and when she died he got a taste of what real life was like. He started to party with us then he got interested in the rest of it."

"You mean white pride?"

"Christian American pride." He puffed up.

"Was Sally Woods in your group?"

"She's only a gal. Women are meant to serve us, not be the boss."

I raised my eyebrows.

"See, white men are chosen by God to rule because we're superior in intelligence and morals. But we let other people into our group if they believe in the cause and if they can help. Just as long as they're Christian. We don't allow no Jews or Catholics or niggers to join. In fact, I don't even know any Jews or Catholics and I don't wanna know any because they represent Satan. They're taking over the government and taxing us to death so they can spend our money on illegal aliens and welfare mamas who use up all the resources that God has bequeathed to the white Christian. The fascists use our tax money to keep themselves in power, and the average American stays so broke and tired that they can't resist or revolt."

He spoke with such fervor that spittle sprayed from his mouth. "The court system is a good example. I mean like here I sit with insufficient evidence against me and I can't even get out because I don't have the bucks Homer does. Do you know how easy it is to manipulate the court? All you need is money, man. And the average person on a jury is so stupid and gullible there's no fairness at all. Ya just gotta look good. But I betcha I could change the course of history here—I know how to play to those suckers. I can make 'em believe whatever I want them to because I got twice their brains without even trying." He took a breath.

I intervened to get him back on track. "Suppose you found out there was a Jew or Catholic among the white Christians?"

"Wouldn't happen." He frowned and shook his head.

"But just suppose? Suppose you didn't know?" I pushed.

He smiled and flexed his eyebrows as if to say he'd enjoy the experience. "We'd deliver justice. We say 'To save white America, kill . . . kick their ass.' "

"Homer isn't white," I pointed out.

"He's white enough. And he can help our cause."

I wanted to say that I bet all of Homer's family's money could help their cause, but asked instead, "Is your group large?"

"Not too big. Not yet. Mostly a few friends locally but we know of other groups and we will eventually form a union and return America to her rightful rulers." He leaned back an inch and turned his head to the left in order to focus on me with his right eye. His hand slipped down and fell on his crotch.

"Was Sally's father in the group?" I tried not to seem too interested.

He crossed his arms and his eyes closed to black slits. "You ain't gonna trick me into telling you nothing that would incriminate me. I know my rights and I think I said enough."

I looked at my notepad.

He ducked his head to catch my attention. "Sorry, miss. Don't wanna hurt your feelings none. But like I said, my attorney don't want me talking 'bout Anerd."

"I understand. I would like to come back again, that is, if the judge says I can." I clutched my notepad to keep my hand from shaking. I needed to get away from him and collect myself.

"Far as I'm concerned, the judge is half Communist. You can come back if Mr. Troutman says so. I trust him." He leaned forward banging the front legs of the chair against the concrete. He slid up the sleeve of his shirt over his right biceps and scratched. A two-inch homemade tattoo of an "A" in a circle decorated his arm, the same as I'd seen on Homer's arm.

"Does your tattoo stand for something?" I shoved my notepad into my briefcase and snapped it shut.

He glanced down at it and quickly pulled down his shirt-sleeve. "Nah. Just my ma's initial. Her name was Annabelle."

I thanked him, buzzed for the guard, and clutched my briefcase to avoid having to shake his hand again. We made polite small talk while we waited. I wasn't going to get the information I needed from Verlan if he knew what I really thought of him.

I walked out of the jail wishing I could take a shower. The clouds had lifted to allow a pale pink swatch of afternoon sun to highlight the harvest colors on the mountain. I took a deep breath of air spiced with evergreen and exhaled through my mouth to cleanse myself of Verlan. My Great-uncle Chester would have called him more vile than vermin and pinched off his head.

I remembered the summer when I was ten and Chester had taken me to Mount Shasta. We stayed overnight in a stone hut near the base of the mountain; for supper we ate a rabbit he'd shot and wild blackberries. We left early the next day to crawl through scree and drag ourselves by ice ax over glacial flows to conquer the 14,000-foot summit. Below, rivers curled down the valley floor through riparian wilderness and golden meadows. White-capped Lassen Peak stood majestically to the south and Mount Jefferson to the north. At the horizon, we saw the curvature of the earth. My great-uncle pointed out the Bolum glacier, an ocean of pale blue ice sliding relentlessly down the northern slope of the mountain overtaking everything in its path. "If you take one wrong step," he told me, "you'll fall ten thousand feet."

On the way down the mountain, when I was so exhausted and blistered I could barely put one foot in front of the other, he said to me, "When you remember this day, remember both beauty and peril." Years later I realized he wanted to teach me awe and triumph, perseverance and stamina. Perhaps he wanted teach me about survival.

Eleven

I was halfway across the street before remembering that my car was in the jail parking lot. I turned around to go back but feeling a little dizzy and shaky, I decided to get something to eat.

Beverly, the bleached-blond waitress, was on duty in the coffee shop where Mavis and I had talked. She poured me hot water for tea and took my order for soup while she made sympathetic noises about how cold I must be in a suit and heels on a day like this. I nodded and murmured politely and mentally tried to recover from my interview with Verlan.

Beverly brought my soup and slopped some of it on the table. A few drops landed on my suit and soaked in before I could grab a napkin to dab it up.

"Oh, I'm so sorry. What can I do to make up for it?" She was all over me with napkins and ice water, which only served to grind the soup further into the fabric.

"It's okay, no problem."

I had just put a second spoonful into my mouth when a man slid into the seat across from me. In the backlighting from the window his face appeared ashen and shiny with a thin sheen of sweat. His eyes were wide-set and a bland blue-gray, his hair an oily shade of silver, and his suit the color of a wet steelhead.

"Laurence Troutman." He reached his hand across the table.

"Cassie Ringwald." I dropped the spoon into my soup and accepted his clammy hand.

"I hear you've been interviewing my client." The accusatory tightness made his voice sound dry and squeaky.

"Yes. Just following orders from the judge." I smiled.

"Well, I'm not happy about it." He smiled back, not from politeness. His teeth were possibly the smallest I'd ever seen on an adult, and gray like the rest of him.

"I hope you understand that I've been retained to help with Homer Johnson's case and I need to get all the information I can get. I certainly don't mean to interfere with your client."

He narrowed his eyes. "Yes, well I wonder what you and Peck have up your sleeves."

Getting defensive clearly wasn't going to help the situation. "Why, whatever do you mean?"

"Knock off the innocent act. You and Peck and Valentine are up to something and as far as I'm concerned I have enough for a mistrial right now." He pumped his fist with insinuated warning.

"Your client hasn't even been to trial yet." I tried to keep my voice even and my facial expression neutral.

"If you mess up my case, I'll be all over you like flies on four-day-old bait." His lips curled into a malicious smile.

I stared at him and didn't speak until I could recover from his threat. My heart pumped a bit harder. "Mr. Troutman, neither Richard Peck nor I have any intention of interfering with your defense of Verlan." I didn't mention that I planned on interviewing Sally, too.

He pounded his fist on the table with enough force to splash more of my soup onto my suit then pointed his forefinger in my face. "Don't let me have to tell you again, you little bi—" He was interrupted by Beverly, who was on me again with napkins and ice water.

I smiled my most gracious and grateful smile at her and turned to him with the sweetest and most supportive tone I could muster. "Mr. Troutman, sir, perhaps if you lose the case, it will be because your client is guilty. And please forgive my impertinence, but you might want to consider working a little harder on your personal magnetism. I mean for the jury, of course. I hear the Dale Carnegie course is quite helpful."

I turned back to the blond waitress who gave me a sympathetic look. By the time I looked back in Troutman's direction, I saw the front door barely miss hitting him in the tail end.

"Mr. Troutman's wife," Beverly whispered, "she's old Jackpot so he thinks he can get away with anything."

I raised my eyebrows. " 'Old Jackpot'?"

"We call her the Princess Di of Jackpot. Her daddy was judge for years and then mayor. Everybody in town has just loved her since she was a little bit, but I don't think anyone likes him much. He's a real ass."

I took another two spoonfuls of soup but my stomach churned and protested. I set down a five and walked to the door.

"Thanks for the information," I said to Beverly. "And for the soup."

She smiled and gave me a wave with her fingers.

The sky had turned a deep shade of gray and was spitting in a half-hearted attempt to snow. I crossed the street to my car and had my hand on the door handle before I caught myself muttering aloud. If I drove home now, I'd have to drive back through the weather to interview Sally Woods. If I stayed, Aunt Liz would be upset but not as upset as she'd be if I had to come back. And who knew what Troutman could do in the next day or two to keep me from getting any possible information from Sally.

I walked back into the jail and stepped over the drunk who by now was sprawled on the greasy linoleum floor. Deputy Martin slumped in his chair and snored softly.

I presented my ID again. He looked as though he'd never seen me before, and then made a point of staring at his watch.

"I realize it's late, sir, but I would like to finish before I drive all the way back to Cedar Gulch." I moved closer to the window.

He looked at me again, and without speaking hunched down so he could see out the window. He stared past me.

I gripped the counter. "Sir. Deputy Martin, I promise I won't take long. It's imperative I speak to Ms. Woods."

"Looks like the weather's coming in. It's gonna get real chilly and you ain't dressed for it. Maybe you oughta hit the road now, young lady." He gave me a fatherly smile.

"I know, my great-aunt is probably worried sick. But I really want to finish now so I don't have to drive all the way back later in the week. I was lucky my car made it this time. It's a bit cranky at high altitude and the heater . . . Well, you know old cars." I chattered on benignly and hoped he had daughters my age.

"Well, it's almost suppertime. I just told her lawyer to come back tomorrow because Sally don't like to miss her meals." He chuckled and patted his belly. "The cook up here's pretty good. Especially his cinnamon rolls."

"Well, I won't keep her from her dinner. In fact she can eat while we're talking. So do you like working at the jail? Have you worked here long? Not that you look like you've been here forever, of course, but you sound like you know everything that is going on around here." I rubbed my hands together then tucked them into my armpits to show him how cold I was, but stood my ground to show him I wasn't going anywhere.

He chuckled and shook his head. "I got a niece about your age. She babbles on a bit, too. I 'spose it's a woman thing. Guess I better let you in before you talk my ear off and I miss my supper, too." He waved me through the door and buzzed me into a tiny interview room.

In the half hour I waited for Sally in the icy room, I wondered if the designer of the Jackpot jail had neglected to install a heating system. I rocked back and forth on the uneven legs of a chipped green tubular metal chair, chewed off most of a thumbnail, and worked a hangnail into a bloody mess. I was sucking on my forefinger when the metal door clanked open and she walked in. Before I could greet her, she burped heartily.

I stood and reached out to shake her hand.

She covered her mouth and giggled. "Pork chops and fried potatoes and onions and applesauce. And sauerkraut. And a cinnamon roll for dessert. I can get you some."

"Thank you, but I just ate." I also had to drive back home with closed windows in a tiny car that hyperreacted to every bump.

She stuck out her hand. "Are you here to see me? I'm Sally Woods."

"I'm Dr. Cassandra Ringwald. I came to talk to you about Homer Johnson." We shook hands. Hers was moist and warm and a comfort to my chilled one.

"Are you his friend?" Her face was eager with anticipation.

"Well, not exactly. But I'm working with his attorney, Mr. Peck, to help him on his case." I motioned for her to sit and she plopped onto the chair.

She had dark eyes, a pink pudgy face, and a turned-up nose. She squinted in order to see me. Her body was waistless, but her breasts were oddly voluptuous. There could be no mistake that she was Anerd's daughter.

"My attorney, do you know him? Mr. Troutman. He said not to talk to anyone, but I don't want Homer to get in trouble." She twisted a strand of hair around a plump pinky and smiled shyly.

"Tell me why not." I leaned my elbows on the table. I felt immediately relaxed with her.

"He's always nice to me. He calls me by my real name when everybody else calls me Miss Sow-y. You know. Like the pig?"

"But Homer doesn't?"

"He always treats me nice. In fact, I think he likes me a little. But I'm really Verlan's girl so there's no chance for me and Homer." Her face was a mixture of confusion and pride.

"How long have you and Verlan been going out?"

"Well, we're not officially going out, but he calls me his bitch—his fat bitch—so I guess I belong to him." She lowered her eyes demurely. "I think he really does like me for more than—you know—just sex."

"Do you ever think of breaking up with him?" I kept my face neutral to hide my pity for her. She really wasn't so unattractive.

"Well, no. Why would I do that? He wants me to be his bitch so I have to do what he says." She verged on defensiveness.

"Does he ever hurt you?" I de-escalated the potential emotional minefield by looking down at my notebook and away from her eyes.

"No, not really. I mean he's slapped me a few times for not wanting sex with him but otherwise he's nice. He takes me places and we have fun." Her words came more freely without the effort of maintaining eye contact.

"Where does he take you?" I kept my tone light and conversational.

"Oh, to meetings and stuff."

"Meetings?" I asked.

"The White People's Brigade. We have potlucks and stuff. Verlan lets me cook when we go."

"What do they do at the meetings?" I doodled squares on my notepad.

"The guys mostly just talk about politics and stuff. But it's a lot of fun and I get to talk to the other girls there about preparations for the coming time."

"Politics? Preparations?" I glanced up at her, then worked at shading in the squares on my paper.

"About how the people will overcome and the Jew-controlled government will fall and the minorities will all be sent back to where they came from. And how we can survive while there is anarchy and all the stores are closed and there are no gas stations and stuff. And we sing, too. A guy named Freddy is a good songwriter and we sing his songs." She hummed a few bars then sang in a high-pitched squeak:

"The white man rides on shining horse, to save the land for thee,
We once were lost in liberal cause, oppressed but now we're free."

She smiled. "Freddy said I could sing good."

I dropped my pen on the floor. "Sally, have you ever heard the song 'Amazing Grace'?"

"No. But let me sing you the second verse." She took a deep breath and the sound erupted out of her.

"The Jewboy, Spic, and Spook will fall, on ground God gave to us,

The blood will spill, we'll give our all, 'til they decay to
dust."

We both startled at the sound of my notebook slapping onto the floor. "My God, Sally, that's pure bigotry. And it's sung to 'Amazing Grace.' "

"What's big-tree?" Her eyes were wide with surprise at my reaction.

"Sally, it's a hate song. It's about killing people. It promotes a race war." Stunned, I struggled to get the words out. "My great-uncle nearly gave his life to save the world from this garbage."

"But if we don't take back our land, they'll take it all away from us." She spoke to me as though she were explaining a simple fact to a small child.

"I'd like to point out that your good friend Homer is a Native American and his ancestors didn't exactly give this county to the white man." I bit the inside of my cheek to control the sarcasm in my voice.

She looked at me blankly. "If it wasn't for us the Indians wouldn't have reservations to live on."

"Well, I guess that's one way of looking at it." I reached down to pick up my pen and notepad. Sally used her foot to push the pen within my reach. I wasn't getting very far teaching her American History 101, much less racial tolerance. "Sally, did you know that the music to 'Amazing Grace' is the same as the music you sang? The man who wrote it was a slave trader who realized he was doing a bad thing and repented by writing the song."

"What does that have to do with me?" She didn't get the connection at all.

"Nothing, Sally. Not a thing." I straightened out my notebook and smoothed the pages. "What can you tell me about your father?"

"He's my dad. I love my dad."

"Why did you want to kidnap him?"

"At first I wasn't serious, but then everyone else wanted to."

"Including Homer?"

"We used Homer's little truck. Verlan didn't want to use his own car in case we was seen."

"How did Homer get involved?" I asked.

"We told him we was going to a WPB meeting and he was invited. He'd been wanting to get in so when Verlan said we could go in his truck Homer said okay."

"What did he know about the plan to kidnap your dad?"

She continued. "Oh, he was there when we talked about it. Verlan said to me that he'd told him about the plan before they drove on up to my house that night."

"So Homer knew?"

"I don't know what he knew. You see I didn't want to hurt my daddy, just to get some money from him. Verlan didn't think he would know who it was until Homer messed it all up." She spoke rapidly and earnestly.

"How did he mess it up?" I twiddled with my pen and looked directly at her.

She wanted to tell me the rest of it. "I guess he froze. Verlan handed him the gloves—so as we wouldn't leave no fingerprints—and Homer just stood there like a dummy staring in the window. I didn't want him to get in trouble and I didn't want anyone to get hurt. But then my pa saw him, and that's how he got arrested."

I scribbled some notes then asked, "How did your dad get into the dump?"

"I don't know." She averted her eyes.

"You and Verlan didn't take him there?" I didn't expect the truth. To admit she knew made the difference between charges of assault and attempted murder.

"No. Verlan put him into the truck bed and just took off. Verlan was so mad at Homer that he left him standing in the front yard like an idiot." Her face and voice belied regret.

"Did you and Verlan take your father to the dump?" I scribbled madly.

"We drove Homer's truck down the mountain to my dad's shop and had sex." She blushed. "Verlan left me there and said he was going to get Homer."

"Did Verlan take your father to the dump? Or both Homer and Verlan?"

She opened and closed her mouth, then shrugged. Loud voices filtered in from the lobby of the jail.

I had a notion my interview with Sally was coming to an end. I spoke rapidly. "Sally, do you know who might have wanted your father to die?"

Her eyes clouded and a single tear fell onto her cheek. "I'm afraid for him. I never wanted him to get hurt or make him mad at me. I wish he came here to see me." She slapped the table then moaned and shook her hand in the air. "I miss him."

"Sally, I get the impression you know more about this." The voices in the lobby were getting louder. I spoke even faster, but Sally was not to be pushed. She nodded numbly and pressed her lips together.

The lobby exploded with shouting and slamming doors. I figured I could get in one more question. "Do you think Homer had something to do with your father ending up in the dump?"

She hung her head and burst into wet sobs. I rooted around in my briefcase and found a tissue. "It's okay to tell me, Sally. I'm trying to help him."

Someone yelled, "I told you I wanted to see her now. Quit fucking with me."

Another deeper voice boomed, "Enough already. I told you to go home."

The first voice hollered, "You let that little bitch in there and not me? I'm Sally's goddam attorney." It was the voice of Laurence Troutman.

"Sally, what about Homer?"

Her shoulders shook with sobs, but she said no more.

The door burst open and Deputy Martin led Troutman into the interview room.

I reached across to touch Sally's arm. "It's getting very late and both of us are tired. I'm really sorry I brought up some difficult things for you, and I hope you'll talk to me again."

She looked up at me through her tears. Her mouth twitched into a tiny smile.

Troutman lunged at me and pulled my arm, but I jumped up and away from him before he got a firm grip.

My knees nearly buckled under his glare. I threw my shoulders back and said loudly, "Thank you for the opportunity to interview your client, Mr. Troutman." I turned to Sally and said even louder, "You've been most helpful, Miss Woods. Thank you for your time, and I'll see you again."

Sally looked back and forth between me and Troutman, bewildered and frightened. "Did I do something wrong? I didn't mean to. What did I do wrong?"

"Nothing, Sally. It's okay." I patted her reassuringly from the end of the table farthest from Troutman.

Troutman's jaw worked up and down, but he looked too furious to form coherent words.

I slid in back of Sally and stood near Deputy Martin, who wore sugar crumbs on his chin, probably from a cinnamon roll. His tired, stale breath had been replaced by the sour-sweet smell of sauerkraut and applesauce. He winked at me.

"I hope you had all the time you needed, Doc." He put his arm around me protectively.

"Yes, thank you. It's time I got on home." I allowed him to lead me out the door.

He slammed the heavy door to the jail cells behind us and looked over his shoulder through the small window. "I never could stand that cocky little prick. Hear he beats on his wife, Connie. That doesn't please folks too much seeing how she's Jackpot royalty."

"Thank you so much for allowing me to talk with Miss Woods." I shook his hand.

"Not a problem for me. And if it pissed off Troutman, all the better." His belly rippled as he laughed.

I bid him good-bye and walked out into the cold night. The wind blew tiny shards of ice through my suit and my feet cramped from the frozen sidewalk. I looked across the street but Mr. Homeless Truck Man was hidden in the shadows of the cab of the Chevy.

I wobbled through the icy parking lot, and had to hold on to the bug's hood to keep my feet from sliding out from under me. I got in and told her, "Come on, little Beetle. It's mostly downhill from here."

Twelve

The house was open when I got home, and the gray-blue light from the television room spilled into the backyard. A few lonely petals hung limply from the branches of the ancient rose that climbed up the white board fence. I came in the kitchen door, set down my briefcase on the counter, and hung my jacket on the hook. A cast-iron Dutch oven sat on the stove. I lifted the cover, and the comforting smell of chicken and vegetable stew made my stomach growl. I turned the flame on simmer to warm it up.

Shouts and jeers echoed down the hall. On my way to the television room I speculated that Auntie Liz might be having a beer bust, but quickly discovered the cause of the ruckus.

Tony and Aunt Liz were having a tea party and watching live wrestling. The gladiators were a tall blond man with a handlebar mustache who was wearing the bottom half of a red and blue matador outfit, and a stout bald man in a leopard skin leotard.

"Grab a cup and join us." Tony offered me a toast with his blue and white china teacup. "How was your day?"

I shook my head. "I'm too beat to discuss it. Suffice it to say my mind hasn't stopped spinning."

"Kill him. Choke him," Aunt Liz screamed at the television and shook her cane in the air. The empty bottle of Pinot Grigio sat next to her teacup.

"Aunt Liz, do you think this is good for your heart?" I gave Tony an incredulous look. He shrugged, and mouthed, "Not my idea."

Aunt Liz didn't take her eyes off the screen. "Best I've felt in years. Used to love to watch wrestling with Chester." She shrieked again, "That's it. Flatten him! Stomp him!" The blond wrestler swung his leg behind the shorter man, tripped him, and sent him sprawling to the mat on his back. He rolled over and tried to get up.

I sighed. "Want a beer, Tony?"

"No thanks." He checked his watch. "I'm on duty in two hours. The tea's good. Have a cup."

"Grab his balls! Get him, get him!" Aunt Liz grabbed the arms of her easy chair and rocked in agitation. The blond wrestler flung himself onto the prone body of the bald one, and bounced up and down in rhythm with the spasmodic efforts of the bald one trying to get up. The scene looked like the mating ritual of giant man-frogs.

I picked up his cup and sniffed. He was indeed drinking tea. "Oh great. You get her all riled up and I have to calm her down enough to get her to bed. Between the wine and the caffeine, she'll never sleep."

Tony shrugged again. This wasn't his problem.

"Now, young lady, I am not a two-year-old." Auntie Liz pointed a bony finger at me and jabbed the air. "I am perfectly capable of getting myself to bed." She patted Tony's hand. "This young man was keeping me company, and we were having a fine time until you came in all crabby. Why don't you go get your supper and leave us be. And don't come back in here to bother us until you're in a better mood."

I turned to leave. Out of the corner of my eye I could see Tony doubling over with laughter. "Fine," I said. "I'm going to bed and I hope you can fall asleep because I'm not going to stay up all night with you."

Auntie Liz's voice followed me down the hall. "You have a bad habit of always needing the last word, young lady." Then, "Nail his ass. Watch out! That's it. *Yessss!*"

I closed the kitchen door to get some peace, eat in silence, and think about the day. The more I learned about the Woods case the more bewildered I became, not only at trying to dig up facts and decipher the puzzle, but also at the depths of ignorance and fanaticism it had revealed to me. It was almost as though Verlan, Sally, and Anerd believed that hatred, destruction, and anarchy were laws of nature as out of control of the individual as the rising of the sun or phases of the moon.

Tony slid the door open after a while. The television was quiet and the house once again restored to dignity. "She's in bed and snoring. Hit the mattress like a sack of walnuts."

"I guess that which doesn't kill her will surely make her stronger." I took a stoneware bowl off the shelf and nodded my head toward the stew pot.

"Hey, she had a good time. That's what counts." He took the bowl and ladled himself some stew. "She was feeling pretty spry today. Asked me to come over to help her make dinner then did most of it herself."

"Good thing we have her and your sister to cook. Between the two of us we'd starve." I set my bowl in the sink. "I know she's lonely, even more so since your mother died. I appreciate you and Maria spending so much time with her. I feel as though I don't do enough, and this case takes so much time—"

"Hey, she's basically my aunt, too. How else can I repay her for all she's done for us. She held Mom together when my dad was killed, and then she was our rock when Mom was dying." He lowered his eyes and cleared his throat.

I reached over to touch his arm. He was trembling. "Do you still have nightmares about your dad getting shot?"

He wrapped one muscular arm around me, then drew me close and held me tightly. His breathing was labored and irregular and his warm, moist breath filtered through my hair. I could feel his heart pounding through his T-shirt. After a moment he pulled back, kissed me on the forehead, and released me. "Thanks for the shrinkage, bud."

He put his bowl in the sink and walked toward the door. "By the way, I heard the guy you rescued left the hospital against medical advice."

"Dang. He was hurt pretty badly, too." I moved my neck from side to side to stretch out the kinks. "I wish I'd had the chance to see him. I don't even know who he was."

"Bruno some Italian name," Tony said.

"Not Bruno Seronello?"

"Something like that. He's from Modoc."

"No way. He's the guy Anerd talked about. Homer's grandmother's boyfriend." Another puzzle to decipher.

"How about that. You should check him out."

"What time do you get off duty?" I twiddled with a lock of hair.

Tony's face did not belie trust. "Six, but I need some sleep."

"How about I pick you up at ten and we can go to Modoc?"

He shook his head and smirked. "Uh-uh, Cassie. Not this time. And tomorrow's Friday. I've got plans."

"Like what, besides sleep? It may be snowing and you know what a hazard I am in the snow." I smiled and moved closer.

"I have a date." He frowned sternly but his eyes twinkled.

"With the brunette? This will be more fun. Besides I need you more than she does. I'll tell you all about my case." I batted my eyelashes.

He laughed at the manipulation. "You're too obvious. Okay, but not before noon. And not in the bug. I'll drive the truck."

"I can always count on you."

"Sucker me is more like it. You owe me." He feigned a punch at my arm.

"Many times over." We'd known each other so long and owed each other so much that I barely felt any guilt.

He grinned and was gone.

I went to check on Auntie Liz to make sure the excitement of live wrestling hadn't triggered a cardiac event. She snorted and stirred and in the moonlight I could see that her eyes opened.

"Are you okay?" I whispered.

"I'd be better if you and Tony were an item. Such a nice young man, and good-looking, too. Maybe if you saw him in his uniform, you'd fall for him."

"Auntie Liz, I appreciate the concern, but I have seen Tony in his uniform many times and yes, he's a babe, but even if I wanted him, which I don't, he only dates bimbos." I smoothed her bedcovers.

"He's an intelligent young man. Why would he want a silly woman?" She pulled her hand out from under the covers and touched my arm.

"I don't know, Auntie Liz. Maybe someday you can ask him." I relaxed under her touch. After today I needed all the contact comfort I could get.

"Maybe because he can't get you." She gave my hand a little squeeze.

"Auntie Liz, Tony and I are good friends. Why would either of us want to complicate our relationship with romance?"

"His poor dead mother and I both knew since the time

you came to visit us when you were ten years old that you were meant to be together. You've both had too much tragic loss and each of you needs someone who will understand and be supportive. Why, when I'm gone . . ."

"Guilt doesn't work with me," I said, which wasn't entirely true, but I wasn't going to let her know it. "And when you're gone, we will still be friends if we don't lose our heads and do something foolish. Besides, you want to fix me up with every man who comes along."

"He's the best of them. I just hope you figure that out someday."

"Yes, Auntie." I pulled the covers up under her chin and pecked her cheek. Before I left the room, I fiddled with the thermostat. "Good night," I told her but she was already snoring. I was glad because the next words out of my mouth would have been that I was too afraid of needing anyone to think about a relationship.

That night I dreamed I was being smothered beneath a man's body that turned into earth and buried me alive. I floated out of my body and looked down to see Tony as a small boy in short pants and an oversized CGPD baseball cap, on his knees, digging with tiny fingers at his father's new grave.

Thirteen

I rearranged my schedule to squeeze in three clients and a telephone interview before noon. I fixed Auntie Liz a huge bowl of cream of broccoli soup and gave her the rest of the box of Saltines before I went over to Tony's and let myself in. He was standing in the kitchen, wearing only red-and-blue striped boxer shorts, and watching the coffee drip into the pot.

"Good afternoon," I said.

Tony groaned and rubbed his eyes. "I can't believe you conned me, again." His face was puffy with sleep.

"I'll get the coffee. You get into the shower." I pushed him in the direction of the bathroom but was intercepted by the ringing of the telephone.

I reached for the receiver but Tony took it away from me with one hand and grabbed me around the waist with the other. We both fell backward onto the sofa.

"Hi. Yeah, sorry about last night. I was, uh, I had to take care of something," he said into the receiver. "Sorry, can't today. I just got up and I have to go on a case."

I wiggled away from him. "Go brush your teeth."

"No, no one," he spoke into the phone. "I mean that was just Maria. My sister." He flipped me the bird while he jumped up and bolted to the bedroom, dodging furniture with the telephone cord.

He came out in two minutes.

"The brunette?" I asked.

He nodded.

"I can't believe you shined her on like that. Why don't you just tell her the truth?"

"Is it your business?" He put his hands on his hip and wiggled his butt in a crude imitation of me.

"No, but as your friend I think it's my business to inform you that you're insensitive and you treat women dreadfully." I crossed my arms, and glared at him.

"Sure, I'm insensitive. Especially when I drive you all over hell in the snow on five hours sleep when I could be with a woman who fawns all over me." He crossed his arms and glared back.

"There's no need for sarcasm."

"Do I treat you dreadfully?" He acted angry that I would think so.

"No, you don't. I wouldn't put up with it."

"Maybe that's why. I'll be in the shower." He yanked a towel out of the hall linen closet and spilled a pile of sheets onto the floor. He yelled from the bathroom, "And remember, while you were out gallivanting around last night I was sitting up and watching live wrestling with your invalid aunt instead of getting *laid!* What other guy would do that, huh?"

Maria stuck her head out of her bedroom door. "Will you two shut up so I can get some sleep? I'm on graveyard."

"Sorry, Maria. I didn't know you were home." I picked up the sheets in the hall and put them back into the closet. "I guess I said the wrong thing."

"Well, kiss and make up and give me some peace and quiet." She closed her door, and I heard her crumple onto her bed.

I poured a cup of coffee for Tony, and added milk and three spoons of sugar. The bathroom door was unlocked and steam poured out when I opened it. I set the coffee on the toilet tank and wrote "sorry" in the condensation on the mirror. Tony stuck his head out of the shower and looked at the mirror. He broke into a grin. "Wanna come in?" He yanked back the shower curtain, I ran out the door just in time to avoid an eyeful.

I set the teakettle on the stove and poked around the living room. Tony's chess set sat on a Mission-style table in the corner. On the chair next to it lay a thick volume on the strategy of chess. I was leafing through it when he emerged from the bathroom with a towel wrapped around his waist.

"Why don't you teach me chess?" I asked.

"Because I think you're already good enough at plotting strategy." He disappeared into the bedroom.

The bookcase behind the table held various books on police science and administration of justice, some junk novels, a section on war—the civil wars of the United States and Spain, the revolutionary wars of America and France, the two world wars and several books on the history of England. I pulled out a slender volume, and hearing the kettle whistle, took it with me to the kitchen.

I fixed myself a cup of tea, and opened the book.

Tony came into the kitchen buttoning his shirt. "What'cha reading?"

"*Henry the Eighth*." I replied. "What a man. Is he your role model?"

"I wish I was that lucky." Tony tucked his shirt into his jeans. "Time to hit the road, Cassie." He flipped the book closed, and handed me my jacket from the back of the chair. "I don't have all day."

I burned my tongue trying to chug the rest of my tea. We hopped into his big red Ford F-250 truck which I had nicknamed the Red Beast. We were halfway out of the driveway when Maria came running out the door with the portable phone in her hand.

"Auntie Liz is on the phone." Maria clutched a beltless pink chenille robe around her and danced on the cold pavement in her bare feet. "Hurry, I'm freezing."

Tony reached through the window, took the phone and handed it to me.

I looked up to see Liz waving from her window. "What's up?"

I could see her lips moving as she explained. "Richard Peck called and said he needs to speak with you immediately. It's an emergency." I held the receiver away from my ear, and her excited voice filled the cab.

Tony groaned and banged his head on the seat back. "It's always a crisis with attorneys. Try to get off the phone in less than an hour." He leaned his head back and closed his eyes.

I shushed him. "Okay, I'll call him."

Richard answered on the first ring. His voice sounded somber and gravelly. "Good, I'm glad I caught you. Something terrible has happened that changes the entire case." He paused for drama which I supposed served him well in the courtroom, but annoyed me. "Homer's bail was rescinded this morning. The district attorney has amended the charges to include first-degree murder."

"Yowza! What happened?"

"According to his wife, Mavis, Anerd went missing last night."

I made noises of incredulity, and Richard continued.

"Mavis called the police after she talked with you the other day. She said that Anerd hadn't returned home that night, and that he was not at the shop. The police searched for him, and a fisherman finally found his truck mired in mud near the Trinity River. There was enough blood in the bed to look like a cow had been slaughtered, but it was human blood of Anerd's type. As we speak, they're dragging the river for his body."

"That's a long shot. The river has a lot of rapids." I vacillated between feeling sympathy for Mavis and Sally, and relief that I wouldn't have to interview Anerd again.

"There's enough runoff that they figured his body could have made it down to the ocean if he didn't get caught on a snag."

"What did Mavis say that made them arrest Homer?" I held the receiver against my right ear and plugged my left one to drown out Tony's snoring.

"She claims that Homer was the ringleader in a plot to murder Anerd, not just to kidnap him."

"And this just happened to slip her mind before now?"

"She said she was protecting Sally, but that she talked to Anerd after Homer was released, and she is sure Homer followed through on the plot."

"Sounds pretty weird to me."

"I think our client is being set up."

I wanted to say I wasn't so sure he didn't deserve it. Instead I asked when I could interview him again.

"The judge is furious that he let Homer out on bail and then Anerd disappeared. You'll have to go to the Jackpot jail. I want to know if Homer's capable of plotting and carrying out not only a kidnapping but a murder. Are you sure you want to continue the evaluation? The stakes are much higher."

"I started it, I'll finish it."

"There's more."

"What?"

The public defender, Laurence Troutman, is having a fit because you interviewed Sally and Verlan. He's trying to get the court order blocked."

“In other words, he’s told them to shut up, and I have all I’m going to get from them.”

“I hope it was enough.”

I hung up and nudged Tony. “Time to go, champ.”

Tony yawned and rubbed his eyes. He pulled out of the driveway, and we headed toward Modoc. “So what’s the plan?”

“We’re going to meet Homer’s grandmother.”

He blinked into the glare of the overcast sky. “I thought she lived in the boondocks,” he said, steering with his knee while putting on his seat belt.

“We have to find Bruno first and I’m hoping he’ll take us to her.”

Modoc County is high desert country in the northeast corner of California with Oregon to the north and Nevada to the east. I figured with minimal heavy weather we’d find Bruno’s place by three and get to Homer’s grandmother’s by four. A steady drizzle soaked the faded meadows east of Cedar Gulch. Water the color of chocolate milk overflowed the banks of Cow Creek. By the time we started up the first summit past the Afterthought Mine, the snowflakes had started to stick to the windshield.

Tony switched on the wipers. “Why do you need to talk to Homer’s grandmother?”

“Anerd, Mavis, Verlan, and Sally all have differing stories about Homer. I’m hoping his grandmother can add some balance and history. The boy hasn’t been exactly forthcoming with the details.”

“Why, besides the money and wanting to impress Richard, are you working so hard on this one?” He turned on the defrost and wiped the misty window with his sleeve.

I thought for a moment. “There’s a vulnerability about Homer. I don’t think he’s as tough as he puts on.”

"So you feel sorry for him?"

"Not exactly. At first I didn't like him at all but now I want to figure him out. For example, he acts as though he doesn't give a damn, but then Sally tells me he's the only man who ever treated her with respect. Not like Verlan. He's one scary dude." I told Tony about my interview with him.

"Must be tough for you hearing all this neo-Nazi rhetoric." He glanced at me.

"It's made me think about Uncle Chester." I looked out the window at the treeless landscape, the carnage of an arson fire that devastated a hundred square miles.

As we crested Hatchet Summit, a small car in the westbound lane hit some black ice and skidded downhill toward us. Tony held the steering wheel with both hands and gently guided the truck around it. "Do-si-do and around we go." He watched through the rearview mirror. "Hot damn." The car spun completely around and centered itself in the westbound lane. "He made it. Now he'll have to go home and change his pants."

"I'm glad you're driving," I said.

"That's my job, to keep you safe."

"You didn't feel used and abused?"

"I couldn't live with myself if anything happened to you." He turned his head away from me and stared out the window in the direction of one of the area's rapidly disappearing lumber mills. I knew he was rebuking himself for the death of his own father.

The sky cleared east of Fall River to reveal Mount Shasta rising solitary and as white as the winter moon above the wild rice paddies.

Tony hadn't spoken in half an hour.

I reached to touch him gently on the shoulder.

He looked straight ahead. "I don't get how something that happened twenty-five years ago seems like it happened yesterday," he said. "I just hope I can be half the cop my dad was. I still have nightmares about him being cold and by himself in that damn coffin. That's why I took the blanket to him. And his cap. I thought I could put them in with him. I just wanted to see him again—like maybe he wasn't really dead."

"You were five years old. Children think magically."

"If I hadn't disobeyed him in the first place, if I'd stayed in the house, he would have never been caught off guard. That nutcase wouldn't have shot him." He flexed his jaw. "He'd be alive and my mom wouldn't have had to suffer like she did."

"You were trying to help him, Tony. It's natural for a child to want to defend his family." As I said it, my heart shattered at the thought that at the age of seventeen I didn't protect my own mother and baby sister from my father. I said more to myself than Tony, "At least my family didn't die."

Tony looked at me and said nothing. He reached for my hand and held it lightly. After a while he said. "Boy, we're a couple of walking wounded. No wonder no one will have us."

"What about the brunette?" I asked.

Tony snorted. "Stephanie? She's a bimbo."

The pass leading to Modoc County is barely two lanes wide and wraps around the mountain like a boa constrictor. Occasionally a crushed automobile carcass emerged from the snow-covered boulders below as a warning to watch for black ice and rocks in the road. When the end of the civilized world comes, a well-placed stick of dynamite or two will block off Modocers from anyone who wants to invade them. If anyone would want to invade them.

As we gained altitude, shallow lakes shimmered from a valley floor framed by snow-capped Shasta and Lassen Peaks. The snow began again and a few more cars tried to dance with us as they slid across the road.

We dropped over the top of the summit to Big Valley, which stretches to the horizon in every direction. The casual observer might think the area to be a wasteland, but we saw antelope, flocks of snow and Canada geese, and even a skinny coyote loping across the frozen meadowlands. We crossed the last pass and the sky cleared to a crystal blue.

Modoc County is forty-two-hundred square miles and home to less than ten thousand old-timers, refugees from smog and traffic, welfare mamas who brave the cold for cheap rent, and Paiute, Pit River, and a few surviving Modoc Indians. The pace is slow and the economy almost stagnant. The drive border to border, east to west or north to south, takes less than two hours but seems like eons. Geological formations, which include black lava flows and multicolored layers of sedimentation, are all there to enjoy—not much flora grows to conceal them.

Few outsiders had even heard of Alturas, the county seat, until a few years ago when the lame duck governor of California paroled a serial rapist there "so he would be in an area where he couldn't hurt anybody." The three thousand residents of the town took exception and within twenty-four hours every shop window on Main Street displayed a picture of the rapist centered in a gun sights. Even the *New York Times* took notice with a full-page article in which a law professor railed about discrimination against "hicks."

I unfolded the directions to Bruno's place given to me by Richard Peck's investigator with the warning that the place was "pretty far out," which promised to be true in more ways than one.

"After we drive through Alturas we head east past Cedarville on what this map refers to as a road." I looked ahead to the two-lane highway that stretched across the high desert and seemed barely wider than a deer trail. "Is this where that young couple got stranded out in the snow with their baby?"

"Yep. Flatlanders. They figured I-5 was closed so they'd take a shortcut through the middle of nowhere during a blizzard. The husband stashed his wife and their baby in a cave and hiked in circles until someone found him. Lost a bunch of toes and nearly died. They made a television movie out of it." He switched the defrost on to high. "No accounting for some people's lack of common sense."

I turned up the heater. "I hope we don't end up making the same mistake." I thought about Homer. Growing up in this wilderness he had been protected from the cruelties of civilization, yet he had been more than eager to leave.

As we reached the Nevada border, the blue of the sky deepened and the temperature seemed to drop another fifteen degrees. I rummaged behind the seat and found a red sweatshirt to throw across my legs.

The blacktop highway was replaced by a shale road that snaked adjacent to the dry lakebed, a flatland of sage brush and jackrabbits, ringed by mountain peaks and the only sign that water had ever graced the pale desert.

"Damn," said Tony, as the truck crunched over black shards of rock. "This road wasn't made for city tires."

The first tire blew out thirty-seven miles either side of nowhere. The spare was thin, and I held my breath in anticipation for the next five miles, and exhaled in resignation when it blew as I knew it would.

Not another car in sight. The map showed what had been a ranch a hundred years ago a couple of miles ahead.

"Our options are to stay with the truck or try for the ranch," Tony told me.

"In other words we either die of boredom or freeze to death. Maybe if we survive we'll at least get a TV movie out of it." My teeth chattered at the mere thought of getting out of the truck.

"The ranch isn't too far and it's not likely to snow. Let's try it." Tony found some stones and lay them on the hood to form the word "ranch" and an arrow pointing toward it. He handed me the red sweatshirt to put over my jacket, and I tucked my hands into the sleeves. I wished I'd remembered my gloves.

We walked over frost-encrusted dry grass, which cracked under our feet. The air, so cold it was visible, bit at my nose and numbed my lungs. "It's freezing. My toes are frostbitten." I examined the bottom of my boot. "I think the leather's wearing through."

Tony finally got tired of telling me to quit whining, and strode a few paces ahead of me to motivate me to keep up.

The sky had turned gray by the time we reached the ranch. There was not only no phone, there was no longer a standing building. Back to the truck, the only bright spot in forever, to wait for whatever.

Tony took the pebbles off the hood and climbed in to the cab. He rolled his windbreaker behind his neck, put his Cedar Gulch Police Department baseball cap over his eyes and rolled the seat back to take a nap. "Someone'll come along. Too cold to do anything else."

I dug through the junk in the truck bed and found an air mattress pump. I hopped down, and with numb and trembling fingers managed to affix it to the air valve on the tire. If I held it in place and pushed on the bladder with my knee I made progress and my teeth didn't chatter as much.

Tony rolled down the window. "Knock it off, Cassie.

You're wasting your energy. Get back in the car before you freeze to death."

I kept pumping until I built up a sweat. Between pants I hollered, "This is why we have men, Tony." He snorted and rolled up the window.

The sun was halfway behind the mountain when Tony jumped from the car and dislodged all my hard work. "Told ya." He pointed to a pale cloud of dust in the distance. "Someone's coming."

A man drove up in a battered green Chevy truck towing a horse trailer. He peered at us as he slowed down and cranked on the emergency brake before he lumbered out of the cab and limped toward us.

"Look to me like you need some help." He was huge, with a wide middle section that tapered at either end. His face rolled like a sand dune covered with purple bruises fading to yellow. He sported a hedgehog hairdo, a European-something accent, a black patch over his left eye, and a Homo National Forest baseball cap. I looked but didn't ask.

He told me anyway. "It's in honor of when queers come out to the desert to go to hot springs." He grinned and revealed teeth that looked as though they'd been used to open beer bottles. "Bruno's the name." His handshake was sandpaper and sweat, and he smelled of garlic and manure.

"Not Bruno Seronello?"

"The same, young lady. And I know you. We been expecting you to come. You're little doctor gal who got me out of jam with skinheads. I am obliged greatly but we talk later. Go on. Into truck." He motioned dramatically with his hands and wobbled over to help Tony load the blownout tires into the back of the truck.

Tony made me sit between the two of them. Bruno turned the heater on high and the three of us choked on gasoline fumes for the next forty miles. The two men insisted on making conversation over my head, adding entirely unnecessary hot air to the stuffy atmosphere. I interrupted to comment on how quickly he'd healed from the beating.

"Indian medicine," he said. "Winema is medicine woman. You meet her and see." Bruno chattered on as though we were the first humans he'd seen in a year. "Only two flats? Guy last week had four. Those city tires get ate up on the shale. Yeah, pickin' up some deliveries. If you hadn't broke down you may have missed me. Grocery truck broke down—only vehicle I got running just now is truck and horse trailer." He must have noticed my jaw drop because a look of concern furrowed his brow. "Now you no worry. I hosed horse shit out of trailer before I put in deliveries."

We drove across the Nevada border and forty minutes later landed in a concrete-block town glimmering the palest pink in the fading sun. Bandon. It should have been called Abandon for all that was there, or maybe Bruno. Everything in the place was named Bruno's something or other. Bruno's Bar, Bruno's Cafe, Bruno's Grill, Bruno's Casino, Bruno's Country Club, and Bruno's Gas Station. Bruno dropped us off at the bar, a dark place with peeling wood-grain linoleum floors, worn red bar stools, and a purple starburst Formica counter with strategically placed divots worn from weary elbows tippling beer. He hollered to someone in the back to unload the horse trailer and then tended to his only two customers.

I called Maria to tell her to look in on Aunt Liz and tell her we were fine. When I returned to the bar I opened my mouth to order white wine, but Tony was faster and wiser. "She'll have a tomato juice." Bruno opened a can, warm from the heat of the sizzling woodstove. He scrutinized the gun in Tony's shoulder holster with the eye that didn't have a patch on it.

Tony asked, "You want me to take the firearm off?"

"Nah, it been worn more than shot." He handed Tony another beer. "These from the house. On me for payback for little gal." He rolled his eye in my direction.

The place smelled of gin and stale sweat. I was glad my blouse was hand wash, not dry-clean only. As soon as I was paid from this job, I promised myself, I'd take a trip to San Francisco to shop at a department store that carried more than Western wear and flannel.

Dinner at Bruno's Cafe was also on the house. Tony buried his head in the plate of homemade meat ravioli topped with a red grease sauce. For a guy whose idea of haute cuisine is a strata of hamburger, Limburger cheese, and Tater Tots, he was in heaven. I picked apart the ravioli and wondered what kind of meat, other than jackrabbit, lived out here. Or, to be more accurate, died out here and from what cause.

Bruno bounced out to pour more of his homemade red wine into our tumblers. His face fell when he saw my plate. "You no like it? I made it myself. Grandmother Seronello's recipe handed down in family."

"Oh, it's very good. I'm just a slow eater."

Tony looked up at me with an astounded expression, and I plunged in wondering just how bad ravioli could taste on the way back up.

After dinner, Bruno joined us for a glass of his wine. "You stay here tonight, my guests in my country club, then we fix tires in morning and get you on your way."

"We came here to talk to Homer's grandmother. Can you take us to her?" I asked.

"She on Pit River Indian Reservation. Not so easy to get there but I can take you because you special friend of mine. But we get tires fixed first." He patted my hand, and tipped his plastic tumbler toward mine.

"Bruno, can I ask you about the night I found you in the

road? Who were those people who attacked you, and why did they want to hurt you?"

"We talk later about it. You had hard day, and now you rest."

I opened my mouth to say more, but Bruno poured some more wine and chattered on about a couple of women who came to his country club and shared a room, setting the entire town of forty-two awash with rumor about their sexual orientation.

Bruno's Country Club was a one-story concrete block tunnel with a flaking composition roof and green metal windows, most of which had been painted shut. Bruno led us to our "suite," which was smack in the middle. No towel rack, no toilet paper holder, green astroturf carpet for what I assumed was easy cleanup with a fire hose, and a petrified mattress. Fortunately I've never been afraid of spiders and lizards. Tony stripped to his shorts, and climbed into bed. I folded the bedspread in half lengthwise, and positioned myself on the underside of it, in my clothes. I hoped the gas wall heater wouldn't asphyxiate us in our sleep.

In the morning we walked to the café where we feasted on crispy fried eggs and sausage done in enough grease to fill a wine vat. The morning waitress was kind enough to find me an antacid before we headed over to Bruno's garage to find the tow truck. Bruno apparently had been inspired to try a different form of architecture—the gas station was variegated tin propped up by sagging two-by-fours.

A body rolled out from under the flatbed truck. Bruno's belly made a scratching sound as it rubbed against the metal of the undercarriage. He looked at Tony from a supine position, winked at me, and spoke out of the side of his mouth. "Sam. They here." I smiled graciously to acknowledge his third wink, or was it his fourth?

I jumped at the automatic weapon blast of auto repair

machinery. A pair of greasy Levis beckoned us from the corner. Sam turned around. Slivers of blue eyeballs embedded in a pudgy face spied me and looked up and down my five-foot-two-inch frame. "Howdy. I'm Samantha." She spat a wad of chew into a coffee tin on the floor, and wiped her chin with her forearm. She blushed. "Sorry," she said, and rubbed her greasy palm on her jeans. "Forgets my manners sometimes with city folk." She shook Tony's hand and nodded toward the tires. "They're shredded. Can't fix 'em so I gotta go to Reno to get some more. We don't got any in stock."

Bruno pointed me to his truck. "Get in the truck and we go now to talk to Homer's grandmother."

Fourteen

"Fandango Pass was major route for emigrants coming to California in wagon trains." Bruno was driving west over the Warner Mountain Range that separates northern California from Nevada. We escaped the ashen desert and began our descent into a valley green with pine trees. Ahead, Goose Lake shimmered in the midmorning sun. Beyond the shallow lake was the unexpected sight of Mount Shasta floating above the horizon.

A short distance past the causeway over the shallow lake, we ascended rimrock to a view in every direction. We rumbled down a dirt road to a compound consisting of aged trailers and a rambling planked wood and mud shack with a rusted tin roof.

"She live in there." He pointed to the shack.

The property was overrun with animals. Donkeys, horses, goats, sheep, rabbits in hutches, doves in cages, dogs of no known breed, and dozens of cats of all colors and tail lengths announced our arrival with various whinnies, barks, mews, bleats, and flutters.

"Oh, my God." I pointed at a black bear that ran out from behind the shack.

"She ain't gone to hibernate yet," explained Bruno. "She get food here." The bear ran across the yard into the trees.

Bruno knocked on the splintered frame and opened the door. "Bruno here," he called out. We followed him in. The structure was a maze of rooms that appeared to have been built as necessity demanded and connected with whatever means available.

We entered the low-ceilinged kitchen and dodged a jumble of implements, some old and some new, and some that appeared to be more appropriate to a barn. Spices and herbs littered the steel countertops and dozens of dried plants hung from the rough-hewn beams and window frames. Half the floor was covered with scaling avocado-green linoleum under reed mats, the other half grease-stained rust-colored peel-and-stick carpet tiles. The gray plank walls looked as though they had been salvaged from a defunct barn. A cast iron woodburning stove served as the range and oven and a forties-era porcelain refrigerator was jammed into a corner next to a pile of burlap bags. I thought that if the occupants really wanted to keep something cold they probably set it outside.

A handsome Native American woman walked gracefully from the back of the house into the living area. She was plump, with round cheeks and pretty black eyes. If I squinted I could see a resemblance to Homer in her jaw and nose. She was dressed in a purple velvet jacket, a long black woolen skirt, and brown plastic cowboy boots molded to look like carved leather. Her hands and wrists were delicate and covered with finely cut silver rings and bracelets heavy with turquoise, coral, and azurite. She wore a squash blossom necklace that was easily worth more than my Volkswagen. When she saw me look at her jewelry she commented, "From a Dineh friend of mine—a Navajo silversmith from near Winslow."

"Arizona?" I asked. "I lived there. Isn't that near where Homer went to school?"

She looked at me suspiciously and turned to Bruno. "What brings you today? I thought you said Saturday."

"This is the young lady and her friend. The one who ran off the bad ones and took me to the hospital." He stepped aside to give her a clear view of me. "And this is Winema Johnson, grandmother to Homer."

She walked over to me and looked intensely into my eyes, then took my hand and held it lightly. She smelled of earth and spice and her skin was brown and smooth. She wore tiny coral earrings, and a small tattoo of an animal adorned her neck. "You did us a great good thing. I have sent you magic and the spirits brought you here for me to thank you."

"I came here to help your grandson Homer. I'm evaluating him for the court." I felt suddenly awkward. I didn't know if she'd heard about the murder charge.

She looked at me for a long time, appraising me, then placed her hand above my chest. "You seem to have a good heart. I believe you do want to help Homer. And I do know he's been arrested again, this time for murder."

I raised my eyebrows in Tony's direction, and he picked up my cue.

He looked at Bruno. "What say you show me the spread?" They left through the kitchen door.

Winema ushered me down concrete steps to the living room. "This was a winter house of my people. I've added on to it over the years."

The walls and ceiling were made of logs packed with mud. Plank shelves lined the walls, crammed with books, ceramic jars, and cattail baskets with geometric designs. Above the exterior doorway, the bottoms of glass bottles had been laid in the mud. Red, cobalt, and green rays of light poured over the fine geometric designs on Two Gray Hills and Yei Dancers Navajo rugs scattered on the sunken earthen floor.

I looked through the window. "You have a beautiful view of Mount Shasta."

"It is sacred to my people. The Modoc believe that the Great Spirit made Mount Shasta from snow he pushed down from the sky. He made a home there and the fire and smoke that came from the vent were from the fireplace he made to warm his family."

A finely carved European corner cupboard held tiny animal fetishes made of semi-precious stones and seashells. I picked up a bear fetish carved of jade with a turquoise, mother-of-pearl, and red coral arrow strapped to its back. "We saw a bear outside, near the house."

"The bears are our ancestors and come to us to cure disease and ensure long life," she explained. She took the fetish from me and held it in her palm. "When he created the earth, the Great Spirit made bears the masters over all. His daughter married the son of a bear who saved her from a storm. Their children were different from spirits or bears—they were the first humans. The Great Spirit was angered that they made a new race and made the bears walk on all four feet unless they are fighting. Only then do they stand on two."

She led me through a low passageway into the dining area. A large board supported on three wooden sawhorses dominated the room. A doorknob-sized hole centered on one side revealed the original purpose of the oak table. Five mismatched chairs were scattered around the room and the floor underneath was made of pitted wooden strips—probably pine or fir—painted ocher. The walls were unpainted gray cinderblock and the window was a large sheet of Plexiglas affixed to the metal window frame with several layers of duct tape. In the corner, a battered brass pot of simmering water rattled on an antique porcelain and chrome wood-burning stove; orange and blue flames flickered behind the mica door. The scent of burning fir and leaves was not at all unpleasant.

Winema pulled out a metal chair and motioned for me to

sit in a pressed back oak one. "What do you want to know about my grandson?"

I had many questions, the foremost in my mind being how on earth he got hooked up with neo-Nazis, but I had the feeling I needed to work up to that one. "Tell me about his family—his mother and father. I know his mother is dead."

She bowed her head and remained silent until I feared I had offended her in some way and my opportunity was lost. Finally she spoke. "That was a very sad time for all of us. How does speaking of the dead help you?"

I felt like a voyeur prying open her soul. "The court will want to know his history, and why he got into trouble. I have to know as much information as possible to tell the judge so he'll believe Homer is telling the truth that he didn't mean to kidnap the man Anerd Woods, much less kill him."

"Would it not be enough if I told you he is a good boy and tells the truth?"

"Unfortunately not."

"Why would it not? The Modoc do not tolerate a liar." She looked so deeply into my eyes I felt the back of my head buzz.

How could I explain the vagaries of the legal system to her? "The judge and the jury will want to know why Homer acted as he did. If they don't understand what kind of boy he is, they will believe that he is lying and that he kidnapped and murdered Anerd Woods. I can't explain his personality unless I know more about him."

She bent her head again and was silent. At last she spoke softly. "It gives power to the evil spirits no matter what I say. My family, my tribe, has suffered so many broken trusts, and to say more about the things that have wounded Homer will make him vulnerable to being hurt again."

I wanted to tell her she could trust me, but the words would have sounded hollow. "I know it's a paradox. To help him we have to hurt him more. I can't explain it, all I know is that it's the only way to keep him from going to prison."

"There is no punishment the white man can give that will please the Great Spirit. Homer will find his power only through the traditions of the native people." She shrugged. "It's all in the past, and should be laid to rest. The people can't hold on to hatred and still be at one with the earth. But if you say so, I guess it will be so. Tell me what you need to know to help my grandson."

"Let's start with his mother." My voice cracked, and I was surprised at the emotion I felt.

"Esther. She was a beautiful young woman. A Wintu from south of here. She lived with her family on the Rancheria, her mother and father were good and loving parents. They didn't drink or gamble and they struggled to raise cattle on the barren land. But she was restless, and wanted to leave her home like so many of our children. They don't respect the old ways because we have not taught them.

"She met my son, Charley, when she was in high school and he had started at the junior college. He was one of the few of our young to stay in white man's school. They fell in love and she became pregnant. They dropped out of school, and married. She was fifteen and Charley had just turned nineteen when she gave birth to Homer. She died in an auto accident." She looked as though she wanted to say more, but shrugged and was silent.

"What about Homer's father? Charley?"

"He was named for an ally of my ancestor, Captain Jack, who fought against the white man's army to protect our homeland in Modoc." She reached over to the table by her chair and picked up a hand-carved pipe and a pouch of tobacco. She pressed a pinch of tobacco into the bowl, and made great ceremony of lighting a match, setting it to the tobacco, and inhaling deeply. Her lips smacked with effort.

"My ancestor, Kientenpoos, was given the name Captain

Jack by a white friend because of his resemblence to a miner by that name. Captain Jack was a peaceful man until the whites took our land without a treaty, and sent us to live with our enemies, the Klamath, who took our timber and fish and seeds. Captain Jack refused to stay there and brought the Modoc back to Tule Lake. The army attacked and the Modoc fled to the Land of Burnt-Out Fires that you call the Lava Beds to live in hiding. Finally, the army sent General Canby to talk the people into giving up. But because they had been betrayed many times before, a renegade Modoc band led by Hooker Jim forced Captain Jack to kill Canby. The army came again and attacked. For two years, the Modoc fought bravely, but when Captain Jack saw the women and children dying of starvation and white man's bullets he surrendered. Hooker Jim and his band betrayed Jack to save themselves. Boston Charley was loyal. He and Captain Jack went to trial without a lawyer or an interpreter. They watched the building of the gallows outside the stockade."

She puffed on her pipe and exhaled. "They knew their fate before the verdict. In violation of ancient Modoc taboos, their heads were cut off and sent to the Army Medical Museum in Washington, D.C. Captain Jack's body was dug from his grave and his head pickled. It was sent to the East as a carnival attraction for an admission of ten cents."

She stood abruptly and walked toward the kitchen. "Would you like some coffee or tea?"

"Um, tea please." I took a deep breath and followed her into the kitchen. "Winema, that's a tragic story."

She pulled teabags from a pine needle basket and placed them into two chipped pottery mugs. She went to the woodstove, scooped boiling water from the pot into the mugs, and handed me one before we returned to the dining area.

She sat across from me at the table so her back was to the window and her face partially obscured by the backlighting.

When she looked at me her eyes glistened. "In the aftermath, the spirit of my people was killed. They were forced into boxcars on a train and sent into exile as political prisoners to Oklahoma, a place they did not know. Many of them died of starvation. The traitors to Captain Jack were set free."

She set her cup on a pine needle coaster and wiped up a drop of spilled water with her finger. "What makes you think my grandson will be any more successful at fighting the laws of the whites?"

At that moment I couldn't bear to look at her. I swirled the tea leaves in the bottom of my cup. When I could speak, I said, "Tell me more about Charley."

"My son Charley has chosen his own path. He is torn between the native traditions and the white man's ways. He has not honored the spirits. The result is a fracture in his soul. He is loving and generous, but dangerous and uncontrollable with drink." She stuffed more tobacco into the pipe and relit it. "Neither Homer nor I have seen Charley in years."

"So you've taken the responsibility for Homer?"

"Who else could?"

"Did you grow up in Modoc County?"

She took a puff and held it for a moment before exhaling. "When I was five the BIA took me from my mother and father to send me to the government boarding school. They shaved our heads and made us wear white man's clothing. They beat us with a belt for speaking our native tongue. They told us that we could take one of two paths. The first path was toward the heavens, and lined with dollar bills. The second path was toward the earth, and ended in hell. This was crazy to us because the earth nourished our families.

"Day by day they stole my spirit. When they finished, did I want to be an Indian? I forgot my parents and what my people used to be. In my mind I saw the pictures of frightening-looking Indians on the warpath, killing and scalping innocents. Why would I want to be like them? When I was fifteen, I became so lonely for my family that I ran away. I was caught by the police and punished, but I ran away again.

"I met Samuel Perelson at a train station. He was a Jew. He had lost his family in a concentration camp. I'd lost my soul to the white man. The difference between us was that Samuel hated the Germans for what they did, but I hated myself for who I was."

Her head fell to her chest and for a moment I thought she'd fallen asleep. When she lifted her head again, she sounded drained. "Samuel took care of me, and we eventually married." She was quiet again while she sipped her tea. When she was done with it, she set down the cup and continued.

"When Charley was a boy we sent him to private school back east. I didn't realize the value of my people until I visited Captain Jack's stronghold, and stood at the railroad where my family was shipped off to an unknown place. By then, it was too late to teach my son his birthright.

"My husband, Samuel, died and left us with money. But what do I need that money will buy? The path I have chosen is to live on my ancestors' land and to honor their traditions. I tried to teach them to Homer but he is confused and does not value his heritage." Her eyes grew blacker. "Without a vision, Homer will be lost to the traditional ways."

I didn't point out that Homer wasn't doing so great with the white ways either. I looked up at her. "How did he get mixed up with the skinheads?"

"When a young man loses his heritage and ignores the spirits, he opens himself to evil spirits." She paused and nodded to my cup.

"No thanks. I'm fine."

"I am an old and tired woman. I have spoken enough for

today. If you cannot help my grandson, then his fate will be guided by the spirits."

She rose from her chair and took her cup into the kitchen. I followed her out the door. There were myriad questions I had yet to ask but she was a private woman and I would need time that I didn't have. Homer's trial was approaching rapidly and I was nowhere near ready to complete my report.

"One more question," I pushed. "Why do you and Homer go by the name of Johnson and not your husband's name?"

"After Samuel died, I called myself Johnson to honor the name my ancestors took when they were taken to Oklahoma. I did not do it to disrespect my husband, but to honor my people."

"What about Homer?"

"That I don't know except that he didn't call himself Perelson after he came home from the Arizona school."

"This question will be the last, I promise. Why did Homer go to the private school in Arizona?"

"It was the wish of his father that he go to a white school to lose the traditional native ways. I did not agree." She turned away from me and walked toward an Airstream travel trailer.

Bruno and Tony stood by the trailer having a chew. Winema and I walked toward them and were nudged by an Appaloosa mare who pulled back her lip and shook her head at Winema. The woman pulled a carrot out of her pocket and held it out for the horse. Winema stepped up into the trailer and the mare followed, sticking her head through the open window and nickering at her mistress for another carrot. Several chickens ran erratically out of the trailer, clucking and dodging the legs of human and horse. She motioned for me to come to the door. The trailer held a bed covered with a woven woolen blanket, a table with playing cards and two glasses on it, and a propane heater. Women's underclothing and men's woolen socks hung from a clothesline strung between the walls.

"This is where I sleep," she said. The only decoration on the wall was a grass dress richly covered with beads and shells. Winema placed her hand on it and without looking at me said, "My grandmother's wedding dress."

"Thank you for your time, Mrs. Johnson." I tried to catch her eye before she stepped out of the trailer but her attention was elsewhere. "I'll do the best I can to help Homer."

"Someday I may add a bedroom to the house. Maybe if Homer comes home." She walked to her shack followed by various creatures looking for a handout.

I followed. "Do you want him to come home?"

"He must first go to the place of the spirits on the mountain for his quest." She saw my puzzled look and continued. "Homer has been troubled since the time of his mother's death. He cannot know his true power until he is healed by the spirits."

"His true power?"

"I believe he is extraordinary. If he realized his spirit power, he could be a shaman."

She entered the shack and closed the door behind her, leaving me staring at old wood bleached by the sun and rusty hinges.

Fifteen

"Was Homer a good child?" On the way back to Bandon, I decided to question Bruno.

"He was nice boy until his mother died."

"Anerd said that Homer had a motive to hurt him because you and Anerd had bad blood. What do you think?" I persisted.

Before he spoke, Bruno whistled a few bars of a country-western tune I couldn't identify. "That old Anerd don't know nothing about it. Homer didn't want to hurt him. Anerd hang with skinheads, he deserve what he gets."

"What do you know about the white supremacists? Why did they beat you up?" I asked.

Tony nudged me and when I looked at him, his expression was incredulous. I gave him a mind your own business glare, and turned back to Bruno.

"I don't think it was them that did it." Bruno drummed his fingers on the steering wheel. "I think it was just some punks. You know, nottin' personal."

I felt a little wounded that I had saved his life, and all he gave me for it was an obvious lie. "Do you know about the skinheads around here?"

"Yeah, I know a little bit."

"What can you tell me?" I stomped on Tony's foot with my boot heel, and he removed his elbow from my ribs.

"Not much to tell," Bruno said. "They're around and make a fuss now and again. They don't like people who are different than them." He looked out the window and began whistling energetically.

I persevered. "I'd really like to know more, because Homer is involved with them."

The old man reached across me to the glove compartment and pulled out a can of chew. He drove the truck with his knee while he packed a good-sized wad behind his lower lip. I glanced over to Tony, who rolled his eyes and mouthed at me, "Knock it off."

Bruno rolled the chew around in his lip, and reached past me to offer the can to Tony. I curled my upper lip in disgust, But Tony took a large pinch and tucked it into his cheek, his eyes on me defiantly the whole time.

The scent of mint-flavored tobacco enhanced the bouquet of male sweat, and diesel. I refused to be intimidated. "So, are there a lot of skinheads around here?"

The chew seemed to give Bruno courage, and he finally began to talk. "Some up here. More around Trinity County. They live up there in the woods and mountains and never meet any other kinds of peoples so they hate them all. They say they're oppressed," he chortled. "They're paranoid is all. They say that other peoples take away their living and their land. It gives them excuse to persecute those peoples they hate and then they don't have to admit that they can't even figure out how to pour piss out of a boot if the directions was on the bottom." He rolled down the window, turned his head back, and spit forcefully.

"Kind of like what greedy white people did to Indians. They call them savages, then stealed their land and killed their buffalos to wipe them out, then sent the childrens to schools to make them forget they was ever Indian. That way the white man can say they do good for Indians so they don't have to admit that they were to blame for murdering them. They say, 'Kill the Indian and save the man.' "

The words echoed those of Verlan: "Kill the Jew and save America."

Bruno shrugged. "Happens over and over to peoples all over the world. Happened in second war with Hitler and then with Stalin and Mao after. Happens now, too."

I guessed at Bruno's age. "Were you in World War II?"

"I was there." His voice was barely a whisper.

"So was my great-uncle, Chester. And he was never the same afterward even though he was a hero and saved many people. I never could understand why he felt so guilty. Maybe because he survived?" The words tumbled out before I could think how different Bruno's experience could have been from Uncle Chester's.

He answered immediately. "Maybe he blame himself for being afraid." He spit the wad of chew out the window, then swallowed hard.

After a few moments of silence I asked, "Given what happened to his grandmother and her family, why do you think Homer is involved with these people?"

"I don't know," Bruno said with a finality that told me the conversation was over.

Tony's truck had new all-terrain tires when we reached Bandon. Sam made out the bill while I thanked Bruno for his hospitality.

Thirty seconds out of Bandon, Tony said, "I hope you're satisfied."

"About what?"

"Bugging Bruno half to death."

"Bugging him?" I asked.

"Maybe you should leave the interrogation to cops. We've been trained for it."

"And I haven't been trained?"

"Look, Cassie, I don't think you want to alienate these people."

"You think I alienated them?"

"Well, not totally. But . . ."

I took a deep breath. "I am busting my butt on this case and no one seems to want to give me a straight answer. Homer's trial starts next week and I am still in the dark about whether he's a good guy gone astray or if he's really malevolent. Or just darn dumb. I go one way, then the next—at first I didn't like him, then after talking to Sally I wasn't sure Homer was even involved with Anerd's kidnapping at all, much less his supposed murder, and now I'm halfway between feeling sorry for him and wondering what his family is trying to hide. I have to present my evaluation to the court in five days. If I can't figure this out I might as well go back to waiting tables in a casino because my professional reputation will be in the toilet. And you have the nerve to tell me to leave the questions to the cops?" I took another breath, and Tony interrupted.

"I was just trying to help. . . ."

"Well that is not the type of help I need."

"What do you need?" He was maddingly calm.

"I need information, and something that makes sense. And I need to eat something. I'm starving." I rubbed my forehead. "Sorry, I'm just frustrated. And after all you've done, I shouldn't take it out on you."

He grinned. "Wow. That's almost an apology. How about I fix you dinner at my place?"

"As long as it's not ravioli. And if you say one word about PMS, I'll shoot you with your own gun."

"Believe me, I wouldn't think of it."

After a moment I said, "Tony, you're an angel to put up with me."

"I know," was all he said.

Sixteen

We reached Cedar Gulch well after dark. Auntie Liz's cottage was dark and I assumed she was in bed. Tony pulled into his driveway, and as I got out of the truck, Maria came running down the front porch stairs.

"Liz is with me," she called out.

"Is she okay?" A pang of anxiety clutched at my chest. "Is it her heart?"

"She's fine and after what she went through this afternoon, I think her heart is stronger than mine."

"What happened?" I ran toward the front door of the bungalow.

"She's sleeping now so don't wake her." Maria grabbed my arm to slow me down.

"What happened?" I insisted.

"She had some visitors while I was at work. She called 911 and as soon as I heard the address I threw my headset to the call-taker and rushed home."

"What visitors?" I pulled away, and had my hand on the screen door before she could answer.

Maria spoke to the back of my head. "She called them hoodlums. They sounded like skinheads to me."

"What?" I turned around slowly, and shuddered.

"They didn't exactly introduce themselves to her."

"Did they catch them?"

Maria shook her head. "By the time everyone got here, she'd chased them off."

I pushed open the door and ran into Maria's bedroom. No Aunt Liz. I plowed into Tony in the hall, and pushed him into the wall to get to his bedroom. Aunt Liz lay on his bed snoring softly, and clutching the stuffed bear given to her by Uncle Chester on their thirtieth wedding anniversary. The bear was dressed in a leather flight jacket, and cap with a USAF insignia on it. When I saw her I choked, halfway between a sob and a giggle.

I backed out of the room and gently shut the door. Tony put his arm around me, and led me back into the living room.

Maria handed me a glass of wine. "I put her in Tony's room because I figured you'd want him to stay with you tonight, at least until they can find these guys."

"What happened?" I asked.

"Apparently she was feeling well enough to cook some supper and while she was heating some soup she heard someone at the door. She answered it, and three men stood on the porch. As soon as she opened the door they were in. They pushed her around a bit, and tore up your office. She asked them what they wanted, but they didn't say. Drugs maybe."

"Drugs?"

"Medications. Lots of people figure if you're a doctor you must have them in the office. Anyway they got belligerent, she stood up to them, and they threatened her. It all ended when she fell on the floor, and pretended to have a heart attack. They ran off, bless their little black hearts, without even calling an ambulance. She called, and half the police department was here within two minutes."

"Oh, my God." I trembled down to my fingertips. "I knew

this would happen. I should never have put my office in her house."

"No sense in second-guessing yourself. It could have been worse." Maria motioned to refill my glass, but I refused.

"I need food and sleep, if that's possible. I have to be able to think clearly and it's tough enough already." I started to head home.

Tony hollered at me to wait up. He grabbed his toothbrush and another clip for his gun, and we walked to my house. The door to my office had been kicked open, leaving the jamb shattered. Papers were strewn over the floor and drawers emptied onto the rug. My computer was on, but the file on Homer was intact and the backup disc was in the wooden cigar box on the top shelf of the tea cart I use as a computer table.

"Looks like Auntie Liz scared them off with the fake heart attack before they got into it," I said.

We straightened up the office and waiting room. Tony parked me at the table, and rummaged through the kitchen until he found the makings of macaroni and cheese. He poured me another glass of wine while he waited for the water to boil, grated cheese and chopped ham while the noodles cooked.

"We need a green vegetable," I instructed.

"Done." He dug through the freezer until he found a bag of peas that he dumped into a pot.

After we ate, Tony said, "I'll take your bed, you sleep upstairs in Liz's bed."

"No way. I'm not getting trapped upstairs if they come back. I'm staying downstairs with you." I followed him back to my bedroom.

Tony lay his jacket over the ladder back chair next to my writing desk. "It's going to be kind of cramped in the daybed." He set his gun on the bedside table and pulled his T-shirt over his head, then sat on the bed and lifted a foot for me to pull off his boot. "I think I deserve a foot rub."

"Think so?" I giggled and swatted at his foot.

"I drove you all over the north state for two days, listened to you bitch at me, and then fixed you dinner. You owe me."

"You're whining." I sat on the floor and pulled his boots and socks. "And your feet stink."

"And now I'm risking my life, *again*, to keep you safe from the bad guys."

"Okay. But only if it will keep you quiet." I dug in. His feet were built like the rest of his body, square and hard.

Tony grunted, and leaned back on the bed with his eyes closed. "Anytime you need a driver just let me know. The foot rubs are worth it."

"I bet Stephanie doesn't do this." I popped the knuckle of his big toe.

"She has other talents." He grinned without opening his eyes and threw the pillow in my direction. "But tonight I'll settle for this."

Having no justification for snapping his Achilles tendon, I kept on massaging. By the time I finished with the other foot he was purring.

I went into the bathroom to put on my nightgown and brush my teeth. When I came back to the bedroom Tony's jeans lay on the floor and he was under the covers. His eyes looked hazel in the amber light and the firm angles of his body pressed against the delicate scrolls of the daybed. The warm rush in my stomach made me reconsider going upstairs, but he opened up the covers and invited me in.

I snuggled next to him for the comfort, and because there was no room to do anything else. He wrapped his arm around me, and I could feel his heart beating against my shoulder blade.

"Don't get too cozy now," I warned him. I didn't sound as stern as I would have liked.

"Just keeping you from falling out of bed." He nuzzled his face into my neck and held me tighter.

We fell asleep in the spoon position. When I awoke in the middle of the night, I didn't take his hand off my breast.

I awoke before dawn with the pressure of Tony's morning erection hard against my thigh. I hopped out of bed before my good sense failed me, wrapped myself in an old chenille bathrobe, then called Richard Peck to tell him about my altercation with Troutman and my visit to Homer's grandmother.

Richard's voice was tight and low. "If this case was looking dismal before, sit down. I have even more bad news," he said. "Jury selection starts tomorrow and rumor is that Verlan is trying to cop a plea for reduced charges by claiming that Homer was the ringleader in Anerd's kidnapping. Get to the Jackpot jail as soon as you can. There's no way Homer is getting out on bail again."

The thought of driving back up the hill to Jackpot made my stomach churn. "How much time do I have?"

"I would have liked your report last week. It's probably only two days before we start with witnesses, and I don't have a good strategy yet. Homer's still not talking much to me or my investigator. Do you think we can try a diminished capacity plea? I'm wondering about his ability to assist in his own defense if he can't even—"

"Not even close, Richard. Sorry. Homer's a bright enough boy, and he's grounded in reality at least in a legal sense. The closest I can get is that he's afraid of what might happen if he tells the truth."

"That's hardly going to fly in front of a Trinity County jury."

"Sorry, I forgot. No one in Trinity County admits fear of anything except running out of beer or ammunition or suffering marijuana crop failure." I looked at my schedule book and remembered it was Sunday. "Give me an hour—I just got up, and I'll see him at ten. Can you arrange it?"

"No problem. And after you return from interviewing him maybe we could go out to—"

Tony's deep voice interrupted. "You want tea, love?" It was an endearment he called his sister and my aunt and for all I knew every woman in his life. I covered the receiver and answered yes, then turned my attention back to Richard. "What were you going to say?"

"Never mind. Sounds as though you're busy. I'll arrange for you to be at the jail at ten. Call me when you finish talking with Homer." The tone of his voice had cooled.

"I'll do my best to get through to him." As I said it, I knew my best wasn't good enough to steer Homer off self-destruct.

I showered and dressed in jeans, a sweatshirt, and Laredo ropers. The weather was miserable and I was tired of trudging through the snow in Jackpot in high heels. In the kitchen, I could hear drawers slamming and pans clanging as Tony cleaned up.

We ran next door and greeted Auntie Liz, who sat at Maria's kitchen table bundled in a flannel robe and a pair of Tony's woolen socks. Maria was working up a sweat starting a fire in the woodstove, and trying to cook Liz's breakfast at the same time. I took over stirring the oatmeal while Tony went to get another load of cedar logs.

"I want you to stay here today, Auntie Liz. I have to go up to Jackpot again to interview my client. I'll definitely be back tonight."

She muttered through her tea, but didn't protest as I had expected. A white-hot light filled the room, and a half second later a thunderclap shook the house.

"Dang." I looked out the window to see a sheet of rain obscure everything more than twenty feet away. A bolt of lightning streaked across the blackened sky and hit a black oak on a knoll above the house. I heard a loud crack and watched the tree split in two. One half hovered in the air then slowly twisted to the ground. The thunder that followed was loud enough to make my ears ring. "Guess I'll be late. I hope this passes quickly."

Tony joined me by the kitchen sink. "You're not taking the bug in this. You'll be washed right off the mountain." He handed me the keys to his truck. "Take a bag in case you get stuck up there. I'd go along, but I'm covering for a buddy this afternoon and can't get out of it. Are you sure you can't put this off?"

I shook my head. "Trial starts Tuesday. Maybe I'll just stay up there until I get the information I need from Homer." I looked toward Maria.

She nodded. "Don't worry. I'll take care of Liz until you get back." She put her arm around my great-aunt's shoulder and squeezed. "We'll keep her over here and she'll be just fine, won't you, Liz?"

Auntie Liz looked up and for the first time I saw that her eyes were glazed and unfocused. I sucked in my breath. "Are you okay, Auntie Liz?"

She looked at me blankly.

Maria tousled Liz's hair. "She's just a bit tired. Sometimes old folks take a while to recover from a shock. Those bad guys gave her a bit of a fright, that's all." Her voice was calm and comforting, but her eyes were dark with worry. "You go on, Cassie. You need to finish this evaluation." She must have seen the mist in my eyes, because she reached over and squeezed my chin between her thumb and forefinger. "You don't have the luxury of feeling guilty right now, so get going."

I kissed Auntie Liz good-bye, and went back to my house

to pack my red plaid overnight bag in case I got stuck in Jackpot. I went upstairs to Liz's bedroom and emptied the buckets we'd positioned under the leaks in the roof. The pillow on the window seat was soaked. I picked it up and ran to the bathroom to throw it in the tub, then took a towel and wiped down the soggy paneling.

I moved the bedside table away from the window and put Great-uncle Chester's picture in a drawer underneath some linens.

"Cassie, are you in here?" Tony called out.

I heard his footsteps on the stairs.

"I'm up here. In Auntie Liz's room."

"What are you doing? Shouldn't you be on your way?"

"I just came up to empty the buckets and protect her pictures from the rain."

He offered me a hand to help me up, and looked around the room. "Boy, this place is a mess, but there's nothing much we can do about it now. Come on, the weather's cleared for the moment, and you need to get going."

Tony carried my bag and briefcase to the truck, and I grabbed a pillow off the sofa in the television room.

"I filled up the Red Beast's tank," he said.

"Thanks." I climbed in, thankful I wasn't wearing my beleaguered blue suit. "You're my best buddy."

He helped me pull the seat all the way forward, then stuffed the pillow behind my back so I could reach the pedals. "Drive carefully. If you need to put it in four-wheel drive, remember to put it in reverse first. Give a call when you know when you're coming back. We'll watch Liz." He shut the door, and waved as I backed out of the driveway.

The first twenty miles to Jackpot were uneventful but when I began to climb through the switchbacks the weather turned nasty. Within a few minutes the rain turned to slush, then to snow. A thick blanket of white covered the trees and I tried to admire the beauty between fits of anxiety. A snowplow came along the other way and the driver drew his finger across his throat, which I took to mean that the road conditions were going to get worse. He pushed a ridge of rocks and ice into my lane. I veered to avoid it, and the truck fishtailed across the slick pavement. I got control just before I slid off the edge. Time to go into four-wheel drive, but where? There hadn't been a shoulder to the road in ten miles, and there wouldn't be until I reached Hatchet Summit in another fifteen.

I slowed the truck to a crawl and looked in the rearview mirror, which revealed only a white cloud of snowflakes. I had to take the chance or risk plummeting over the side.

I skidded the truck into the center of the road so at least two wheels would get traction on the plowed part, pushed the four-wheel drive lever, and threw the truck into reverse. I braked as the transmission caught, congratulated myself for only slightly grinding the gears and not bumping into anyone, then got back into first and pulled as far to the right as I could. A logging truck barrelled down the highway toward me a half second later, skidded around the curve, and blasted his horn at me.

I waved, and returned his scowl with a smile.

By the time I reached the summit the snow was thick enough to conceal the trees at the edge of the road. I had the feeling that I wasn't going home that night.

Seventeen

The truck rumbled into Jackpot just after noon. I found a parking place near the clock tower and wedged the Red Beast between a Volvo and an aging Cadillac with tail fins and a flat tire. Deputy Martin was on duty again. I wondered if he ever went home or just ate cinnamon rolls and slept on his stool. He recognized me right away.

"Why, it's the doctor lady. Yeah, got a call you wanted to see Homer. Let's see now." He got on the intercom and punched a few numbers. "Where's Homer Johnson at? Well get his ass down to the interview room."

He took my driver's license and went through the drill of examining it without really looking at it. "That Homer fella is a strange one if you ask me. Sure don't seem to like being locked up much."

"I don't imagine most people do."

The deputy handed me back my license. "Some do. Three hots and a cot is better than having to earn a living for some of them. Homer's been waking up at night hollering." He shook his head. "Last night his cellmate got a little enthusiastic about telling him to get back to sleep, so we had to move Homer into the holding cell for psychs."

"Thanks for the warning. I'll ask him what happened."

The buzzer signalled me to push open the door. Within a few minutes, I was face-to-face with Homer.

"Thanks for driving all the way up to talk with me," he said. "I hear the weather's pretty bad." His right eye was blackened, and nearly swollen shut.

"Your trial starts this week and I still don't have enough to write up a decent report on you. What happened to your eye?"

"Nothing."

"Nothing? You just woke up that way?" I slapped my briefcase on the table and pulled out the chair. The familiar screeching of its legs on the concrete sent a ripple up my spine.

"Yep." He crossed his arms and leaned back against the wall.

"That's not what Deputy Martin told me." I motioned for him to have a seat.

He lifted the chair from under the table and gently set it down. He sat and held on to the table while he balanced the chair on two legs. "He wasn't there, was he?"

I shook my head. "Homer, to be perfectly honest, I don't understand your bad attitude, and furthermore, I don't have time for it. I need to get the real story this time and I need to do it today because your trial will probably start Tuesday or Wednesday and I am up against the wall." I didn't care if he knew I was annoyed with him. What difference would it make at this point?

He drew back. After a moment he replied. "I guess I act that way because everyone expects me to. I know I'm in trouble. Mr. Peck told me to cooperate with you." His eyes warmed up, and he became the likeable, friendly Homer again.

"Good. Then let's get started." I was happy to get a hint of insight from him.

He sat forward and leaned his elbows on the table. "Did

you hear that Verlan's going to come out against me? The rumor is he'll say I was the ringleader and that I killed Anerd."

"Did you?" I showed less sense than curiosity by asking.

"No!" He reached out his hands to me, and dropped them palms-up to the table. "I have no idea who killed Anerd, that is, if he's even dead."

"I don't think the district attorney would have charged you with murder if there wasn't enough evidence to presume he's dead. But let's get to that later. What really happened on the night Anerd was kidnapped? Why were you at his house?"

"Mr. Peck wants you to say I didn't understand what was going on." His black eyes looked directly into mine, and I saw Winema in them.

"Homer, you're not stupid and I know full well that you knew what was happening."

"Can't we just say I have diminished capacity? That I'm unable to help with my defense?"

"That wouldn't be true. The fact that you know what the term means is a good indication you don't have it. And I don't believe you're unable to help. Unwilling is more like it and I can't understand why."

He hung his head. After a long pause he looked up at me. "I can't tell you. I can't tell anyone." His eyes filled with tears and he looked up at the ceiling to get control.

"At least tell me what the nightmares are about."

His head jerked toward me. "How do you know about them?"

"Waking up screaming is a clue." Wrong response, he was finally cooperating, and I was being sarcastic.

"The ghost comes to visit me. I see his face, and he's angry."

"The ghost?"

He nodded.

"That's what wakes you up?"

"Sometimes I'm already awake when I see him." Homer's eyes were bright and wide.

"What does he tell you?"

"He stares at me."

"Then what about the vision scares you?"

"I don't know," he whined. The tiny room felt closer, and the smell of his anxiety was stifling.

"How do you know the vision is a ghost?"

"Because he vanishes when I try to talk to him."

"Homer, I don't know what you're trying to prove, but this will not make you qualify for diminished capacity." I couldn't disguise my frustration.

"No, I mean it, really. He tells me I need to sacrifice myself to please the Great Spirit and to become a man."

I sighed. "Let's try something else, Homer. Tell me about your relationship with Verlan."

His expression hardened then gave way to resignation. "I met him at a party. We got drunk together and later we started hanging out."

"Why did you hang out with such a scumbag?"

"I didn't want to be an Indian."

It was probably the first honest thing he'd said to me.

"And why not?"

"They're losers." The vexatious Homer was coming back.

"Your grandmother Winema is a loser?"

"Look at the way she lives. In a damn shack with animals running all over."

"And Verlan's place is better?"

"At least it's a real house."

"Your grandmother told me that you were never taught about your culture."

"Why would I want to know?"

"She told me she believes you have the potential of becoming a shaman."

He snorted. "She wants me to go on some damn quest to atone for my disrespect of the spirit world."

"What does that mean to you?"

"I'd have to go out to freeze and starve in the boonies for five days, and build rock piles, and use a stick to scratch my face." He sneered. "Oh, and I'd call spirits to get some kind of answer. To what fucking question, I have no clue."

"Tell me about your father."

"He's a loser, too. I haven't seen him since my mother's funeral."

"So to summarize, self-hate is the reason you hang with the white supremacists."

"Shut up. That's not true and you know it."

"I know how you sound to me, Homer. If Verlan is so wonderful, why is he setting you up for the murder?"

Homer glared at me. "I don't know," he said coldly.

"Think about it. Maybe he wants to save himself, and you're a convenient scapegoat."

He frowned and said nothing.

"Okay, Homer. Truce. What was your relationship with Sally?"

He glowered for a moment, then softened. "I wanted to save her from Verlan. He's mean to her. And so was Anerd."

"Have you ever had sex with her?"

"No."

"Could you if you wanted to?"

"I don't care what anyone says. She's not like that."

"Did you join the White People's Brigade to impress her?"

"I joined the WPB because I wanted to and because I believe in their cause."

"I don't believe you, Homer. I'd like to know the real reason you're on self-destruct."

He scowled, his lips twisted in defiance. "Does it make any difference? Does anything I say make a difference? It's a one-way track for me, and there's no getting off the train."

I thought of boxcars full of Homer's ancestors sentenced to starve in a hostile land. Was his collaboration with a hate group his only hope to be someone important? Or a means of survival? If so, he wasn't likely to cooperate with me. In frustration I left the interview with every intention of telling Richard Peck that I couldn't help his client.

Eighteen

The lobby of the Jackpot jail overflowed with people. I walked to Deputy Martin's cage to hand him back my temporary ID badge.

"Visiting hours," he said, rolling his eyes. "I get to do the honors because of my experience with animal control."

Until his comment made me smile, I had been unaware that I was clenching my teeth. "How's the weather out there?"

"Worst I've seen since eighty-six. I hope you don't plan on driving down the hill."

"I came prepared. Could you tell me a good place to stay for the night?"

"Not much choice 'round here in winter. All the cabins at the lake are closed up for the season. 'Bout the only place open is the Yellow Inn." He leaned forward, squashing his belly into the counter. "I wouldn't advertise that I was a female traveling alone."

"Thanks, I'm okay." I grinned at his avuncular protectiveness. "I used to wait tables in a casino. I can handle a few rednecks."

"The inn's just up the highway a half mile. And you call down here if need be." He handed me a Trinity County Sheriff's Department card with his name on it.

"Tell that gal at the switchboard to put you through to Martin. That's me. Dale Martin."

"Thanks. Are there any restaurants open?"

"Pizza parlor and Jo's Coffee Shop nearby. Pizza place closes at five this time of year, coffee shop stays open 'til seven."

"Where do all the cops go for coffee and doughnuts at three in the morning?" I teased.

"Where do you think?" He raised a toast to me with a half-eaten cinnamon roll.

A gust of wind whistled through the double glass doors to the lobby. One slammed open, and a blast of snow and ice shot through the room. A baby-faced skinhead kicked the door shut with his foot, and glared at the rest of the startled visitors. His eyes settled on me. A smarmy leer slid over his face. At first glance he appeared to have no incisors, but as his lips parted I could see that his teeth were green with decay.

"Gotta go. I'll be back tomorrow." I turned back to Deputy Martin.

"Take care running the gauntlet." He looked past me and glowered in the direction of the young man. "Skinheads and deadheads, Trinity County's finest."

I turned and waited for a zonked-out fiftyish hippie with shoulder-length dreadlocks to move his feet. He stared at me with bloodshot eyes that didn't seem to focus. I cleared my throat. As he slid his feet under the plastic chair, the smell of burning leaves floated off him. Given the blizzard, I doubted he'd been tidying up his yard this morning, and hurried past him to avoid getting high from the fumes.

The skinny woman next to him, his wife perhaps, looked no more than twenty and only slightly less stoned. She smiled at me, and I gave a half smile back.

Her hair was matted and greasy and she looked as though she'd slept in twigs and weeds.

The next three chairs held young children of indeterminate gender who followed me silently with their eyes. The eldest looked about seven years old and wrapped its arm around a toddler with snot running from its reddened nose to its fever-blistered mouth. The third child looked at me with huge brown eyes and plucked at a bald spot on its head.

The skinhead at the door stepped into my line of sight. His right ear was pierced with studs from the lobe to the cartilage and each of his eyebrows were pierced with metal hoops. The post from the stud in his nose stuck out his nostril.

"You're the prettiest one here," he said.

"Thank you," I said, and reached for the door handle.

He reached across me, nearly sideswiping my chest. He pulled the door open, forcing me to step back to miss it. The sleeve of his workshirt pulled up and I saw the tattoo of an A on his forearm.

"What does that mean?" I pointed at his arm.

He stuck out his tongue and waggled it to show a silver stud piercing the gray meat. He clicked the stud on his teeth. "Anarchy."

"Oh. Thanks," I said, and walked through the door into the blizzard.

By the time I found Tony's Red Beast, two inches of snow covered it and the street was nearly empty. Even though it was only four in the afternoon the streetlamps bathed the town in a pale green haze. I scraped the snow off the windshield with my bare, hands, wishing I'd remembered to bring gloves. By the time I climbed into the cab, my fingers were wrinkled and blue, and I had to sit on them for a minute to thaw them enough to hold onto the steering wheel.

I'd left the truck in four-wheel drive and when I pulled out of the parking place, its transmission groaned in protest.

The truck crept down the highway, snowflakes smacking into the windshield with such force that I expected to hear it being blasted away. Instead, there was only the squeak of the frantic windshield wipers, the muffled crunch of the tires on the new snow, and the deathly quiet of the town.

"It has to be pretty bad if the Jackpotters won't go out in it," I told the Beast.

I reached Jo's Coffee Shop, where I'd spoken with Mavis Woods. I slowed to turn and an instant later decided I didn't want to talk to anyone else today. I kept driving to the Yellow Inn, a renovated Victorian that, bathed in the green streetlamp, took on a iridescent chartreuse hue, and reminded me of a sixties restoration nightmare. The driveway was obscured by snow. I could park on the street and get shoved off by a snowplow or take a chance.

The truck shuddered down a slope. Its tires went *rat-a-tat-tat* over what were probably the wooden planks of a bridge over the creek that ran parallel to the highway.

I pulled up as close to the front porch as I could, and jumped out into a snowdrift that reached to my knees. I high-stepped to the porch and hung on to the rail to steady myself on the slick steps. I skidded to the front door, and twisted the doorknob.

The door was locked.

I banged on the leaded glass window. No answer.

I slid to the porch rail, and looked up and down the street. Not a soul in sight. Just when I thought it couldn't get any worse, the electricity went out and the buildings along the street faded into a gray mist.

By the time I trekked back to the pickup, my stomach began to growl. If I didn't eat right now, I would faint or worse, get a massive headache.

I ripped everything out of the glove box in hopes of finding one of Tony's candy bars. Nothing.

At the thought of cinnamon rolls and spending the night

in the same room with the bestudded skinhead, I leaned on the horn of the truck and waited. Not a peep from the Yellow Inn. My only option was to go back to the jail. I retraced my tracks onto the highway, and crept back through town.

Two blocks later I saw the only light on the main street coming from the pizza parlor. "What the heck." I pulled in. The boy at the counter was about seventeen, and with the exception of unruly red hair, he was the most normal-appearing person I'd met in Jackpot today. He was scrubbing the counter by the light of a kerosene lamp. He looked up at me in surprise when the bells on the front door jingled. His name tag read Todd.

"Wow, how'd you get here? I mean, may I help you, ma'am?"

"Can I still get something to eat?" I forced myself to smile to conceal my intent to rip off his arm and eat it raw if I had to.

"Sure," he smiled. "The pizza oven is gas so it's still working. What would you like?"

"How about a pizza?"

"Sure. What kind?"

I looked at the menu. "How about a vegetarian pizza?"

"Okay." He took out his pad, and scribbled on it. "Except we're out of peppers and mushrooms and tomatoes and onions. And olives."

"What do you have?"

"Let's see." He opened the door to the walk-in refrigerator and held up the kerosene lantern to peer inside. The rest of the room was plunged into darkness for a moment.

He poked his head out and his eyes sparkled in the yellow light. "We still have pepperoni. And anchovies."

For the first time all day I had an easy decision. "Pepperoni then."

"One Jackpot-style vegetarian pizza, coming up." He grinned and set to work.

The blizzard raged while he prepared my pizza. When he popped it into the oven, I asked, "Is there a place for me to stay tonight?"

"The only place that's open off-season is the Yellow Inn."

"Been there, done that. No one's home."

"Really? Let me call her." He reached for the phone on the wall and dialed. While he waited, he spun the cord like a jumping rope, slapping it on the counter and sending specks of corn meal and flour skittering toward the sink. I got the impression this kid would probably do well with a more intellectually challenging job.

Finally he spoke into the phone. "Aunt Fran? Yeah, where were you? There's a lady here who needs a place for the night. Okay, I'll let her know."

He hung up. "She was out chopping firewood, but she's back now. She said she'll fix up a room for you." He continued wiping down the counter. "Are you up here for the Indian's trial?"

"How did you know that?"

"Why else would anyone come up here during a blizzard? I mean, it's not like Jackpot is on the way to anywhere." The statement seemed to have deeper meaning for him. "Are you a witness?"

"I'm a psychologist, and I may be testifying."

"Wow, the psychologist lady. I thought about becoming a psychologist. That is if I can save enough money to get out of this place and go to college."

"You'll do it if you want it enough. I did it by waiting tables."

He smiled. "Then there's hope. Cool." He sprayed some cleaning foam onto the stainless steel refrigerator, wiped it, then stood back to check for missed spots. He dabbed at a few places then wadded up the paper towel and lobbed it into the garbage can. "So who do you think really killed Anerd?"

"How do you know he's dead?"

"Because no one ever disappears around here who doesn't turn up dead. If they turn up at all. Besides, you can't live with no blood."

"Good point. What's your theory?"

He leaned on the counter with his elbows and cradled his chin in his hands. "He was too fat to throw in the Trinity River. At least in one piece. It's not very deep up here, even with the runoff, and he'd show up real quick. The woods at this time of year would be treacherous, and even King Kong couldn't have dragged him very far. Anyway he'd be found as soon as the snow melted. Hmm." He scratched at a pimple. "Based on rumors at school and my sixth sense, I'd guess he's in the dump in Cedar Gulch. At least part of him."

"That's a thought. He almost didn't make it out of there the first time."

"If they had any smarts they would have dumped him there on the day the scrapers were working." He nodded toward some spigots on the wall. "Want a glass of wine? It's on the house."

I nodded. "White, please. The scrapers?"

He filled a clear plastic tumbler, and handed it to me across the counter.

"Those humongous machines that load dirt. They are *scarrrry*." He gave a mock shudder. "So I know this is probably confidential, but do you think the Indian did it?"

"What do you think?" I took a sip of the wine. It was cold enough to hurt my teeth. "Thanks," I said.

"Well all I can say is that Anerd had a whole lot more enemies than some Indian he met once or twice."

"Enemies? Like who?"

He guffawed. "Like the entire town. He managed to rip off or piss off just about everyone. The only people who liked him were his daughter, Sally, and his wife. And the whole high school knew he wanted to get into Sally's pants but basically was too chicken, so he'd set her up with football players and then watch them do the dirty deed."

I wrinkled my nose. "Gross. Do you think Sally had something to do with his disappearance?"

"The only thing I can figure is that the Indian might have wanted to protect her from Anerd. But Sally loved her daddy and got real mad when anyone bad-mouthed him."

"What do you know about Mavis?"

"Most people like her. I guess she's okay."

"How did she react to Anerd? I mean he was horrible to their daughter."

"She's pretty meek, at least on the surface. I mean if it bothered her so much, why didn't she leave him? It's not like she would be broke, with her job and half of the business. My aunt says some women just love their man so much they put up with anything." The buzzer went off in the midst of his adolescent supposition.

"Pizza's done. Let me box this up for you so you can get on over to my aunt's house before it's completely dark." He opened the door to the oven and pulled out the pizza, slid it into the counter, sliced it deftly, and slid it into a box. "There you go, ma'am."

I had just pulled out my wallet when the bells on the door jingled. The kid's eyes widened, and his smile faded. I turned to see the bestudded skinhead from the jail walk in the door with a taller one behind him. They sauntered up to the counter, thumbs hooked through the belt loops on their black jeans, crotches thrust forward, and rancorous attitude all over.

The pizza kid said to me, "That's okay, ma'am. I'll catch you tomorrow. I already locked the cash box, and I can't open it." The last sentence was loud enough for the skinheads to hear. "You go on now, ma'am. Don't worry about it," he said in a lower tone.

I backed away from the counter. The second skinhead

was the one who had come to my house and offered to change the tire on my Volkswagen. He wore black from head to toe and had a new silver-colored cap on his right incisor. I smiled at him, intent on defusing the impending confrontation.

"How's your tire?" He looked at me up and down with his ice-blue eyes.

"Got it fixed. Thanks for asking." I didn't call him Tinsel Tooth.

He moved closer to me. I backed up, and bumped into the guy from the jail. He clicked his tongue stud against his teeth and shimmied closer to press his pelvic region against me. My fight or flight response kicked in on top of my need to eat. Watch out, Mr. Studly Dude, I thought, although I was armed with only a scorching hot pizza.

The pizza kid looked at the tall one. "Freddy, if you guys want a pizza you better order one now because I have to turn off the oven."

"Nah, we just want beer," clicked Studly. "Maybe the little cutie here would have a few with us." I could feel his stare boring into the back of my head at the same time my fingers felt like they were blistering from the heat of the box.

"Sorry, buddy, we're out of beer right now." The pizza kid's voice was intensely apologetic. "How about some nice Chablis wine?"

I swallowed a giggle and took a step to the side. Both skinheads stared with slackjaws and furrowed brows at Todd the pizza kid. He was smiling most helpfully at them, but when he glanced at me, his eyes gave a hint of concern.

"Here, why don't you have a taste. I'm sure you'll like it." He grabbed a plastic tumbler and filled it from the tap on the wall. I took the cue and walked backwards toward the door. I exited just as Todd forced the tumbler onto Freddy Tinsel Tooth and insisted he taste.

After I hopped into the cab of the truck, I threw the hot

pizza box on the seat. My fingers were red and tingling. I had an urge to stick them in the snow but not knowing how long Todd could forestall the skinheads, I ground the truck into reverse and did a two-point turn onto the highway. Opening the pizza box with my right hand, I pulled out a slice and took a big bite, ignoring the sizzle as a piece of pepperoni made contact with the roof of my mouth. The steering wheel of the Red Beast reacted slowly, which was good because I was wobbling all over the road.

After missing the Yellow Inn the first time, I turned around in the middle of the highway to go back. The proprietor had placed a kerosene lamp on the porch. I found the driveway just as I swallowed the last of my third slice.

I pulled around back and sat for a moment while enjoying the rush of glucose to brain. "Who needs drugs when there's pizza?" I said aloud.

Fortified, I pulled out my bag from behind the seat, locked the door, and trudged through the snow carrying my red plaid bag in one hand and the pizza box in the other. My legs were weak with cold and fatigue by the time I reached the porch. I set down my suitcase and climbed the stairs, set the pizza by the front door, and went back to retrieve the suitcase. By the time I got back, a woman had opened the door and was staring at the pizza box. She bent down to pick it up.

"That's okay, ma'am. I'll get it." I reached down, swooped it up, and bashed into the door jamb.

She held open the door. "I apologize for the door being locked before. It's usually open but the latches are getting weak and the door tends to blow open in the strong wind." The woman was the archetypal plump and matronly country woman. Her hair was gray and pulled into a bun and her glasses were perched on the end of her nose. Her eyes were soft and brown with thick straight bovine eyelashes. Small wood chips tumbled from her hair as she slowly and gently bent over to pick up my suitcase with an ease that belied her age.

"Nice to meet you." She reached out a plump hand. Her grip was strong and sure.

"I'm Cassie Ringwald. Thanks for opening up."

"Not a problem for me at all. I wish you'd called before you came—would have saved you the trouble the first time."

"Next time I will. Is Todd your nephew?"

"Yes. I'm raising him up." She added, "Many of the people up here are related."

I didn't tell her that I'd already guessed many of the parents in Trinity County were their own siblings.

She carried my bag to a room in the back on the second floor. "I'll put the rest of your pizza in the kitchen. Breakfast will be ready at seven tomorrow morning. Any dietary restrictions?"

After the pizza I couldn't claim to be a delicate eater. "Whatever you have is great."

The phone rang and Fran answered it in the kitchen. "Yes, she's here safe and sound. You know the rules about school nights. Well, okay, just this once." She hung up shaking her head. "That boy. He won't be home until late because he's going to study with a girl he likes."

"By candlelight?"

"I suspect that's the very reason he chose to go over there tonight."

The room was cozy, with a four-poster bed and crocheted bedspread. A log burned in the tiled fireplace and the room smelled of cedar. The pink roses on the wallpaper were the same shade as the picture and crown moldings, and the door and window moldings were the same cream as the wainscotting. A reproduction of an antique phone sat on the bedside table.

I unpacked and washed up, snuggled into the down comforter, and called Maria.

"The doctor said Auntie Liz is just fine," she told me. "She's already asleep and she had dinner."

"Tell her I'll be back as soon as the weather breaks. It's a blizzard up here."

"We're at flood stage down here. Hurry and finish your work. If you don't get a new roof soon . . ."

"I know. The entire house will collapse."

"We'll keep changing the buckets. I haven't seen weather like this since the storms of '86."

"So I've heard."

"Give my brother a call. He said he wanted to speak with you."

I hung up and called Tony at the police station. He was filling out a report.

"Glad you called," he said. "I've got this worked out. Next break in the weather, I'm going to get some of my buddies up on your roof and do some major patchwork until we can get it fixed right this spring." He seemed way too cheerful.

"Tony, you don't have to do that. I'll hire someone." I wanted to talk about Homer and Todd and the skinheads. "This kid I talked to, Todd, thinks Anerd's body ended up back at the Cedar Gulch dump. Maybe you guys ought to go check it out."

"Yeah, right. In this weather. But why should you hire someone to do the roof when we can handle it? And why didn't you tell me it was that bad? I would have gotten a loan for the money. The entire roof will have to be stripped. Some of those trusses don't look so hot either."

"Tony, I haven't had the best day."

"I'm only trying to help you."

"I ran into a couple of skinheads at the jail. One of them is the guy who showed up at my house."

"You want me up there?"

"No. I'm okay." I didn't want to ask him to do any more for me. "I'll call the bank when I get back to see if I can get a loan to fix the roof."

"Right, Cassie. You already tried. They won't give a loan to an old lady and a shrink with a brand new practice."

"Tony, I'll figure it out. I don't want you to handle this for me. I'm a big girl . . ."

He wasn't listening. "I can get the materials for close to cost from my uncle in Sonoma. I guess I know what I'll be doing this summer."

I was getting annoyed. "Fine. But if you really want to help me, check the dump for Anerd." The interaction was making me more determined to break Homer down and get enough information to testify in court. I needed the money, and I needed to take care of the roof myself. I was never going to be as dependent on a man as my mother had been on my father.

Tony chatted for another minute or two and when he got no response from me asked, "You all right, Cass?"

"Just fine."

"Why do you need me only when it's convenient for you?"

"Because I can manage my life on my own." I didn't like him getting into my head, especially when he was right.

"That's why you're up there in my truck."

"Oh. Oh, oh," I sputtered. "That's low."

The phone connection crackled.

"You want it both ways, Cass. Okay, I'll try not to be such an ass next time. Instead I'll let you drive your VW to Jackpot in a snowstorm. You might make it without falling off the mountain. And instead of staying the night with you, I'll teach you how to shoot the .357 so you can protect yourself against the bad guys. And rather than fix your roof, I'll lend you a hammer. Anything to make you think I'm a nice guy."

"Enough already. Why do men always feel compelled to fix a woman's life?"

"That's our primary purpose on this planet. You should take it as a compliment." He was being sarcastic.

I couldn't help but giggle. "Okay, you made your point, but I wish you could understand. . . ."

"This isn't just about you, Cassie. I need to take care of Aunt Liz, too. It's her house." I could hear him tapping his pen on the counter. "Someday you're going to find yourself in a situation you can't talk your way out of. Then maybe you'll appreciate me."

The phone crackled again. "Sounds pretty bad up there," he said.

"The electricity's already gone out."

"Phone will be next. You stay safe. If those skinheads . . ."

And the phone line went dead.

Nineteen

I hated arguing with Tony and the effort made me crave pizza. My T-shirt served as my sleeping attire so I slipped on my jeans and pulled my boots up over the cuffs, wrapping the laces around my ankles and tying them loosely. I lit a fat bayberry-scented candle off the mantle and walked as softly as possible down the stairs.

Fran was nowhere to be found. Having no idea if other guests were in the house, I resisted my temptation to explore.

The kitchen was in the back of the house and fairly well preserved. It was in turn-of-the-century style, with the exception of a side-by-side refrigerator-freezer and a gas stove. I found my pizza on the slate countertop and opened the box. Five pieces left. The cheese had congealed in the coolness of the house and the pepperoni was dry and stiff. I stuffed a slice into my mouth and looked for something to heat up the rest over a fire. I gave up with two slices left. My stomach was beginning to complain anyway.

A huge ski jacket hung from a hook, and I put it on intending to put it back when I went up to bed. I found a hand-painted ceramic cup in a glass fronted cupboard and went to the sink to get a drink. While I sipped at the ice cold tap water, I looked out the kitchen window. The blizzard seemed to have no intention of slowing down. Eerie shadows were cast over Fran's white blanketed yard—there must have been a bright moon above the storm to account for the diffuse light. I looked toward the truck. There was already an inch of new snow on the Red Beast. I put the cup in the sink and wondered if I would be trapped in Jackpot until the spring thaw.

As I turned to go back upstairs, I noticed movement near the truck. I tried to tell myself that my imagination was getting the better of me, then tingling with paranoia, I blew out my candle.

Two forms holding powerful police-issue flashlights ran around the truck and pulled at the door handles. When they couldn't get in they ran to the front of the truck and yanked on the hood. One ran out of my line of sight and came back with a short crowbar. They stuck it under the hood and jerked up on the crowbar until the hood popped open. Both of them bent over the engine.

One of them pulled something out of the engine and tucked it into his jacket. Then they walked directly toward me through the deepening snow. The taller of them opened his mouth and a shiny silver tooth sparkled in the dim light. The shorter turned his head and I saw the glint of metal in his nostril. The skinheads, Tinsel Tooth and Studly Dude were coming into the Yellow Inn.

My intuition told me they weren't houseguests.

I ran out of the kitchen and down the first hall. "Fran, Fran," banging on doors, I fumbled in the darkness.

Finally I heard someone moving behind a door. Fran's soft woody smell floated out when she opened it.

"Someone's coming in. Skinheads."

"Now calm down, young lady. I'm sure there's an explanation. Jackpot's not Cedar Gulch. It's safe here."

"They just disabled my truck. They took something out of the engine."

"I'm sure they meant no harm—"

Her words were interrupted by someone kicking in the front door.

I grabbed her arm, but she just shook me off.

"Now that's just ridiculous. They could have knocked." She pushed past me, and stomped down the hall.

The picture started to come together. Studly at the jail, Tinsel Tooth at my house, the assault on Auntie Liz. "I think they may be here because of me."

"Oh, don't be silly." She forged ahead, and I followed.

Fran confronted the skinheads in the living room. They shined their flashlights directly into our eyes, blinding us. The silhouette of Fran's plump thighs showed through her flannel nightie.

"Freddy. Buddy. What do you want?" she asked them. She was holding a baseball bat at her right side.

"How come you got the blond bitch here?" Freddy-Tinsel Tooth said.

"I'm running an inn. She's a guest. What business is it of yours?" Fran held her left hand in front of her face to shield her eyes from his flashlight.

"Don't you know she's fixing to blow this town apart?" Buddy the Studly Dude clicked.

"That's none of my concern," Fran said firmly. "I'm sure she'll do what she was hired to do and nothing more."

How did everyone seem to know so much about me and the purpose of my visit to Jackpot?

"She's been hired to say the fuckin' Injun didn't kill Anerd," Freddy snarled.

"That's not true," I said. "I was hired to evaluate him, not to give a particular opinion one way or the other." The skinheads glared past Fran to focus on me, the subtlety of my argument lost on them.

"We know why you're here." Freddy moved toward us. "And we don't want you saying Homer didn't do it."

"What do you have against Homer?" If Fran and I could escape, we'd have to flee to safety in the freezing cold.

"Because." Buddy looked toward Freddy.

"Because he's an Injun." Freddy nodded with authority.

"But I thought he was part of the White People's Brigade."

They stopped cold. From the expressions on their faces, I wondered if they'd ever thought about that, if in fact they'd ever thought at all.

"He was a fuckin' wannabe," Freddy said. "That pussy Verlan wanted him in, not no one else."

"I didn't know." I took a breath.

Fran stared at the men. "Suppose Homer didn't kill Anerd?"

Buddy scowled. "It don't matter who done it as long as the Injun takes the fall. We don't want no Injuns in the WPB."

"Oh. I see." The field of suspects had just opened up, and as far as I was concerned Homer had walked into the clear. Now, I wanted to know who was Homer protecting and why, but if Freddy and Buddy had their way, I might not get the chance to find out.

"We gotta make sure you don't get to talk at the trial," Buddy said. "We gotta take you to our place. Then when the trial's over we'll bring you back."

"That's called kidnapping," I said. "It's a federal offense."

"Ain't no feds around here," Freddy growled.

"There weren't at Ruby Ridge either. At least at first." I wasn't making headway.

Freddy began to threaten me. "You ain't gonna talk at that Injun's trial." He shook his finger in my face. "We don't want no trouble from you. You'll do perxactly what we say."

He whacked his flashlight across the back of a chair. The wood cracked and the arm flew across the room.

"You'd better think carefully about this," I said.

He grabbed my arm and twisted it behind my back. "Get in the fucking truck." He pointed at Fran's baseball bat. Buddy ripped it from her hand and walked out the door.

Fran looked stunned. She remained immobile.

"You say one word and you're both dust." Freddy pointed his finger in her face. "Remember. One word."

Trying to fight him off would be stupid. He had a clear physical advantage, and I couldn't take the chance of another elderly woman getting beaten.

Besides, I was more afraid of them than I would have been someone rational. They were unpredictable and dangerous, they were driven by hate and anger and ignorance. They were unpredictable and dangerous. What choice did I have but to go with them?

Twenty

The vehicle was a well-worn former Cal Trans one-ton truck with dually tires on the back. A bumper sported a sticker that pronounced: "Bad cop, no donut." Another read: "Stop honking, I'm reloading."

Freddy opened the driver's side door and shoved me in. I landed on a spring in the seat where the upholstery had worn through to the stuffing. The men climbed in on either side of me.

The truck's glove box was held closed with a paper clip, and there was an opening in the dash where the radio should have been. I accidentally stuck my boot into a hole rusted through the floorboard. The only fully intact item was the brand-new rear window gun rack, which held a shotgun and a .22 rifle. Probably used for poaching deer, I thought.

I pulled my foot out of the hole in the floor and clutched my arms as close to my sides as possible to avoid touching either Freddy or Buddy. When we were on our way I asked, "Who are you?"

Freddy snarled, "We know who you are and you don't need to know who we are."

"Okay, that's fair enough." I braced my heels against the drive shaft hump.

Freddy drove over the little bridge onto the highway. I

hoped he'd miss and we'd end up in the creek, a premature end to our journey. But then he might take out his frustration on Fran, and I couldn't cope with that.

The headlights swung over the road and revealed a few stranded cars, which were rapidly taking on the appearance of large snowdrifts. We drove through town, past the courthouse and jail. I tried to look into the jail lobby to see Deputy Martin but the electricity had not come back on and the building was dark. No other cars were on the road as we headed up into the hills.

"Where are we going?" I moved my right foot to the driver's side of the hump to avoid the snow that sprayed up through the hole in the floor and soaked my boot.

"Told you. Our place." Freddy had become even more terse.

I smiled at Buddy.

He smiled back.

"Who's in your group? Besides both of you and Verlan?"

"Don't tell her nothing," Freddy warned.

"Why not? It's not like it makes a difference. She's just a woman. What's she gonna do about it?" Buddy coyly used his thumb and little finger to twist the stud in his nose.

"She don't need to know any more about it than she knows. And if you tell her too much, I'll have to hurt her."

"But she's a white woman. We can't hurt her none." Buddy raised his eyebrows. I was surprised he could, considering the weight of the studs.

"I'll hurt her if I have to. Now shut up." Freddy braked hard and stopped opposite a stranded car. He jumped out with a small crowbar, crossed the freeway in three strides, and forced open the trunk to yank out the spare tire, which he rolled across the road and tossed into the back of his truck. He went back to the car, reached in, and with the crowbar tore the radio out. He left the car door open, trotted back to the truck, and handed me the radio. "Hold this, bitch."

He put the truck into gear and drove off. "She's a Injun lover and probably a nigger-Jew lover, too," he continued, referring to me.

"She might like us if we tell her why the WPB will save the white race."

"Like the bitch is gonna listen." Freddy slapped the flat of his hand against the steering wheel, making a cracking sound with his ring. I thought it odd that he wore such a heavy ring on his forefinger and looked closer. He had no forefinger—the first digit on his right hand was his middle finger. An image tugged at my mind.

"You know it is a free country." I made small talk with him. If he thought I understood his politics, maybe he'd leave me alone. "You and the rest of the WPB can think and do whatever you want as long as it's not illegal."

"Yeah, but like you said, at first there weren't no feds at Ruby Ridge." He clearly didn't want to talk anymore.

"Oh, I imagine they've learned their lesson by now." I looked at his bland face. None of his features were remarkable with the exception of the ice-blue eyes. A fuzzy memory in the back of my head told me I'd seen him before he came to my house with the offer of fixing my flat tire, but something about him was different. The image seemed to stick behind my right eye.

I turned back to Buddy. Psychologically, he was the weaker of the two, and perhaps I could use him as an ally to set me free. "Why did Verlan want Homer in the WPB? I thought your philosophy was to exclude minorities."

"You sure do use some big words. I like smart women." He leered at me.

Just my luck. I turned away, and kept my mouth shut.

But Buddy was in the mood to share. "Verlan liked Homer because he came from money and all. Besides, he's got some white in him and he's not like a nigger color."

I refrained from saying that Homer's white blood was Jewish.

"Besides," Buddy continued, "Homer's good-looking, and Verlan figured we'd use him to attract women."

"He's a fucking spy," Freddy interjected. "Anerd said so after he was got out of the dump."

"A spy?"

"He wanted to take control over the WPB, and get all the power," Buddy said. "Him and his partners."

"There's rival factions in the White People's Brigade?" The notion seemed so silly. This was not Chicago or Miami. How much power could there be in Trinity County?

"Yeah," said Buddy. "Homer betrayed Anerd."

"How?"

"Okay, bitch," Freddy said. "You wanna know, I'll tell you. Let's just say the only way things are gonna be made right is if Homer is out of the way. And if he doesn't get hanged, I'm gonna beat him to a pulp."

And then the memory struck me between the eyes. Bile and pepperoni stung my throat, and I had to cover my mouth to keep from vomiting. Not only had Freddy the Tinsel Tooth shown up at my house, he was the leader of the skinheads I'd seen assaulting Bruno with baseball bats. He was the one who had threatened me by drawing his middle finger across his throat. I hadn't recognized him because he'd shaved off his horrid Hitler mustache and goatee.

I panicked inside. Could Freddy have figured out that I was the person who saved Bruno on that night of terror? His ruthlessness and potential for violence were even greater than I'd feared, and now he was taking me where no one could find me. Keep calm, I told myself. Talk your way out of this.

Buddy kept chattering. "Yeah, things have gone to shit

since Anerd disappeared for the second time. We don't know who's in charge."

"I know who's in charge," Freddy said. "But to keep it that way, Homer's gonna die. And whoever else gets in our way."

I had the sinking feeling I was one of them.

Twenty-one

We turned off the highway and drove up a steep road with more potholes than a minefield. Freddy maneuvered the truck onto the shoulder. I shut my eyes as we teetered near the edge. We rocked back and forth. I kept bumping into Buddy in spite of my efforts to stay in the middle. I opened my eyes to see the road tilted at a forty-five-degree angle. After an eternity, the truck crashed into a hole in the bank and I was thrown against Freddy. He turned the steering wheel sharply to the right and we landed hard but level. If I had been any taller I would have sustained a head injury from smashing into the ceiling.

Freddy drove up to a single-wide trailer under a wooden frame topped with a rusty tin roof covered with a foot of snow. I jumped out of the truck, and landed in snow up to my thighs. Buddy reached out his hand to help me to the trailer steps.

Freddy took all three steps in one leap, grabbed a hatchet leaning against the railing, and swung it twice to whack a log into kindling strips that he piled into the crook of his arm. He opened the trailer door and threw the wood onto a cinder block hearth, then lit a kerosene lamp and piled the kindling and a log into the steel drum that served as a woodstove. He wrapped a magazine into a cylinder, poured some liquid from a red gas can on it, stuffed it into the stove, then took a wooden match and threw it into the door. It exploded, shooting a blue flame a foot into the room.

Grinning at his handiwork, he used his foot to slam the makeshift stove door shut. I could see he was not a patient man.

Freddy shut the front door and locked the deadbolt from the inside with a key that he put in his pocket. He went to the kitchen and popped the top off a can of beer.

The trailer was a combination of poor white trash revival and neo-Nazi chic. The dining room table, a throwback of steel and Formica, was covered with handguns, catalogues for law enforcement supplies, and a copy of the *Anarchist Cookbook*. I cleared off a pile of *Soldier of Fortune* and *Hustler* magazines from one of the chairs and piled them next to an orange Naugahyde couch detailed with round burn holes from cigarettes and irregularly shaped wounds from other flammable materials.

I leafed through the *Anarchist Cookbook*, the most sophisticated of their reading materials.

Buddy sat in the chair next to me. "We learned how to make drugs but we don't take them."

That was a good sign, because neither Buddy nor Freddy could afford to lose any more of their gray matter.

Buddy continued, "We want to know how to make drugs because when the race war comes we want to give them to the niggers to make them so they're too stoned to fight."

"Really? Some people think the CIA beat you to it."

He gave me a baffled look. "Anerd told us that was his idea. But we use the book to find out about weapons and such."

I hated to tell him that if the WPB had to rely on the *Anarchist Cookbook* they probably weren't the threat they aspired to be. Still, that didn't mean they couldn't hurt Homer. Or me.

"You want something to drink?" Buddy asked. He walked into the kitchen area.

"Some tea would be great."

"Ummm. I don't think we have any." Buddy pawed through the cupboards. He looked back at me and shook his head.

"That's okay," I said. "I'll just go to bed."

"You'll sleep out here on the sofa bed." Freddy pointed Buddy down the hall. "Hit the hay. We gotta be in Jackpot early to see Homer."

Buddy made a move to open the bed, but Freddy shoved him in the opposite direction.

I lay on the unopened Naugahyde couch, and wrapped myself in the ski jacket I'd put on at the inn. If they fell asleep, I could try to get away. I drifted off to the smell of gasoline fumes. My last conscious thought was thank God I'm a white woman.

I woke up to the full moon shining in my eyes through the living room window. The Milky Way made a lacy veil across a cloudless black sky, and the Big Dipper was rising, the stars of its bucket pointing to red Betelgeuse on Orion's shoulder.

I clutched the ski jacket around me and tripped over the block hearth on my way to try the front door. The deadbolt held tight. I went back to the couch, leaned over, and yanked at the aluminum window. It groaned but didn't budge. I tried again and it opened a crack.

Suddenly, out of the darkness, a voice said, "I wouldn't do that. It'll make Freddy mad."

I just about jumped out of my skin. Buddy stood three feet away from me, smiling, his studs glowing in the filtered moonlight and his dingy, threadbare junior size Jockey shorts bagging off his butt. He was bare-chested and his left biceps sported a jailhouse tattoo that in uneven letters said: USMC.

"I needed some air." I bit my lip, and tried not to look at his skinny white legs.

He shut the window. "It's cold out. Why don't you come on back in my bed. I'll keep you warm."

"Uh, gee. I'm really flattered but, you see, I'm engaged." I lowered my eyes, and prayed he'd believe me.

"Oh." He sat on the couch. "Gosh, that's too bad. I mean it's too bad for me." He picked up a *Hustler* and leafed through it.

I sat on the hearth and pulled up my knees. My right foot grazed the hatchet Freddy had used to chop kindling. I wiggled my boot over it, then casually reached down as though to tie my shoelace.

"You look just like her." Buddy held up a glossy centerfold beaver shot.

I tried not to gag. "I love my fiancé very much and I could never betray him."

"Oh." His shoulders slumped and he closed the magazine. "Do you sleep with him?"

I drew my left hand to my throat in feigned shock. "Of course not. It wouldn't be proper." I tightened my right hand around the handle of the hatchet and pulled it toward me.

"Sorry." He moved a bit closer to me and dropped the *Hustler* on the floor in front of him. "Then you're not the type of gal who sleeps around before getting hitched?"

"Certainly not." I bit my tongue and silently added, "With the likes of you."

"Then maybe there's a chance for me. I want to marry a virgin."

Great. Damnation no matter what I told him. "Well, you'd have to take that up with my fiancé. I don't think he'd approve of your attitude." The hatchet rattled against the bricks. I sipped my boot toe under the blade to muffle the sound.

Buddy looked at me for a long while. "Well, alls I can say

is that it's a real shame that a looker like you's already spoken for."

"Why doesn't a nice boy like you already have a girl?" I smiled and balanced the steel blade on my foot.

"Ain't many to be had. At least nice ones. Most of 'em are sluts."

"Oh. Too bad." Maybe I should have told him I'd screwed the Seventh Fleet, and had every disease ever diagnosed in a ship's infirmary. "So you know Sally? Verlan's girl?"

"Sure do. She done just about every guy in Jackpot. But we don't hold it against her or nothing. Some bitch that looks like that's only good for practicin'." He shook his head. "But not for marryin'."

"I heard that her father set her up."

"Anerd?"

"Yes. To sleep with the boys on the football team." I slid the hatchet over my foot and lifted it beside me.

"I dunno. I never played football."

"What did Sally's mother think about Sally's sexual proclivities?" I had a good-enough grip to smash the hatchet between his eyes.

"You mean did she like it?" His eyes had the sparkle and intelligence of pancakes.

"Yes."

"I guess she didn't think too much of it. They never got along real well."

"Really. I thought Mavis wanted to protect her daughter."

"Alls I know is that old gal would holler a lot at Sally and call her a slut and stuff."

"That's awful. How about Anerd. Did you like him?"

Buddy puffed up and crossed his ankle over his knee. The effect was not as masculine as he seemed to think it was. "Anerd started the WPB. He got both of us into it and a whole bunch more guys, too. Some real important people in Jackpot."

"Why do you belong to it?" The handle of the hatchet was becoming slick with my sweat. I gingerly let go and wiped my hand on my jeans.

"Nothing else to do 'round here."

"How about finding a job?"

"Who'd hire me?" He shrugged.

Good point, I thought. "What made Anerd want to start it?"

"He wanted to protect the white people from the threat to America. That and he got a new computer and got on the Internet and found other groups that believed the same. He wrote to some of them on the E-mail to get ideas."

The log in the woodstove crackled in a final burst before settling into embers. I inched away from the heat, scooting the hatchet before me. "Is that what Anerd told you?"

"Yeah, that's what he told everyone. He even said that he's give his own money to the Brigade because he believed in the cause." In the dim light, Buddy's face looked splotchy and yellow.

"Really? How else did you raise the money?"

"Some of us sell drugs. I don't like that so I collected on old debts for him."

"Oh?"

"Yeah, like from people who owed him money but didn't want to pay him. We'd go and collect what they owed—sometimes we'd repossess the stuff."

"How did you know it was his stuff?"

"Because he told us which of it was his stuff."

"And then what did you do with the money?"

"We gave it all to Anerd because he knew about business. He bought guns and other weapons and lots and lots of ammo."

"Where does he keep all of it?"

"I could get into trouble telling you." He looked into my eyes and smiled. "Well, all right. He has a garage in a hidden place. Hardly anyone's seen it. But I have." He puffed up even more. "He took me there one time but he didn't let me look inside because he said it would be too dangerous if I was caught and tortured. But when the time is right we'll all go there and start the race war."

"And you think Homer wanted to take over the WPB because he planned to start a race war?"

His eyebrow studs undulated in the moonlight. Buddy chuckled and leaned toward me flirtatiously. "How about you and me play a little game and then maybe I'll tell you."

"What game?" Please not strip poker, I thought as I gripped the hatchet.

"You ask me some questions and I'll tell you if you got it right."

"Like Twenty Questions? Okay. Why did Homer want to take over from Anerd?"

"It actually wasn't Homer, it was someone else, and Homer was going to help."

"Who besides Homer wanted to take over from Anerd?"

"I'll give you a hint. It's someone Anerd knew real well. You gotta guess the rest."

"Okay. Is it about money?"

"Yep."

"About power?"

"Yep."

"Hmmm. What else?"

Buddy clicked his tongue stud on his teeth. "It's about revenge."

"Revenge? Revenge about something Anerd did?"

Buddy nodded.

"Who would want revenge?" According to Todd the pizza kid, it could be just about anyone. "Revenge for a business deal?"

"You're getting real warm."

"Did Anerd take this person's money?"

The skinhead laughed aloud and said seductively, "You are gettin' hot, babe."

I ignored his insinuation. "But hasn't he done that to many people?"

"Depends on who you ask about it."

"There must be another reason this person wants revenge."

"Maybe there is."

"Jealousy?"

"Maybe." He winked at me.

"Trying to protect someone they love?"

"Maybe." He winked twice.

What other reasons did people want revenge? "What does this person have to do with Homer?"

Buddy smiled.

Who would benefit from Homer's conviction? "There's more to getting Homer locked up than plain old racial hatred, isn't there?"

Buddy laughed out loud. "I sure do like a smart chick. Why don't you ask that old boyfriend of yours to let you try a real man?" He flexed his skinny arm and exposed the tattooed A on his forearm. He stuck out his tongue and flashed his stud. "This here little toy drives the babes wild."

The thought of his parts within a mile of me made me cringe. I pulled the hatchet onto my lap under the ski jacket. Buddy was saved by the thudding of Freddy's bare feet on the vinyl flooring.

"What the hell are you doing? I thought I told you to get to bed." He thumped Buddy alongside the head, causing him to wince and bite down on his tongue.

"Ow. Leave me alone. I was talking to the doctor chick."

"Well, you can talk to her some other time. Get your scrawny ass back in bed." He glared in my direction. "And you quit trying to stir things up."

When they had gone I climbed back onto the couch and snuggled into the ski jacket. Who was Anerd's rival? Someone who had reason to resent him, someone who had the bad end of a business deal, someone who wanted revenge. Someone who would be hurt by Homer's conviction. As far as I could tell, everyone wanted Homer in jail. But not his grandmother, and not Bruno. My thoughts drifted into dreams of a grizzled man-bear pursued by a pack of hairless dogs.

The sound of pots banging wakened me. Freddy was throwing sausages into a cast iron skillet. They sizzled and bounced as they hit the hot pan. A plume of grease spiraled to the ceiling to join the rancid brown stain from previous meals.

I sat up, laced my boots, and squatted in front of the woodstove. There were enough embers left to ignite some kindling. After the twigs smoked and burst into curling orange flames, I took a cedar log from the hearth and pushed it into the stove, then slammed the door shut with my elbow.

The hatchet lay under the couch where I'd set it. For the first time I noticed rust-colored stains between the blade and the handle.

Freddy was in the kitchen, dressed in full camouflage and army boots. His head and face gleamed from being freshly shaved and he smelled of Old Spice. He was burning eggs to a crisp in the sausage grease.

"Need some help?"

He grunted and swiveled the handle of the pan toward me. I turned down the heat and shook the pan to loosen up the eggs.

"So you two are going to see Homer today?"

"Trial starts today." He slammed open a cupboard door, pulled out the last few slices of a loaf of white bread, scraped vainly at some blue-green mold, and slapped the bread into the toaster.

I scraped the eggs from the pan onto a white ceramic platter. “I thought it was only jury selection.”

“We wanna see who’s on the jury. It might be someone who needs some education.”

“Oh. And what do you plan to do with me?”

“Leave you here. You ain’t going far without us.”

“Oh,” I said. “Would you mind bringing in some more firewood before you leave?”

“Goddamn it. You ain’t gonna be one of them whiny bitches, are you?”

“Am I whining?” I cracked some more eggs into the pan.

“You’re already telling me what to do and you ain’t even been here a day. You wanna know why I don’t have no women here? Well, that’s why. They whine all damn day long.”

“Sounds like you didn’t sleep too well.”

“Not with you and Buddy there yakking all damn night. Speaking of the little asshole, go get him up.”

“Just as soon as I’m finished with the eggs. Do you like them over easy?”

“I don’t fucking care.” He stormed down the hall and pounded on Buddy’s door. “Drop your cock and get out of bed, you horny bastard.”

Twenty-two

Buddy waddled down the hall pulling on his khaki fatigues and scratching his crotch. The right side of his face was reddened and wrinkled from sleep, and a stubble of black whiskers covered his face and head. He pushed part of the mess off the table onto the floor, and sat on a metal chair. I handed him a plate with a crunchy fried egg and two links of burnt sausage.

"I sure like a gal that can cook." He beamed at me.

I glanced under the couch where I'd shoved the hatchet. "Thanks," I told him.

Freddy grabbed the platter with the rest of the eggs and sausage from the counter. The toast popped up and he stuck a knife through two slices and dropped them onto the eggs. He stood at the counter, smashed the toast into the eggs, and shoved the mess into his mouth along with a bite of sausage.

"That's okay," I said. "I'll eat after you two have gone to town." I didn't so much as elicit blank looks.

Freddy finished his plate in three more bites and burped heartily.

"When will you be back?" I asked.

"Shut the fuck up." Freddy scowled over his shoulder. "Goddamn women yak all the time." He slammed the plate into the sink. "Let's hit the road." He looked at me. "I want this place cleaned up by the time we get back."

Buddy jumped up, mouth full of sausage. "You be okay?"

I nodded. "I'll be fine."

He pulled a brown bag out of his pants pocket. "I got you something to make you want me to hurry home." He held out the bag to me, and when I crossed my arms he put it on the table and grinned and waggled his tongue stud at me. It clicked on his chipped yellow teeth.

Freddy slung a Caterpillar baseball cap over his scalp and punched open the door with his fist. "Can't you think about anything besides your puny pud, fuckwad? I'm outta here."

Buddy ran after him pulling on his boots. He reached the door, tripped on his laces and sailed off the steps face first into the snow bank. I would have laughed if he wasn't so pathetic. The two skinheads climbed into the truck and rolled backwards down the hill to a flat spot. Tinsel pulled a two-point turn. His license plate registration tag was a crudely drawn forgery on the lined side of a 3 × 5 card. Within a minute the truck was out of sight. Its rumble decreased in pitch until it faded out altogether, leaving me in total silence. I was caught between relief that they were gone and an apprehensive loneliness. Not even a bird chirped. Suppose the scumbags didn't come back? Then again, suppose they did?

Tony had warned me about getting myself into a mess I couldn't talk my way out of, but I hadn't had much choice with this one. If I'd resisted at the Yellow Inn, I'd be here anyway and Todd the pizza kid's Aunt Fran would be hurt. Or worse. I hit my head and tried to squelch the seed of fear that threatened to germinate. I analyzed their personalities aloud.

"Freddy's antisocial behavior comes from bitterness at being cheated out of what he thinks are his rights. His violence stems from a sense of entitlement, a belief he's justified in stealing, terrorizing, kidnapping, brutalizing in reparation for the discrimination he's suffered at the hands of the government and minorities. If there is one blessing, it was that he may ignore me if I don't antagonize him.

"Buddy can be managed for a while but he could be dangerous as Freddy. He interprets both my attention and my coolness to him as signs of interest. He's an erotomaniac, the type of guy who'd think he's justified in keeping a woman captive because he believes she's in love with him." I couldn't assess just how irrational he might become but my gut told me it didn't look good.

With my return to reason, I closed the door. Freddy was right. The place needed cleaning but I had other plans. I started with the bedrooms.

Freddy's bedroom smelled stale. The warped paneled walls were covered with posters of army tanks, submarines, and muscular half-naked skinheads. If I ran into him again, I'd avoid discussing the homoerotic theme of his decor.

His closet was a jumble of camouflage and khaki. A pair of army boots hung by their laces from a nail. Gray hairs were encrusted in the dried blood on the soles.

I covered my nose with my sleeve and kicked the clothes out of the way to uncover a pair of snowshoes and a canvas backpack with a Confederate flag embroidered on it. I pulled them out and threw them into the hall. On the shelf of the closet I discovered a rifle case. I stretched up to reach it, withdrew the rifle, pulled back the bolt, and opened the chamber to see a shiny brass casing. It was loaded. I set it in the hall.

Freddy's dresser drawers were heavy with artillery. He was either stupid, or assumed I was, to leave me here alone. Regretting that I hadn't taken Tony up on his offer of shooting lessons, I hauled out a semi-automatic pistol similar to his law enforcement one. I pulled back on the slide as I'd seen Tony do, noted the round in the chamber, let it snap closed and flicked the safety on. I put it on top of the snowshoes.

I kicked away the sleeping bag on the bed. The mattress was bare, but an antique Prince Albert tobacco can under the bed held a wad of twenties. I put it back, then pulled it out again, took the bills and stuffed them in the pocket of my jeans. If anyone else lived in this wilderness I could try to bribe them to take me to town.

Buddy's bedroom was across the hall. He had actually made his bed, but I couldn't resist checking out the lump in the middle. A gun maybe? I pulled back the covers and discovered a pair of Jockey shorts stuck to the sheet and the smell of fresh semen. I turned my head and pulled the covers back up.

A curling photo of Buddy holding a black lab puppy had been wedged into the window frame above the bed. In the background a stern-looking, plump woman held a small child. I wondered what his mother thought of her son's facial adornments.

Buddy's possessions were piled onto unpainted shelves nailed to the particle board wall. I found a Red Wing shoe box that contained a pair of small leather gloves and a pile of chemical gel pocket warmers, the kind that get hot when squeezed. I filled a pocket of the ski jacket with them. Another box held an array of military Distinctive Insignia that rattled as I set them back on the shelf. Ironic, I thought, that Buddy and Freddy cherished artifacts of the government they wanted to overthrow.

I stepped over the snowshoes and the pistol to get to the kitchen. The last greasy blackened sausage link lay in congealed fat in the frying pan. I ate it in two bites while I rummaged through the cupboards. An open bag of stale beef jerky and the remnants of a bag of cracked M & Ms were all that was left in the pantry. I put them into my pockets.

The refrigerator was bare except for some sour milk, a flaccid brown banana, several six packs of Lucky Lager, and a third of a bottle of Jack Daniels. I peeled the banana and gagged down the mushy flesh.

I gathered my survival gear and squatted next to the stove. My options were to wait for the skinheads and hope for the best, or try to get to the highway. The sky was clouding up and even inside the trailer the temperature was cold enough to make my breath mist. I thought about Bruno and Auntie Liz and Todd the pizza kid's Aunt Fran and Freddy's poor frustration tolerance. And Buddy's strange passion.

I went to the table and opened the brown bag he'd given me. A ripped sheet of three-ring binder paper was folded into fourths on the top. I unfolded it.

The penciled note was written in a smudged third grade scrawl.

"Kan't wate to git bak an fuk yoo and mak yoo buk wif joy. Luv Buddy."

Inside the bag were a dozen purple, yellow, and silver cello packages. Condoms. Buddy the Studly Dude had been thoughtful enough to offer me a selection. Did he think he was going to use them all in one night? "Thanks, Bud," I said. "You just made my decision simple."

I put the snowshoes and pistol into the backpack, hoisted the pack and the rifle on my shoulder, and walked into the snow. Ten feet away from the staircase I reconsidered and climbed back up the stairs to the trailer. I grabbed the bag with the condoms off the table.

I trudged down the driveway in the tracks of the truck. The memory of my hike with Uncle Chester up Mount Shasta gave me courage, but within a quarter mile I staggered under the weight of the rifle. I tried to switch shoulders but skidded on ice and slid on my bottom into a pothole. The rifle barrel gouged my calf.

Wincing with pain, I staggered to my feet but fell again.

I unstrapped the rifle and stashed it behind a digger pine, rationalizing that the best I could do with it anyway would be to whack someone with the stock, because the recoil would shoot me to the moon. I took the pistol out of the backpack and put it the pocket of the jacket, and sat on the shoulder of the road and strapped on the snowshoes. After tripping and falling on my face a couple dozen times I got the hang of walking like a drunken duck.

I set off parallel to the road and listened for sounds of Tinsel's truck. When the sun had risen higher I chewed on a piece of jerky and sucked on a handful of snow. My stomach cramped from the cold, and I berated myself for not packing water. I squeezed one of the heat packs and slipped it inside my shirt next to my belly.

I walked for hours but it seemed like days. By the time the sun began to sink behind the mountain, the thought of running into Freddy and Buddy made me jump at the sound of the snow crunching under my feet. I turned away from the road in what I calculated to be the direction of the highway, then put another of the heat packs inside the jacket and contemplated how many toes I'd lose to frostbite. I ate some more jerky and prayed I'd find shelter for the night before I froze. I counted. One hundred steps before I allowed myself to rest, and then one hundred more.

The unexpected movement in the shadow of the manzanita made me yelp. The bear wasn't more than two yards away from me. She reared on her hind legs.

I shouted more in surprise than calculated defense and reached for the pistol. She waved her paws and took a step in my direction.

I hollered, "Go away." I pointed the pistol at her chest and pulled the trigger. It didn't budge.

She took another step toward me and fell to all fours. Her head cocked like a dog listening to a master's voice.

The image of being charged and eaten alive by a starving

bear made my hand shake so badly I couldn't dislodge the safety. I pulled the glove off with my teeth and clicked off the safety.

I pulled up the barrel and pulled the trigger. Boom. The pistol discharged and flew out of my hand. I blew backwards into the snow and hit my chin on my knee. A tree limb crashed down near my head.

The bear loped a few yards away, then turned her head over her shoulder and stared at me.

"Go away," I rasped.

She turned to face me and watched me struggle to my knees.

"I'm warning you. I'll shoot." I dug through the snow with numb fingers to find the pistol.

She sat and cocked her head.

I found the pistol buried in a foot of snow and then saw my glove. The bear was licking it.

"Go away and leave my glove alone." My tone worked well with disruptive clients but clearly not with bears.

She twitched her upper lip and sank her teeth into the leather. She shook her head and propelled the glove in my direction. I could almost reach it.

I aimed the gun at her. She curled her lip and butted the air with her nose, a gesture more a sneer than a threat.

"Aren't you supposed to be hibernating?"

She stared.

I put the safety back on and slipped the pistol into my pocket. One of my snowshoes had fallen off and I retied it while I kept my eye on the bear.

My heart was racing by the time I got to my feet. The bear turned and ambled away, leaving a trail in the snow. I gasped and coughed. Twenty yards down the hill she turned back around and plopped her butt in the snow. She scratched her belly with her hind leg, yawned, then stood and strolled off.

She had to sleep somewhere. The black clouds in the

north threatened more snow and cautioned me not to be fussy. I picked up my glove and followed in the bear's tracks down the hill and around a copse of junipers.

The remaining sliver of white sun illuminated the rusting tin roof of a log cabin buried to its windowsills in snow. I slid down the hill and burrowed in the snow but exhaustion and the cold made me too weak to free the door. I leaned against the rough logs and pushed on one of the windows. It creaked. I leaned on it with my shoulder and popped it open.

Behind me I heard the faint grumble of Freddy's truck straining up the road. I hopped in the window and looked out to find the bear.

She had vanished into the dusk.

Twenty-three

The cabin smelled of mold and smoke. I poked around in the fading light until I found a plastic bag containing a box of matches. I lit a rolled-up newspaper and dropped in into the potbellied stove. I considered starting a wood fire, but decided against risking Freddy seeing smoke.

A sleeping bag lay over a willow chair next to the potbellied stove. Before I wrapped myself in it, I shook out the ripe, musty residue from the various species who had used it before me. The filth made me sneeze until I doubled over. I settled into the chair and munched on the rest of the jerky and candy while I prayed the morning light would reveal an easy way to the highway, or at least something to eat.

The sounds of scratching and tiny feet scurrying across the wood plank floor woke me. Mice. I tucked the sleeping bag protectively under me and pulled the jacket over my head.

I dreamed I was imprisoned under bodies in a boxcar. Uncle Chester peered through a crack to find me. He broke through the slats with a hatchet and pulled the dead out onto the frozen ground. When he reached for me, I turned into a bear and ran into the forest.

The silhouette of the mid-morning sun glaring through the cold gray sky awakened me. I tried to sit up and winced when a million needles shot through my back and legs. I couldn't tell which parts of me were asleep and which parts were frozen stiff. My nose felt as if it were impacted with hailstones. I was starving and urgently thirsty.

The cabin was colder than the bottom of the river during the spring thaw. I dragged the sleeping bag with me while I poked a stick of kindling into rustic cupboards and peeked behind the mildewed newspapers and mouse droppings that lined the shelves. I wondered if hantavirus was active below freezing.

The closest I got to food was a half-empty can of refried beans with the gray scum of dead mold clinging to the sides. I was tempted to pick through it but having my standards, scraped out as much of the gunk as I could, and cleaned the can with snow. I sipped more as it melted in my hand. For the main course I gnawed the only fingernail I hadn't chewed to the nub.

I pried open the window and threw the snowshoes and backpack with the can in it outside. My tracks from the night before were nearly covered with new snowfall, giving me hope that Freddy and Buddy wouldn't be able to track me. I pulled myself up to the sill as high as my waist and ungracefully somersaulted head-first into the snow bank.

The bag of condoms fell from my pocket onto the snow. The memory of a rowdy eighth-grade birthday party for which I'd earned a spanking from my father gave me an idea. I unwrapped a red condom and blew on it. It tasted like crude oil. I stuffed snow into it and squashed it until it melted. The major problem was that a handful of snow melted into a tablespoon of water but I managed to stuff the red one and a black one before my fingers turned blue. I tied them and put them inside my jacket.

I looked in the direction I had last seen the bear. Her tracks had disappeared. The ground sloped, then dipped into a depression lined with the skeletons of river oaks and cottonwoods as far as I could see. A question from an intelligence test came to mind. "What would you do if you were lost in the forest in the daytime?" I strapped on the snowshoes and followed the frozen creek bed down the mountainside.

Newly discovered leg muscles shrieked in agony and my back threatened to collapse completely. I skidded down the snow-covered ice mostly on foot but occasionally on my backside. About the time my legs began to shake so hard they couldn't support me, the ice cracked and my knee plunged into icy water. The shot of adrenaline sent me scrambling to the rocks lining the stream. I shook my head to keep away the image of my decomposed body being discovered by a fisherman in the spring. The good news was that I didn't have to melt snow for drinking water anymore.

The water I scooped up in the can chilled me to the bone. I had to get it to body temperature. I kneeled at the bank and tried to fill condoms but only succeeded in sending a green one and a red one writhing downstream like deflated fish. Next I tried to pour water from the can into a blue condom with raised studs (for my pleasure) but ended up with more water outside than inside. I finally took a sip from the can and spit it into the mouth of the condom. The technique worked. I filled up a half dozen, tied them, and tucked them into my jacket. My lips were cracked and my teeth felt as thought they would shatter from the cold, but I had water.

I wobbled like a toad on stilts down the stream bank, and managed to fall only once, popping a condom. By the time the sun was overhead, the rumble of snow tires and chunka-chunka of chains indicated that the highway was nearby and I allowed myself the luxury of sitting on a rock to gather my strength. I drank water from two of the condoms, unable to decide if the worst part was the oily taste of the lubricant or drinking my own spit.

Drenched with sweat and chilling rapidly, I pushed myself

up on quivering legs and forced every step while I concentrated on the image of a hot bath. The muffled scrape of a snowplow guided me toward civilization, or at least as much of it as Trinity County could offer.

The highway was cut into the rock cliff forty feet below me. The slope continued to a steep canyon on the other side of the road. There were no paths and the only footholds were a few struggling scrub oaks that hadn't yet decided to die and hundreds of tall skinny twigs growing straight out of the cliff. Poison oak. I considered jumping and hoping for the best but if the skinheads were on the prowl and I broke an ankle—or worse—I'd be dust.

The ground shook from a passing logging truck. I pitched a rock at it and hit the top timber. The rock ricocheted off onto the tarmac and bounced into the ditch adjacent to the road. The truck driver downshifted but kept going.

I considered plan B. I pulled out the gun and braced myself against a tree. I fumbled with the safety, my fingers trembling not from fear, but fatigue. A rumble of tires interrupted the stillness of the forest and I leveled the gun over the highway and squeezed the trigger. Bang. The recoil pushed me into a rock. A jolt of pain shot down my leg, but at this point I was thankful for all the adrenaline I could get. The car below sped up and passed me in a blur.

Okay, so shooting a gun wasn't the most brilliant move. Even in Trinity County most people wouldn't stop to check out the commotion, unless of course they wanted to shoot back. I put the pistol back in the pack. On to plan C.

I pulled out my arsenal of condoms and set them on the ground. Four water-filled ones left and more if I could stuff them with snow. Another car came around the corner and when it was below me, I dropped a purple condom. It hit the highway and burst after the car passed. The car didn't slow down. I calculated the correction I'd have to make.

A drone of tires increased in pitch as another vehicle came

around the corner from the east. I wrapped my arm around the tree and leaned over the cliff to drop the condom as it came around the corner. Just as I let go, I choked back my yell.

The red blob scored a direct hit onto the windshield of Tinsel's truck. I jumped back but not before I saw Studly's shaved head poke from the passenger window and look back at the cliff. The truck slowed but kept going. I didn't know if he'd seen me.

I lay shivering in the snow and mud for a few moments while I waited for them to come back. While my heart stopped pounding, I convinced myself they wouldn't.

A whirring sound of tires told me that another vehicle was approaching from the east. I pushed myself back to a sitting position and wrapped my legs around the tree. The car passed before I could get into position to drop another condom. I got ready for the next car.

A slow drone of tires approached from the east at the same time I heard a rumble from the west. I held a condom in each hand and braced against the tree.

A sky-blue Mercedes just like Richard Peck's rolled around the turn. I dropped a green condom and, fearing I'd missed, recklessly lobbed a heavier blue studded one. The green condom bounced onto the hood of the Mercedes and blew apart, sending a spray of water onto the windshield. The extra weight of the blue one propelled it on a wild trajectory across the highway. It flew through the open driver's side window of the oncoming truck and exploded right into the side of Freddy's face.

The Mercedes eased to a stop and pulled off onto a gravel turnout. Tony, dressed in plainclothes, jumped out of the passenger side and scanned the cliff.

My cry was eclipsed by the screech of Freddy's brakes as he slammed the truck to a stop in the oncoming lane. He jumped from the truck leaving his door open. He scooped up a rock, ran across the highway and banged the rock on the roof of the Mercedes. "You shitheads wanna start something? What the hell you throwing at my truck?"

Tony shouted, "Back off."

Across the highway, Buddy was standing on the running board of Freddy's truck with the .22 pointed at Tony.

"Oh my God." I fumbled in the backpack until I felt the pistol. I pulled it out and clicked off the safety. "I'm up here," I shouted.

The skinheads and Tony looked up at me.

Freddy smashed the rock against the windshield of the Mercedes and a cracking sound echoed down the canyon as the glass shattered. "Goddamn bitch. Shoot her, Buddy."

I knew he wouldn't. I aimed back at him. "Put the rifle down, Buddy. I don't want to hurt you."

Buddy lowered the rifle.

Freddy charged back across the highway. "Give me the goddamn rifle, you fucking putz."

Tony pulled his service revolver out of a shoulder holster, and crouched behind the Mercedes. He screamed, "Cassie, get the hell out of there. Run."

I would have been lucky to work up to a slow crawl. I kept the pistol aimed at Buddy. "I'm okay, Tony. You get the tall one, the other one won't hurt me."

"Damn it, Cassie. Run." He maneuvered for position. I could see Richard lying prone in the front seat of his car.

I scooted behind the tree for more cover but my legs weren't going anywhere else.

Freddy yanked his rifle away from the shorter skinhead and took aim at me. "Fucking cunt bitch."

"I wouldn't do it," I hollered back. I heard the rumble of a logging truck approaching from the west.

Tony popped up from behind the Mercedes and took the police stance, ready to fire. "Drop it," he shouted.

The ground shook and the rumble raised in pitch.

Freddy was oblivious to the noise. He aimed the rifle at Tony and insanely started across the road.

The truck rounded the corner as Freddy crossed the center line. It veered to miss him and plowed into the open door of his truck. Freddy dove across the westbound lane under the Mercedes. The door of the pickup wrenched from its hinges and spun into the air, the rusty metal glimmering softly in the diffuse sunlight. The logging truck fishtailed and managed to regain control but not before the tail end of it smashed into Freddy's truck and pushed it over the edge into the canyon.

The echo of Buddy's scream down the canyon made me want to throw up.

Twenty-four

The door to Tinsel's truck landed on the pavement with a metallic clang, bounced, and spun into the ditch. Across the highway, sprays of snow shot into the air as the vehicle smashed into rocks and flattened trees on its way to the canyon bottom. After what seemed like hours, it splashed into the creek. Silence prolonged by horror lingered over the canyon before being punctuated by intense human activity.

Tony dragged Freddy out from under the Mercedes by his feet and restrained him with a knee between his shoulder blades. He cuffed the skinhead at the same time he shouted to me, "You okay, Cassie?"

"I am now. How do I get to the road?"

"Hang on. We'll get you."

The skinhead hollered, "Fucking bitch. You did it now. You're gonna pay."

Tony yanked him up by the collar and smashed his face into the pavement.

"What's the matter, asshole? Haven't had enough road rash for today?"

The logging truck driver ran up the highway, glanced at Tony, and ran to the edge of the road to look down the canyon at Freddy's truck. "Fucking-A. What the hell was that asshole doing in the middle of the road? I sure as hell hope no one was in that truck."

"There was a guy. Any sign of him?" Tony ran across the road and looked down. He shook his head. "I doubt he could have survived."

Richard came out from his Mercedes holding his cellular phone. "I called the Trinity County Sheriff's Office. Reception's pretty bad up here but I think they got the message."

"Richard, show Cassie where the road is at." Tony started down the canyon, followed by the truck driver.

Richard walked east around the turn and after a few moments I heard the smooth leather soles of his wingtips slipping and scraping on the rocks. I looked up to see him hanging onto a tree, his face red, his glasses misted, and crescents of sweat in the underarms of his suit.

"This way," he panted. "You missed the road by a few yards." He smiled weakly and I wondered if I would have to help him down.

Until I tried to stand up, I didn't realize I was shivering violently. I sat down hard and looked at Richard. He reached out his hand.

"That's okay, Richard. I can do it." I pulled myself up with my arms and clung to trees on the way down to the highway.

He offered his arm to me again but I waved him off, not from pride but because if I slowed down, I'd fall down. I made it to the Mercedes and collapsed in the backseat. The leather creaked as Richard sank into the front seat.

He looked over the seat at me. "How are you doing?"

"I want some food and a bath. Then I'll be just peachy."

"Food we can do. The bath will have to wait." He reached over and pulled open a small cooler on the floor of the backseat. "We figured you might be hungry when we found you." He extracted a plastic bag and opened it. "Smoked salmon."

I moaned. "How did you know?" I ripped off a chunk and stuffed it into my mouth.

"I have a bottle of Sauvignon Blanc, too, but you should probably warm up first."

"I'll be your expert witness any time," I mumbled through the salmon, then hiccuped.

Richard reached under the front seat and pulled out a thermos. "How about some tea? Earl Grey." He poured me half a cup of steaming tea.

I sipped on it to quell the hiccups. Suddenly I became intensely sleepy and laid my head back. The image of Buddy plummeting over the edge went through my mind before my conscious thoughts floated away. When I opened my eyes, Tony was looking down at me. The echoes of sirens harmonized up the canyon.

"Hi." I pushed myself up.

He did not look happy. "Cassie, next time I tell you to run, you run. I cannot keep my mind on what I have to do if I'm worried about you. Damn it. Don't you remember that's what got my father fucking killed?"

Richard sat with his hands on the steering wheel, looking out the cracked windshield and studiously ignoring us.

I glared back at Tony. "Watch your language, please. I've heard enough of the 'F' word for about two centuries."

"Fine, we won't effing discuss it." He slapped his open hand on the roof and swung into the passenger seat.

We waited in silence for the ambulance and sheriff's deputies to arrive. I sat back in Richard's Mercedes and looked at the attorney's stylish haircut, manicured nails, and well-cut suit. I savored the scent of smoked salmon, Earl Grey, and leather upholstery and thought about how he gallantly climbed the hill to rescue me in his perfectly polished wingtips. So why at this moment was I attracted to Tony with the jarhead hairdo, rough manner, occasional streaks of temper, and God knows how many sexual conquests?

"Life sucks," I said.

Neither of them turned around.

Twenty-five

"I think Bruno was Anerd's rival," I said to Tony and Richard.

We sat in the Mercedes watching the setting sun burst through the cracks in the windshield. Grim shouts rose from the direction of the canyon.

Tony looked over his shoulder. He was over his anger at me but I knew I'd get another lecture later. "I don't know, Cassie. Bruno seemed like a regular guy to me."

"Studly—or Buddy—or whatever his name was said Anerd's rival was close to Homer and wanted revenge for a business deal. Bruno is basically Homer's grandfather and he got the raw end of a deal from Anerd. And Freddy was the leader of the gang that beat Bruno up."

"Well, I don't think your Buddy is going to be talking about it in the future." Tony leaned over to look out Richard's window.

A Trinity County sheriff's deputy in a green jumpsuit ambled across the highway to where we were parked. He leaned casually against the car door, the Kevlar of his bullet-proof vest tapping against the steel. He craned his neck and pulled the vest away from his chest a fraction of an inch. His face was damp with sweat. "Found what was left of him." He nodded toward me. "I don't think you want the young lady here when we bring him up."

He turned and hollered to another deputy carrying a black body bag. "We're gonna need a couple of bags. Tell the ambulance driver we don't need him, and bring some of those flares out. We're gonna need 'em to see." He turned back to Richard and Tony. "Take her on back to town before it's pitch dark." He winked at me. "Looks like you could use some chow and a nice bubble bath, miss. We want you all fixed up nice when we take your statement."

I was too tired to tell him he was a chauvinist, so I smiled at him instead.

He spoke to Tony. "The other skinhead's being booked. We'd appreciate any help you could give us down at the jail." He started to walk away then turned back. "You're Officer Mesa, right?"

Tony nodded as he got out of the car.

The sheriff's deputy grinned. "That tip you gave us was right on. Dispatch just radioed for a few guys to get down to Cedar Gulch. Woods's head was just located at the landfill down there. Looks like it'd been chopped off and wrapped in a garbage bag. Guess that means our department and yours will be up all night in the rain looking for the rest of him. Pretty gruesome day, huh?"

"Thanks for the info," Tony said as the deputy walked off.

Richard sighed. "That's par for this case. I guess the good news is that not much else can go wrong." He chuckled and shook his head. "Thanks, Tony. But please don't do me any favors in the future."

I felt a little guilty. "It's my fault, Richard. If I hadn't told Tony about Todd's theory, maybe Anerd's head would have never been found."

"I suppose it's better the truth is out." He rubbed his temple. "I guess we can always appeal."

Tony opened my door and held his hand out. "That was

Todd's theory about Anerd being in the dump? Maybe that kid oughta be a cop instead of a shrink."

"Maybe."

"You want to ride in front?"

"Is this your way of apologizing for yelling and swearing at me?"

He sighed. "Get in front, Cassie, and quit being a pain in the butt."

I took his hand and let him help me out. He pulled me close to him and wrapped his arms around me, enveloping me in the smell of his sweat. He kissed me on the forehead. When he let go, I began to tremble. I hopped in the front seat and poured myself a cup of tea from the thermos while I chattered to Richard. I was not going to let myself cry yet.

"So what do you think about Bruno being Anerd's rival?"

Richard started the car. "Not much. That gives my client more reason to want to hurt Anerd." The deputy directing traffic motioned him forward and he pulled into the eastbound lane toward Jackpot.

I thought for a minute. "That doesn't mean Homer knew. Maybe Bruno killed Anerd." I took another sip of tea. "Bruno talked to me about being afraid. Wouldn't that be justifiable homicide if he thought the skinheads, led by Anerd, would hurt him or his family again?"

"Cassie, you're grasping at straws. You're trying to make connections that probably aren't there. And Bruno isn't my client anyway."

"Well, who else could have killed Anerd? Verlan and Sally were in jail when he disappeared."

"I'm not sure it matters. I'm concerned about keeping Homer out of prison, not solving the mystery of the skinhead gang in Trinity County. All I need from you is to show that my client didn't have the mental or emotional capacity to conceive of a plot to kidnap and kill Anerd."

"I can't testify that he has diminished capacity. I'd be lying. But maybe if we figure it out, we can clear Homer."

"Whatever you need to do, Cassie. But the trial could start as early as tomorrow and I'll need your testimony by Thursday."

His unspoken suggestion that I needed to establish my priorities was clear. "I'll get up early and talk to Homer before court tomorrow. How was jury selection?"

"What can I say? Anerd brought a good deal of money into this community and there's a number of folk who don't like minorities, and especially minority skinheads."

I rolled my head against the seat back. "This does not sound good at all. I'll talk to him again, but if he refuses to tell me anything, can you work out a deal with Max Valentine? He seems like a reasonable guy."

Richard laughed. "Didn't you know? Mr. Nice Guy District Attorney wants to be a judge. A stepping stone for the governor's office I imagine. He would just love to get a conviction like this under his belt before the election."

"What about Laurence Troutman? Is there any way of convincing him to help Homer? After all, it could help Sally and Verlan, too."

Richard snorted. "Troutman is about the most difficult man I ever met."

"But I bet Sally won't testify against Homer. She said she didn't believe he would murder her father. Troutman must know that or why would he have been so furious when I spoke with her? And Homer is protective of her. I don't believe either one of them would hurt Anerd—Sally because she loved her father, and Homer because he wouldn't hurt Sally."

"And Laurence Troutman will claim that Homer killed Anerd to protect Sally from him. And that Sally is lying to protect him."

"He would say his own client would lie?"

Richard shook his head. "Oh, I'm sure he'll present her as some innocent victim blinded by love. And she's so dumb, she'll fall into it."

"Homer gets upset at the sight of a trapped housefly, for goodness' sake. In spite of his attempt at showing an attitude, I doubt he'd have the guts, or heart, to kill anyone."

"Then you will have to use that in your testimony. The only thing we may have in our favor is your ability to convince the jury that Homer couldn't kill a fly."

Twenty-six

By the time we reached the Yellow Inn, the rain had turned to a drizzle that melted fissures into the snow and sent rivulets of icy water down onto the asphalt of Aunt Fran's driveway. Tony helped me out of Richard's battered Mercedes and brought me to the porch.

Aunt Fran answered the door. "We were so worried about you. Nothing like that has ever happened here before. I'm so sorry. . . ." She hugged me and led us into the kitchen.

"I'm just glad the power is back on and the phone works." My first priority was to call Auntie Liz to tell her I was okay.

Maria answered the phone at Tony's house. "She's doing much better but she's just headed to bed."

"Let me talk to her anyway." I needed to hear her voice.

Auntie Liz came on the phone, her voice tired but stronger than when I left her. "Did Tony and the other young man with the nice car find you?"

"I was sitting there waiting for them."

"Were you hurt?"

"Not a bit. Thanks to Uncle Chester and what he taught me I was just fine." I had an image of Uncle Chester's apoplectic ghost watching me suck melted snow out of red and blue condoms.

"That's good dear. I was afraid those bad boys who came into my house would try to get you, too."

"Don't you worry. They can't hurt us now. You go on to bed and I'll be back in a few days."

I hung up, praying her ordeal hadn't hurt her permanently.

Todd sat at the oak table, eating. "Want some?" He handed me a slice of pepperoni pizza.

"Of course." I joined him at the table.

Aunt Fran poured coffee for Richard and Tony and put on the kettle for tea.

Todd jabbered through half a piece of pizza. "So, did the skinheads take you to the Trailer of Armageddon?"

I sucked on a piece of pepperoni. "How did you know about the trailer?"

He swallowed and smacked his lips. "What do you think I do after the pizza parlor and my homework's done? Watch one of our two crummy television stations?"

"You explore?" A string of cheese fell onto my chin and I wound it around a finger and stuffed it into my mouth.

"I know just about every acre in this county. I was hiking up there last summer and found the trailer. What a dive."

Tony cupped his hands around his coffee mug. "Todd wanted to come with us. With his detective skill, we should have let him."

"Yeah, but all I got to do was give directions. You got any soda, Aunt Fran?" He tipped his chair back and without standing up, opened the refrigerator door.

Tony said, "Half the county was looking for you. I found the trailer yesterday afternoon but you'd already left it. I followed your tracks until dark and then again this morning but lost them just after that little cabin. The sheriff had already arranged to bring in some tracking dogs." He cleared his throat. "Then Richard was kind enough to drive me around after court."

"Hey, it wasn't a kindness," Richard countered. "I was frantic all during jury selection."

"I was afraid to stay too near the road. When I got to the river, I walked on the ice for a while. Until I fell in." My body went limp.

"You must be exhausted." Fran poured my tea into a delicate porcelain cup painted with tiny violets and set the matching teapot next to me. "Let me turn down your bed and get you into a nice hot tub." She wiped down the counter and admonished the men before she left. "You boys leave the questions for tomorrow after Cassie gets her rest."

"Thanks for finding me, guys. I don't want to think about the alternative." I pushed back. "By the way, how's your truck?" I asked Tony.

"Those idiots took out the distributor rotor. It was a simple thing to fix."

Fran led me down the hall while I balanced the teacup on its saucer.

I woke up shivering in the lukewarm water of the tub. I got out and wrapped myself in the fluffy towel Fran had set out for me. I ate the chocolate truffle she had laid on the bedside table, pulled up the down comforter, and dreamed of bodies floating facedown in streams.

The next time I opened my eyes the house was silent and gray with the first light of dawn. I dressed and fixed some tea and toast. Aunt Fran came into the kitchen and made noises about how I needed a proper breakfast. I shushed her and asked if I could borrow her car. She handed me the keys and pushed a fruit scone into the pocket of my jacket.

I arrived at the jail before seven. Martin, my favorite deputy, was eating his usual meal.

"I need to see Homer before the trial starts today."

"I heard that boy's in a bigger mess and really needs your help. He's eating now, but I'll see what I can do." He pushed a button on the intercom and slid a hot cinnamon roll dripping with melted butter through the window opening. "In case you got away without your breakfast."

"Thanks." By the time he called me back to the window, I had finished it.

Homer walked into the interview room with his head lowered and his hair falling over his face. He pulled out the chair and sat facing away from me.

I leaned over the metal table. "Your trial starts today. Richard wants me to testify tomorrow. I figure this is about your last chance to talk to me."

"You mean about my last chance to save my ass."

"That's one way of putting it."

"I don't think you get it." He lifted his head and looked at me. Both his eyes were swollen purple and red.

"Homer, who did this?" I slapped my hand on the table more out of anger than shock.

Homer closed his eyes and said nothing.

I lowered my voice enough to get his attention. "Was it Verlan? Or how about his pal Freddy with the metal teeth? The one who beat up your grandfather."

"My grandfather? He died when I was little."

"Okay, your stepgrandfather, Bruno."

He jumped up so quickly that his chair fell over and clattered against the cement floor. "Why can't you just mind your own business? Don't you see it gets worse every time you get involved?"

"I'll leave you alone if you tell me one thing."

He rolled his eyes to the ceiling. "What?"

"Did Bruno kill Anerd?"

"What the hell are you talking about?"

"Your skinhead friend Buddy told me Anerd had a rival. Bruno fit the description."

"Buddy's dead."

"I know. I saw it happen. Is Bruno Anerd's rival?"

"Bruno didn't have any beef with Anerd except to protect my grandmother and me from him. Anerd's skinheads beat him up as an example if you hadn't figured it out yet." His voice was derisive. "And they're gonna kill me and maybe you, if you don't back off."

"Homer, it's painfully obvious that your strategy of not talking hasn't worked so far. What makes you think more silence will make them stop?"

"Look, if I get out they'll never find me again." His eyes were narrow and black.

"And if you get sent to prison because you didn't cooperate?"

"At least I'll be away from here. I'll be in a place where no one knows me. Or my family." His eyes grew even blacker and seemed to recede into the inflamed skin swollen around his features.

"Did the skinheads beat Bruno to keep you from snitching on them?"

"Isn't it obvious?" He hung his head and his demeanor changed from hostile to helpless. "Please, just go away. Tell Richard you can't help me and don't testify for me."

"So you won't talk because you are protecting your grandmother and Bruno?"

He nodded.

"And others?"

He nodded again.

I sighed. "Okay, Homer. I'll go away. But I can't promise you I won't be back."

On the way out I stopped at the front and spoke with Deputy Martin. "Isn't there anything you can do to protect him? Why can't he be in the psych cell?"

"We can't put him there when we got real psychs. We offered to keep him in his cell during meal and exercise times but he refused. Prisoner's rights, you know. They'd just find another way to get him anyway. It don't take too long to rough somebody up. Just a half a minute or so if the guy doesn't fight back."

"Do you know who did it?"

Deputy Martin shrugged. "It's not too hard to guess, but the boy won't say nothing, and we can't catch 'em. All we can offer him is medical care."

"But they could kill him."

"Well, that ain't gonna happen. Hell, killing him'd take all their fun away. But don't worry, now that the trial's started we have an excuse to keep him isolated." He shook his head. "That boy got himself hooked up with some real assholes. Hope he learns his lesson."

Deputy Martin certainly didn't make me feel any better about it, but that wasn't the worst of my problems. I drove Fran's car back to her house and prepared myself to give Richard the bad news.

Twenty-seven

Richard was on his way out of the Yellow Inn. He looked at me. "Any luck?"

"Did you know he was beat up again?"

"My client appears to be bound and determined to take the fall for Anerd's kidnapping, and probably his murder as well." He straightened his tie and brushed an imaginary piece of lint off his sleeve. "Tony brought your laptop. I'd appreciate any report you could write today. Bring me the disc. We'll get it printed out at the courthouse." He swung his briefcase onto the passenger seat. "See you after court," he said, and got into the Mercedes.

Tony was sitting at the kitchen table watching Todd devour oatmeal from a bowl big enough for a Rottweiler. He looked at me. "I see why you and Todd get along so well."

Todd and I looked at him blankly.

"The way you eat," Tony explained.

Todd dove back into the bowl.

"I don't like oatmeal," I said.

"I meant the quantity and frequency."

"Oh." I turned on the heat under the teapot, sat down and pulled out the scone Aunt Fran had stashed in my pocket. "Richard's not exactly the warm, friendly guy who hired me. He looks as if his only friend ran over his favorite dog."

Todd poured more milk on his oatmeal and slid a plate and the jam jar toward me. "You'd be that way too if your Mercedes got smashed up." Milk sloshed out of his mouth and dribbled down his chin as he spoke.

Tony handed yellow paper napkins to Todd and me. "Richard's not used to losing. That's the reason he hired you."

I smeared raspberry jam on my scone but my appetite was suddenly gone. "I know. I'm afraid I let him down."

"It isn't your fault if some wannabe skinhead won't co-operate," Tony said. "Maybe someone ought to slap him upside the head to help him get motivated."

I ignored Tony's surge of testosterone. "If I had spent more time talking with Homer rather than running all over the state to interview his family, maybe he would have trusted me more."

"He's made his bed." Tony probed at a molar with a tooth-pick. "Some people just decide they're gonna be assholes."

"But Homer's not that way. He's not a jerk, he's keeping quiet to protect his family."

Tony spat out a sliver of wood. "Yeah, well he's doing a real good job of it."

The tea kettle whistled. I jumped up to take it off the stove. "When the sheriff's deputies brought Homer to my office before his bail was rescinded, I almost thought he would talk. But I took such a dislike to him I lost my pa-tience. It's my fault he won't trust me now."

Todd dumped the contents of two more packets of instant oatmeal into his bowl. "Is there enough water for me?"

I poured water into a mug and jiggled the pot. "You can have the rest, but put some more on because I'm going to want a pot. I have to get busy on this report."

"Why didn't you like him?" Todd asked.

"Like who?"

The teenager lifted the blob of oatmeal and plopped it

back into the bowl, kneading it with the back of the spoon like bread dough. "The Indian. The one you're supposed to write the report on. You know, Homer?"

"I'm not sure how much I should be sharing this with you. You know, confidentiality?"

"Oh, come on. Like I don't know what's going on around here. Besides, it's public domain."

Tony raised an eyebrow. "Smart kid." He jammed another toothpick between his teeth.

I turned to Todd. "Okay, when I first met Homer he had a nasty attitude and shoes decorated with swastikas."

"So? You must see lots of people who are weird and nasty. Especially for evaluations. Why did he bother you so much?"

"What is this, therapy?"

Todd shrugged and grinned.

I thought a moment. "I guess what really got me angry was that Homer was so detached. I mean, I would think someone with his background wouldn't have anything to do with such evil. After all, his grandfather, the one who was married to his grandmother Winema, was Jewish."

"What changed your mind about him?" Todd poured a cup of milk into his bowl.

"His grandmother loves him, but so do grandmothers of ax murderers." I poured some milk into my cup and watched it swirl and flow into the blackness of the Earl Grey. "He's willing to sacrifice himself to the skinheads to protect his stepgrandfather, Bruno. But I wonder if Bruno did away with Anerd." I stirred the milk into homogeneity with one of Tony's unused toothpicks. "I guess the thing that changed how I felt about Homer was when he expressed how much he cared for Sally, and how protective he was of her. He's the only person I've met who talks about her like she's a human and not a pork roast. He seems vulnerable when he talks about Sally."

"So now you want to help him and he won't cooperate."

"That's about it. I shouldn't have been so judgmental in the first place. I should have seen beyond the façade."

Todd took a bite of oatmeal then waggled his spoon in the air. "So now you do. And why does he have this façade?"

"Do you mean what was his agenda for getting into the White People's Brigade?"

"Yeah."

"To save Sally?"

"Maybe. Or maybe he wanted to get inside information so he could bust them," Todd said.

"You've been reading too many novels, kiddo. Homer's not that calculating. He's too naive. He wants to be accepted, not bust people."

"But the issue is that you want him to talk to you."

"Richard hired me because he thought Homer was set up and didn't have the psychological makeup to plot a kidnapping. His psychological test results pretty much proved that. But if he won't tell anyone what really happened, the jury won't believe whatever I have to say."

"So get him to cooperate."

"It's so easy for the young."

"Think of it this way—what's he want?"

I didn't have to think about it for long. "To protect his family. To protect Sally."

"So as you said, he's being quiet to protect them."

"Now all I have to do is convince him he will protect them better by talking to me. And I think I know how to do it." I raised my hand and he gave me a high five. "And you will make a good psychologist."

I met Todd for an early lunch at the café to plot the afternoon's strategy. He wolfed down his sandwich while I ate my soup and flipped through my notes. "I'm about three quarters done with the report on Homer," I told him. "I can finish the rest before you get home, then we can go to the jail."

"So which one is it going to be?" Todd slurped on a root beer float.

I looked up from my notes. "Which one is what going to be?"

"Tony or Richard. Which one are you going to go for?"

"What are you talking about?" I took a sip of tea, and looked back at my notes.

"Well, both of them look at you like they'd jump your bones if you breathed hard."

I leafed through pages to find a note on Freddy. "So which one do you think I should go for?" I dog-eared a corner to remind myself to go back to it later.

"Richard's rich. He could buy you a bauble or two. Go for him and get him to buy you a Jaguar and take me for a spin."

"Sure, Todd. I'll get right on it." I found the section I wanted. "You know, Freddy said Anerd had a rival. Well if it's not Bruno, who else would it be?"

"I'll check it out." Todd shoveled a huge spoonful of root beer–covered ice cream into his mouth. "But on the other hand, chicks definitely get the hots for guys like Tony. He's pretty smart, too."

"What?" I was beginning to get annoyed. "Todd, we have lots of work to do. We can talk about my love life later. Besides, Tony has a girlfriend."

The teenager raised his eyebrows. "Oh, yeah? Well how come he never calls her or talks about her? And if she's such a girlfriend, why does he drool all over you?"

"I couldn't tell you." I flipped back a few pages. "What do you think Mavis's angle is in this? I wonder if she's as protective of her daughter as she makes out or if she has some other agenda?"

Todd twirled a mound of ice cream onto his tongue. "Maybe she's just a sportin' woman."

"Mavis? What would she sport?"

"No, I mean Tony's so-called girlfriend. Maybe she's just a sport fuck."

"Young man." I tried to sound stern and not giggle. "Watch your mouth. Besides, that's an adolescent fantasy driven by raging hormones—grown-up men don't think like that."

"Wrong." He grinned. "All guys think like that—grown-up men just won't admit it." He stirred the rest of the ice cream into the root beer and sucked up the mess with his straw. "So what do you think?"

"I think I'll have a root beer float. Want another?" I signaled for the waitress. While we waited, I instructed Todd, "See if you can find out from Sally what her relationship with Freddy and Buddy was. There's something else going on here. I just can't believe that Homer is taking all the beatings just because he's trying to protect his family. If you can get her to tell you, find out who's been beating him up and why. I suppose she knows. It's a small jail."

"I'm also gonna ask her who was there and what was said when Anerd's kidnapping was supposed to have been planned."

"Excellent thinking. If you get that out of her we'll be doing great." The waitress brought our floats, and I nodded thanks.

Todd used his forefinger to dam a trail of foam. "So does Tony ever bring this chick over for dinner to your house, or hold her hand while they're taking a walk, or somehow act like he's going out with her?"

I sighed. "You're fixated on my relationship with Tony. No, the only time I see her is when she leaves his house in the morning. She must go over there after he gets off work." I ate a bite of ice cream too fast, and winced when it sent chills up my forehead and scalp. "Now that you mention it, I've never seen him kiss her—he waves good-bye and she walks herself out to her car."

"You know why a guy won't kiss a gal like that?"

"Because he's afraid he might get carried away?"

"Not even close. It's either because he doesn't want her for more than screwing, or—"

"Yes?" I sucked ice cream foam off my spoon.

Todd gave me an evil grin. "It's because he just came in her mouth."

"Yuck. I can't believe I'm discussing kinky sex with a seventeen-year-old." I widened my eyes in mock horror. "I'll probably get arrested for contributing to the delinquency of a minor." I ripped the top off the paper straw protector and blew it across the table. It hit Todd in the forehead.

He laughed until he snorted root beer and then we both laughed some more.

Twenty-eight

At first I thought the knocking was a woodpecker.

I was sitting at the dining room table at the Yellow Inn processing words on my laptop when it dawned on me that the sound came from the front door. Tony had driven back to Cedar Gulch to help find the rest of Anerd's body and to check on Auntie Liz, Aunt Fran had gone grocery shopping, and Todd had gone back to school to take an American history midterm.

That left me to answer the door. Annoyed I saved the first eight pages of my report on Homer and found the next section of my notes before I got up to open the door.

The first thing I noticed about the woman standing on the porch was that she was tall. The second thing I noticed was that she was exceptionally well dressed. Halston suit, well-cut leather pumps, Gucci handbag, designer sunglasses. And a bruise the size and color of a small eggplant on the left side of her face.

I stepped back to allow her in. "Can I help you?" A silly question—she'd needed help before she arrived here.

"I heard Dr. Ringwald was staying here. I'd like to make an appointment. Are you her secretary?"

I was tempted to tell her that a secretary needs to take dictation and orders and that I wasn't particularly good at either one, but I bit my tongue. "I'm Dr. Ringwald. Let me get my appointment book."

She pulled off her sunglasses and followed me into the parlor. She blinked when I pulled back the curtains. The facial lines of chronic strain and too many suntans became visible in the light from the bay window. The pale coral frost lipstick she'd painted on a fraction wider than her ungenerous lips looked cheap on her. The gray tweed suit jacket was well tailored but frayed around the buttons and worn at the shoulders. Her shoes and bag were scuffed, and a black snag of thread from her skirt snaked down her left leg.

The only brightness on her, aside from the bruise, was the red rims around her gray eyes.

"Are you going to be okay? Do you have a safe place to go?"

She nodded numbly. "I'm fine." She clearly wasn't.

"Have a seat. I'll get you some tea." I led her to the settee and guided her onto it. "Just a minute." I ran to the kitchen and set the kettle on the range, cranking the gas up to high.

By the time I got back she had slouched backwards, a faded rag doll against Aunt Fran's aging upholstery. Her eyes focused on the wall at nothing in particular. I pulled up a side table and poured her a mug of chamomile.

After a few moments she pulled her eyes away from the wall and brought the mug to her lips with a shaky, delicate hand. She sipped cautiously and winced at the hot tea on her tongue. She quickly set the mug down, leaving a crescent of frosted coral on the rim.

For the first time, she really looked at me. "Sometimes I feel I can't go on. Now is one of those times." Her accent was faintly East Coast, Boston probably. She crossed a slender leg at the ankle, and rolled her weight to her right hip, grace in the face of adversity.

"How did you know I was here?" I asked, trying to pay

attention to her and not the clock that reminded me I had less than an hour to finish my report for Richard.

"I got your name from a friend. She said you were the only female psychologist in five counties and that you were up here on a case. I wanted to talk to a woman."

"What happened?" I leaned forward and fixed my eyes on hers.

"I told my physician that I bumped into a kitchen cabinet. It was a lie, of course." She took another sip of tea, cupped her hands around the mug, and looked down into it. The ligaments in her neck cracked.

The wall clock struck a quarter past the hour. I suppressed the urge to question her. Pushing wasn't going to make her talk, and if I told her she needed to wait until next week to see me, she might lose her courage altogether.

She finished her tea and set the mug on the table, then sighed again and recrossed her ankles, the right over the left.

"It was my husband. He's the one who hurt me." She touched the bruise on her cheek and winced. "He's hit me before but on the arms or chest—never where the bruises were visible like this one." She suddenly opened her eyes wide, startled, as though she'd just realized she'd left home without her underwear. "This is all confidential, isn't it? I mean, I haven't paid you but I would like to retain you."

"Absolutely. Anything you tell me stays in this room. That is, unless you tell me otherwise."

Her face relaxed. "I'd still prefer not to tell you my last name. At least not yet. My husband is . . . I have to protect. . . ."

I nodded to reassure her. "What about a first name?"

"Constance."

"Okay, Constance. Can you tell me more about what happened?"

"Connie."

"Pardon?"

"Call me Connie. I keep hoping every time will be the last, and he promises me it will be. But it's not." She laughed self-consciously. "Obviously, or I wouldn't be here. I've tried everything." She ran her fingers through shoulder-length graying blond hair and bit her bottom lip as though to prevent the story from spilling out of her mouth too quickly. "Do you mind if I smoke?"

Under the circumstances I decided to allow her to do whatever would relax her. "Let me find an ashtray." I ran to the kitchen and rummaged through the cupboard before I decided to let her use an old ceramic saucer.

"Here you go, Connie."

She had already lit up and was inhaling deeply when I came back in. She took the ashtray and exhaled through pursed lips, making a slight whistling sound. The smoke rolled into my face. I was immediately besieged by an uncontrollable attack of sneezes. I pinched the bridge of my nose, but try as I might, I couldn't stop. I grabbed a paper napkin, blew my nose, then walked as steadily as possible to the window and fumbled to open the latch.

By the time I looked back at her through watery eyes, she was staring at me the way a society matron might look at a beggar who'd called her a whore. She crushed the cigarette forcefully into the saucer and set it with a clunk onto the end table.

"You should have said something. If I'd had any idea you were allergic, I would have never asked to smoke."

She stood up and looked down her perfectly sculpted nose at me. "I should go. Maybe I can call you for an appointment later. Do you have a card?"

I went to the dining room and found a card in my computer case. I returned to the parlor and handed it to her.

She held the card between the two fingers she had used to hold the cigarette, waving it in the blue haze above her head. "What do I owe you?"

I was caught between embarrassment and vexation that my kindness was perceived as ill-mannered. “We’ll let it go for now. Would you like to schedule something before you leave?”

She smiled strangely, smugly. “No. I’ll call.”

I showed her out and closed the door. In my attempt to rescue the woman, I had lost an undeclared competition of moral superiority. I suppressed the urge to run after her and pound her into the street. Instead, I took out my aggressions on the laptop keyboard, and completed the report on Homer just as Todd walked in the door from school.

Twenty-nine

"So when did you start smoking?" Todd sniffed the air in the parlor as he swung his backpack onto the Eastlake gentleman's chair.

"I didn't. Someone came to visit while you were gone."

"Who?"

"Todd, there are some things that are truly not your business."

He looked wounded for two seconds, then went into the kitchen. "I need to make me a sandwich before we go. Want one?"

"Just a half. We ate two hours ago."

He made turkey, cheddar, and cranberry sauce sandwiches on whole wheat and popped them into the microwave.

"By the way," Todd said, "the rumor at school is that Mavis will testify this afternoon against Homer."

"I'm not surprised. I think Laurence Troutman has already got Verlan set up to give Homer the kiss of death." I nibbled at my sandwich. "That gives me an idea though. Do you have an extra diskette?"

Todd finished his sandwich and went to his room to get me another diskette. "You can print that on my machine." He cleared the table while I added a few lines to my report.

"I'm going to leave this diskette at the courthouse anyway." I winked at him and picked the last bite of turkey off the bread. "As soon as I finish this we can leave for the jail."

Todd swooped up my plate and dumped the scraps into the garbage, and slipped it into the sink of soapy water. He pulled out his calculus book and began his homework.

I completed the finishing touches when Aunt Fran walked in the back door with an armload of groceries. Her nephew ran to the car to get the rest. Fran put the milk away and attacked the dishes in the sink. She picked up the mug my visitor had used and wiped at the lipstick stain with the dish-rag. "Ugh. What a tacky color. No one in town but Connie Troutman uses that shade."

Todd bumped open the door with three sacks of groceries and a cello bag of grapefruit hanging from his arm. "So that's who was here. Has the ass—I mean, has her husband been hitting on her again?" He piled the sacks onto the counter and gave me a smug look.

Fran chastised him. "Well, I heard they were having problems, but you shouldn't spread rumors, young man."

"Time to go, Todd. Don't you have to be at work this afternoon?" I put a diskette into my jacket pocket and held the door open for him.

Todd drove Fran's car to the courthouse and dropped me off. "I'll meet you in the jail lobby at five. That'll give us a few minutes to talk afterwards."

I walked into the front door of courthouse. Mavis stood at the counter and ignored me. "Excuse me, Mrs. Woods, I have this diskette for Mr. Peck."

After she finished cleaning her typewriter keys with a tiny brush, she turned to me. "I shouldn't be seen talking to you. I plan to testify in Homer's case."

She'd apparently gotten the word from Troutman not to talk to me.

"That's fine, but Mr. Peck needs this report printed out for Homer's trial."

She hesitated. "What do you want me to do with it?"

"Just give it to Mr. Peck, and I'm sure he'll get it printed." I almost added it was confidential but didn't want to press my luck. I handed her the diskette. She took it and put it under the counter.

"When do you testify?" I asked.

"I'm on call. It may be as early as this afternoon."

"Well I may be gone by tomorrow if Mr. Peck doesn't use the report. If so, thank you for all the help you gave me. I know this has been an ordeal for you."

She looked at me numbly and nodded.

As I left I looked at her reflection in the glass door. She had pulled out the diskette and was reading the label on which I had printed "Homer Johnson. Forensic Psychological Evaluation."

The decor of the sole courtroom in the Trinity County Courthouse might be described as crumbling Victorian. The plaster walls were last repaired sometime before the Vietnam War, and the varnish on the wood paneling was ragged and yellow. Nonetheless, it had more character than the sterile modern courthouse in Cedar Gulch.

No one had actually told me I couldn't observe Homer's trial, but as the expert witness, I was unsure as to whether I would be allowed to listen to other witnesses' evidence. So I sat in the back and waited for Todd.

I pulled Tony's baseball cap down over my eyes and slouched in the back row of wooden folding chairs. With my jeans and flannel shirt I blended in with the rest of the Trinity County crowd. Maxwell Valentine, Trinity County's district attorney, looked right at me. He gave no sign of recognition, and he didn't have the bailiff throw me out. So far, so good.

Valentine was in the midst of his opening argument. He

looked handsome, professional, sexy. The yellow stripe in his tie brought out the golden highlights in his transplanted hair, his sky-blue shirt reflected the hue of his eyes. He was at least as well dressed as Richard Peck, half a head taller, and far more commanding in presence. The type of guy who could convince both men and women of just about anything. Presidential material.

"And the prosecution will show that Homer Johnson began plotting to kidnap Anerd Woods from the time he met him," Valentine said. "For his money, to take away his daughter, Sally, and to prove himself to be a man."

The argument didn't really make sense. If Homer wanted to take away Anerd's daughter, why would he kidnap her father after meeting him one time? But from Max Valentine's lips it sounded completely logical and convincing.

"Homer Johnson failed in his first attempt to kill the victim. He kidnapped him and buried him in the Cedar Gulch dump. Only by the grace of God was Anerd Woods discovered and revived in order that he could name his attacker. You will hear from Vernon Smith, the Caterpillar operator at the Cedar Gulch Landfill, the words Mr. Woods spoke. 'The Indian did it.' And who other than Homer Johnson would that Indian be? The same Homer Johnson who manipulated the victim's daughter to act against her father. The same Homer Johnson who convinced his friend Verlan Crumm to take him to the victim's home so he could attack an old man while he was eating his supper. The same Homer Johnson who, when released on bail, returned to the victim's home and this time finished the job of murdering a helpless old man." He pointed dramatically to Homer. "The same Homer Johnson sitting there without a care in the world that he killed a husband and father." He shook his head.

Homer looked back with blank darkness.

Max finished his opening argument by leaning on the

banister to the jury box. He gazed deep into each of the jurors' eyes. "I ask you to do the right thing, and I believe you will be able to act on your consciences and convict Homer Johnson of kidnapping and murder in the first degree." They responded with nods and thoughtful looks. He sat down with a look of reproach in Homer's direction.

He hadn't mentioned the White People's Brigade.

The woman sitting next to me whispered, "My, ain't he just too good-looking? If Max Valentine wins this trial, I hear he'll be elected judge." Her buckteeth strained to escape multicolored plastic braces. "My second cousin works at the capitol, in Sacramento, she's an aide to an assemblyman, and she says both the Republicans and the Democrats are already looking at Max for the state legislature."

"Really?" I nodded and tried to discourage conversation because I didn't want everyone in the courtroom looking at me.

Richard stood, awkward and plain compared to Max Valentine. He introduced himself to the jury. His name elicited snickers and comments from the observers in the courtroom.

The woman next to me continued to gossip. "My second cousin, her name is Lucille, she works for Assemblyman Joseph . . ."

I glared at the woman. She shrank into her chair and shut her mouth. The judge banged his gavel and pointed it at the observers. "Order." They stopped giggling.

Richard ignored the rude comments and continued. He extolled Homer's character, his naïveté, and promised to show that he was incapable of plotting the nefarious deeds with which he'd been charged. His argument was cogent and meaningful, but compared to Max Valentine, Richard reminded me of a little gray bird. Not to mention he was an out of county defense attorney who drove a Mercedes instead of a pickup with a rifle rack.

We're screwed, I thought.

Max Valentine called his first witness.

The court clerk swore him in and told him, "State your full name and have a seat in the witness box."

"Verlan Ferrell Crumm." He climbed up the steps to the witness chair. When he sat, the chair creaked. He smirked, and rocked back and forth, his hands splayed across the armrests.

Max Valentine began his examination of Verlan by asking him how long he'd known Homer.

"Known him pretty good for quite a while. Can't say exactly how long." Verlan looked directly at Homer while he spoke.

Homer shook his head and Richard scribbled on a notepad.

Max immediately asked Verlan about the night Anerd was kidnapped.

"Yeah, old Homer drove us on up there in his truck. You see"—Verlan winked at the jury—"I was with my girl Sally and we wanted to make out. So Homer said, 'Let's go on up to her house and I can have a few beers while you guys get it on.' He meant me and Sally could get it on. I personally didn't reckon Anerd would be there."

Max stood with a leg propped on the step to the jury box and boomed, "And tell us what you know about a plot to kidnap Anerd."

"Well, sure." Verlan drummed his fingers on the wood part of the armrest. "I heard Homer talk about it, I mean we all did. He wanted Anerd's money. But, you know, I don't think no one believed he do it." He leered at a blond juror.

"Tell us what happened."

"Well, me and Sally was making out in the truck and next thing we know Homer was in the house. We heard a bunch of hollering and Sally got scared that her pa—Anerd—would catch us so we hightailed it outta there. I don't know what

Homer did after that except he told me later that he robbed Anerd and put him in the dump."

Homer gasped and Richard shot out of his seat. "Objection, Your Honor. Hearsay."

Max Valentine smiled at the jury as though he had nothing but sympathy for Richard's feeble effort to hide the truth.

"Objection sustained," said the judge. "The witness will please comment on only what he saw or heard directly." He turned to the jury. "The jury will disregard Mr. Crumm's last statement about what the defendant said to him."

I looked at the jury. They appeared to disregard the judge's last statement.

"Do you believe, Verlan, that Homer had the capacity to murder—"

Richard jumped up. "Objection—"

"Withdrawn." Max smiled graciously. "Have you ever seen Homer harm someone?"

"Sure." Verlan's veneer of sincerity was transparent. "I've seen him get into a lot of fights. You know, Indians drink and fight all the time."

"Was Homer Johnson drinking the night of Anerd's kidnapping?"

"Don't Indians always drink when they get free beer?"

Several of the jury members covered their mouths to hide snickers.

"No further questions for now, Your Honor." Max strode to the prosecution table and sat.

The judge asked Richard if he wanted to cross-examine Verlan.

Richard rose and walked to the witness box. "Isn't it true, Mr. Crumm, that you are testifying for the prosecution against my client Homer Johnson in exchange for a plea bargain regarding the charges against you in the kidnapping of Anerd Woods?"

Verlan looked uncertainly at Max Valentine. Max nodded and Verlan said, "Sure. But I didn't do nothing."

"Isn't it true, Mr. Crumm, that you knew Homer for only a short time?"

Verlan looked at Max and back at Richard. "No."

"You say he was drinking on the night the victim was kidnapped?"

Verlan nodded. The court reporter looked up and the judge said, "Aloud, for the record, Mr. Crumm."

"That's what I said."

"Then how do you explain the fact that Homer's blood alcohol level was zero?"

"I dunno. Maybe he put someone else's pee in the jar. I just know I saw him drink."

"Objection, Your Honor." Max stood up. "This witness is hardly qualified to testify about blood alcohol levels. If Mr. Peck wishes to call in an expert witness on the subject, I'd be glad to agree to a continuance."

Richard waved him off. "Withdrawn, Your Honor. I'll discontinue this line for now."

The judge looked at the jury. "Disregard the last question."

Max looked even more smug.

Richard continued. "Do you belong to an organization called the White People's Brigade that tried to recruit Homer Johnson? Remember, Mr. Crumm, you're under oath."

"Never heard of it and if it was for white people, why would they want an Injun . . ."—Verlan tried to look sheepish and respectful—"I mean, an Indian, you know—Native American type?"

Richard sighed. "Isn't it true, Mr. Crumm, that you were the ringleader in the plot to kidnap Anerd Woods?"

"Well, if I was the ringleader like you say, why would Anerd tell everyone that Homer did the kidnapping? I mean he was there when it all happened, weren't he?" Verlan gave Richard a defiant look.

"Then how on earth did Homer get Anerd into his truck to take him to the dump in Cedar Gulch?"

Verlan looked baffled. "Huh?"

"Didn't you testify that you left Homer at the Woods's residence and took off with Sally Woods?"

"Yeah, I guess I did."

"So how did Homer get Anerd's body to the dump with no vehicle?"

"Uh, I guess he took Anerd's truck."

"You're testifying that Homer took Anerd to the dump in his truck then drove back to his home where he waited for the police to find him?"

"I guess he was lookin' for the money. Maybe he thought if he shoved Anerd in the dump he'd tell him where the money was and then he went to get it."

Three of the jury members nodded in understanding.

Richard looked at the jury then said to the judge, "No more questions, Your Honor. For now."

Verlan stood down with a glare at Richard. He winked as he walked by Max, but neither the judge nor the jury saw it.

The next witness was Mavis Woods.

She sat primly in the witness box. She wore white gloves and a pillbox hat in lieu of her red scarf and looked as though she'd stepped out of a fifties women's magazine.

"Mrs. Woods," Max Valentine's voice was like silver, "I realize you must be devastated by your husband's death and the legal proceedings. I'll be as gentle with you as possible and I'm sure the defendant's attorney will do the same." His eyes panned the jury as he turned to smile at Richard. "Tell us in your own words what you know about the kidnapping of your husband."

Mavis's voice faltered as she spoke. "All I know is what I heard. I didn't ever think he'd do it."

"About whom are you speaking?"

"Homer Johnson. That man there." She pointed to him. "I didn't think he'd do it."

"Do what?"

"Hurt my husband. Anerd. Why would anyone want to hurt Anerd?"

"And would anyone want to hurt Anerd?"

"The only person I know would be. . . ." She lowered her head and wiped an eye with her gloved hand.

"Who would it be?"

Mavis murmured. The court reporter asked her to speak into the microphone.

Mavis leaned forward and placed her hand on the rail of the witness box. "The man who was Anerd's rival and enemy."

"And who was that?" Max covered her hand with his and looked into her eyes. His head twitched toward the jury box then back to Mavis.

Mavis raised her head and cried, "He is Homer's grandfather." She pointed again. "His name is Bruno Seronello. He has always been jealous of Anerd's success and he would do anything to hurt us."

Richard shook his head and rubbed his forehead. Homer sat perfectly still.

"And what makes you believe Homer was involved in your husband's kidnapping?"

"Because I heard him talking about it with my daughter, Sally, and her boyfriend, Verlan."

"What did he say?"

"He laid out a plan to kidnap Anerd for his money and put him in the dump."

"Why didn't you go to the police?"

"I did. And they said it wasn't enough because nothing had happened and to get more evidence. So I did and I'm prepared to reveal my proof. I only wish I'd gotten to the police before my dear husband disappeared the second time."

Richard stood. "Objection. I was not made aware of this evidence during discovery, Your Honor."

Max Valentine turned to the jury with a puzzled look, shrugged, and turned to the judge. "This information is new to me, too, Your Honor."

Why did I get the impression it wasn't at all new to him?

The judge looked at Mavis. "Mrs. Woods. What is the nature of your evidence and why didn't you reveal it before today?"

"I was afraid. For my safety and the life of my daughter. You see"—she gave the jury an ominous look—"Sally's not quite right in the head. She gets confused and . . ."

The judge leaned toward her. "What is the nature of your evidence, Mrs. Johnson?"

"I have three and a half hours of tape recordings on which Homer Johnson plotted the kidnapping of my husband. He tried to convince my daughter and her boyfriend and me that we could do it without harming Anerd. I went along with it only to get the evidence. And then, when he was released on bail he came to my house and threatened to murder me if I told anyone. Instead he murdered my husband."

Richard slapped the table. "Objection!"

"Sustained." The judge turned to the jury. "Unauthorized audio or video tapes are not admissible in this courtroom and you will not be permitted to hear them. You must base your judgments about this case only on your opinion of the veracity of this witness."

I knew the tapes wouldn't be admissible.

I also knew from their looks that the jury didn't care. They'd already made up their minds.

The judge made noises about adjourning for the day and it was time to meet Todd. I slipped out the back and trotted down the hall. Todd pulled up in his car just as I walked down the steps.

"What did you get from her?" I asked as I fastened my seat belt. I didn't want to think about what had happened moments before in the courtroom.

"Well, the good news is that Sally remembered me even though I'm a year behind her in school."

"And the bad news?" I held my breath. What was the other shoe?

"And the bad news is that she liked me and thought I was cute." He shuddered dramatically.

"Todd, what else?" I punched him lightly in the arm.

"Do you want the best news?"

"Yes, what is it?"

"She totally spilled the beans about her mom and Homer." He looked over his shoulder to pull into the street.

"Wow! Good job. What did she say?" I pulled my notebook out of the glove compartment and looked up to see Laurence Troutman crossing the street directly in front of Todd's car. "Dang. Don't attract his attention." I bent down as though I was reaching for something under the seat.

"He can't keep me from talking to Sally, or Verlan, or anyone for that matter."

"True, but he can sure try to make things difficult. And he seems to have made everyone afraid to talk to me."

Todd swung the car past Troutman and pulled onto the main road. "Sally doesn't want to testify against Homer but her mother is making her do it."

"Why does Mavis have it in for Homer? I understand she wants to protect her daughter, but why not blame it on Verlan? Or Freddy with the Tinsel Tooth?"

"By the way, his full name is Freddy Steele."

"Well, I guess it's better than Freddy Aluminum." I leafed through my notebook to the page on Sally. "Here it is. Sally said Freddy was the one who wrote those horrid racist lyrics to the tune of 'Amazing Grace.' "

"He was three years ahead of me in school. Picked on me from day one of my freshman year."

"I bet he thought you were a real cutie." I told Todd about the homoerotic pictures on Freddy's wall at the trailer. "I bet he had dreams about your tight little behind."

"Yuck. Okay, you got me back," he said. "I won't talk about Tony's girlfriend anymore."

Todd signalled left and turned onto the highway. "Sally said that her mother was not only in the room when they talked about the kidnapping, she gave them suggestions and told them where to find the money."

"Mavis?"

"Yep. And there's more. Mavis is gonna testify the same as Verlan that Homer was the ringleader."

"She just did. They both did. But believe me, Homer does not have the criminal mind to figure out such a plan. However, I'm beginning to wonder if Mavis does. I think my plan to give her the modified diskette on Homer's evaluation just backfired. She didn't back down, she upped the ante."

"Yeah, well you're gonna have to convince the jury of that because so far it sounds like the prosecution is two for three and I'm not so sure Sally won't buckle under, too."

Todd pulled up at the pizza parlor and handed me the keys. "I can walk home if you need the car."

I looked at the gray sky. "I'll come pick you up if it starts raining again."

Aunt Fran was preparing dinner when I got back to the Yellow Inn. She handed me an apron and pointed me to a butcher block that held a bunch of carrots and a vegetable peeler. "Your young man Tony called."

"He's not really my young man." I took a bite of a carrot and began to peel the rest. "What did he say?"

"Well, whoever he is, he said he'd be back up tonight after he gets off work."

"That won't be until midnight."

"Well that's what he told me."

"It probably isn't such a bad idea if Tony stays here." Richard had walked in the door. He slapped his briefcase on the table and sat down, the slowness of his movements revealing depression and fatigue. "As if this trial wasn't going badly enough, Freddy Steele has just been released on a half million dollars bail."

"How did he manage that?"

Fran cried out. "We're not safe with him out." She looked at me. "Cassie, you have to go someplace where he can't find you."

"What about the sheriff's department? Can't they send someone to check on us?"

"They are more than willing to watch for any trouble, but with only four deputies on duty for the entire county, they can't make any guarantees." Richard took off his glasses and rubbed his eyes. "You'll have to go back to Cedar Gulch, Cassie."

"What good will that do? Freddy knows where I live. And I can't protect Auntie Liz from him. Besides, I'm making headway with Homer's case."

"Then Tony and I will have to take care of you."

It was unlikely that Richard could protect me from Freddy the tinsel-toothed homicidal maniac, but I thanked him anyway.

Richard offered to put up Fran and Todd at the nicest hotel in Cedar Gulch.

"Not on your life," she said. "And if I know my nephew, he'll refuse to budge if there's any excitement involved." She went to call him to tell him to run out the back of the pizza parlor if Freddy showed up.

After dinner I gave Richard the report I'd printed out on my letterhead on Todd's machine. "Here's the official version of Homer's psychological evaluation."

"Official version?" he asked.

"Yes."

I didn't want to confess that in the report I gave to Mavis I mentioned that when I'd interviewed Sally she told me she wouldn't testify against Homer. Or that I added a creative fiction or two.

"Funny, I never got a copy from the courthouse."

"I'm not surprised."

Tony arrived just after eight, having traded shifts with a buddy. We drove to pick up Todd from the pizza parlor.

"Aunt Liz is fine. She'll stay with Maria until this is over and you're safe."

"How did Freddy get out of jail?"

"Apparently Laurence Troutman showed up with the bail. But he's not who came up with the money to get him out."

"Who did?"

"That's a mystery. Troutman wouldn't say, and none of the deputies up here has a clue."

"Who would get Freddy out and not Sally or Verlan? I mean, if the person is involved with the WPB, wouldn't they get his friends out, too?"

"Not if they couldn't make sure Homer got convicted. Look at it this way. Sally's protective of Homer and therefore useless. Verlan screwed up Anerd's kidnapping, then got caught. Freddy is ruthless. He successfully kidnapped you, had the balls to assault me, and probably beat up Homer in jail. Whatever the agenda is, Freddy has the best chance of following through."

"But how many people in Trinity County have that much cash to blow on bail?"

Tony turned in to the pizza parlor parking lot. "Not too many of them. I'll keep asking around."

Todd looked through the window at the headlights and took a final swipe at the countertop. He threw the rag under the sink, pulled the keys from his pocket, locked the door, then hopped over a puddle to get to the door of Tony's truck.

I scooted next to Tony, and Todd climbed in next to me.

"Hey, man. Cool wheels. Ever thought of fixing it up and entering it into an antique truck show?"

"Hey, kid. It's paid for, and it runs." Tony grinned, and put the beast into reverse.

"Well it's a lot better than what I'm gonna be driving. If I ever get a car. Tuition at the University of California costs more than Richard's Mercedes."

"So find out who bailed out Freddy, and make a deal."

"Sure, Cassie. Then maybe I can open up a tattoo parlor specializing in swastikas."

That evening, the five of us—me, Tony, Todd, Fran, and Richard—prepared to defend the Yellow Inn. Tony unloaded a small armament from his truck. The sight of him loading weapons and the seductive creak of his firearm leather made me think about the night he stayed in my bed after Auntie Liz was assaulted.

Todd grunted in my ear like a rutting buck. "He's hot stuff, Cassie." He dodged my attempt to slug him.

Todd and I checked all the window and door locks, drew the curtains, put sheets up over uncovered windows, and turned on all the outside lights. Richard brought his cell phone from his car and took the bedroom nearest the back door. Fran made the living room sofa into a bed for Tony. Fran and I were to sleep upstairs. We all tried to get Todd to come to upstairs with us, but he dug his deer rifle out of a cabinet and put out a sleeping bag for himself in the kitchen.

"Whatever you do, kid," Tony told Todd as he demonstrated tactical maneuvers, "don't get excited and shoot me in the back with that rifle."

We dimmed the inside lights and waited for Freddy. Richard read my report and reviewed his notes in his room, Fran and I drank tea while she educated me about the inhabitants of Jackpot, and Todd and Tony plotted at chess and discussed women in the heavily curtained dining room.

At one point I heard Tony tell Todd, "Some women are like those preauthorized bank cards you get for free in the mail. You get what you want without working for it. Others are like buying a Rolls-Royce on credit, and you have to spend forever filling out the paperwork to get anywhere. But most of the time you get a lot more in the end. It just depends on what you want."

Todd added, "But one way or the other, they're gonna make you pay it back anyway." The two sniggered in conspiracy.

I looked at Fran. "Tony's corrupting your nephew."

She shook her head and smiled. "Boys will be boys no matter how much we try to pound civilization into them. It's good for Todd to have a man he can talk to. I can't give him the male attention he needs."

She poured me some tea. "I've had Todd since he was eight. Almost ten years now. He's been a delight and a handful. Too smart for his own good sometimes."

"He's a wonderful kid. I have a sister about his age. I haven't seen her in more than ten years—ever since I left home." I turned my head away and looked at the ceiling to stop the stinging in my eyes.

Fran patted my hand. "You must miss her."

I nodded and thought of Auntie Liz's prodding me to do

something about it. I spent a moment rebuking myself for sins of omission and stupid mistakes.

Fran chattered to fill the silence and help save my crumbling dignity. "It's so hard when families are separated—death, divorce, desertion. I'm just glad I've been able to see Todd grow up. I never had children of my own." She stared at her folded hands. "Todd's father, Brian, my youngest brother, was a firefighter. He was killed when a ceiling collapsed on him while he was fighting a house fire. Todd was just six."

After a moment I swallowed and asked, "What happened to his mother?"

"She got into drugs after Brian died. We don't know where she is now."

I looked back at her. "Funny how people behave under adversity. Tony's father was a police officer killed in the line of duty when Tony was a small boy, but both he and Todd seem to have turned tragedy into opportunity. So many other people blame the world and become what Tony calls professional victims."

"Like Verlan and Freddy. And Sally. All of those young people could have chosen different paths but they chose evil over good. Especially Freddy and Sally. Sally, the poor thing, isn't very pretty, but her father was well off by Trinity County standards. At least well off enough to send her to college. Now Verlan's not too bright but Freddy is just a spoiled kid whose parents moved up here from San Francisco."

"Could they be the ones who gave the bail money?"

"You might think so except that they completely disowned him when he got into the neo-Nazis. There wasn't much of that white pride nastiness around here before he came and got the young people all stirred up."

"Could Freddy be Anerd's rival?"

"That's a thought. I just don't know, but it's certainly something to contemplate."

Richard came down the hall and interrupted us. "I'd like to compliment you on your report."

"Thanks." I looked up at him for a moment. "I have to confess something."

His eyes twinkled behind his lenses. "About being in the courtroom today?"

"Yes." I couldn't actually admit to him that I'd altered the report. "Do you think Valentine was truly surprised about Mavis's tapes?"

"Of course not. He's not that sloppy. But this way he gets the information to the jury without having to worry about the truth of the matter. No matter what is on those tapes, the jury will believe that Homer was the ringleader because they will never hear taped evidence to the contrary. Beautiful strategy on Max's part."

"Is it hopeless for Homer?"

"I hope not. This report is actually quite informative, Cassie. I knew you'd do a good job. Whether it will help or not, I don't know, but the picture you painted of Homer is certainly not one of a young man who would plan to harm a person, much less be able to carry it out."

"So, am I going to testify?"

"I think so."

"Good, I'm ready." I told myself to buck up and turn this one around.

Thirty

My heart thumped out of my chest before my eyes opened. The wind whistled and a tree branch tapped at my windowpane. Downstairs sounded like a guerilla ambush, feet thudding, weapons clicking, hushed voices. I hopped out of bed and bumped into Fran in the hallway. Against male advice and common sense, we ran down the stairs.

Tony stood in a shooter stance at the side of the front door, revolver in ready position. He yelled to Todd, "Cover the kitchen door."

The clock in the parlor struck two.

The porch creaked as the visitor paced to the window then back to the door. The footsteps were heavy and slow and I knew they didn't belong to Freddy.

The visitor knocked. "It's Martin, Deputy Martin."

"Tony, I recognize his voice," I called out. "He's okay."

Tony relaxed his stance, brought his revolver down, and peered through the window. Martin held his badge up for him to see.

Tony opened the door and let Martin in. "We're just a bit goosey." He put the gun into the holster and shook Martin's hand. "Tony Mesa. Cedar Gulch PD. We spoke on the phone earlier. Thanks for stopping by."

"Just came over to check on you. Doing overtime anyway. As usual. No sign of Freddy?"

"Not a peep. But we're prepared."

"So I can see."

Aunt Fran walked into the parlor and fluffed the back cushion of an overstuffed chair. "Have a seat."

"Can't stay long." When Martin sat, the chair groaned and air poofed out of the pillows. "Wanted to tell you Homer Johnson is in the infirmary."

Richard stood at the hallway. "What now?"

"Who did it?" I asked.

"We didn't find him until after Freddy was released so it could'a been him. That Steele boy has brought nothing but trouble to this county, bringing that Nazi crap up here." He took a cup of coffee and an oatmeal cookie from the plate Fran offered and nodded his head in thanks. "Homer took a shank to the gut, and a few kicks to the head."

Richard and I gasped in unison. I lowered myself to the sofa. "Is he . . . ?"

"He's gonna be okay. That is if we can keep him from getting beat up again." He shook his head then took a bite of cookie and a sip of coffee. He chewed and sipped and talked. "He still won't tell us who stabbed him and no one else will either."

I glanced at Todd. "Then we'll just have to find out some other way."

Richard ran his fingers through his hair. "I want to talk to my client. We'll have to get this trial postponed until he recovers." His slacks and shirt were rumpled from three hours of attempted sleep. He put on his suit jacket and picked up his briefcase.

Deputy Martin wiped cookie crumbs from his chin and stood up. "My thinking is that the sooner you get it over with, the sooner you can get him outta this county."

Richard looked at his watch. "If I don't do something,

those skinheads are going to kill my client." He headed toward the door.

I softly asked Todd, "What do you have in school tomorrow morning?"

"Nothing I can't miss. What time do you need me?"

"As early as possible."

"Wake me up at six."

Richard left for the jail with Deputy Martin, who left instructions to call him if Freddy so much as drove past the Yellow Inn. The rest of us slept fitfully through the storm, waking with every creak of the old house.

Thirty-one

Richard returned at five in the morning. I dressed and tiptoed downstairs to find that everyone else had been awake for a half hour. Fran was brewing tea, Tony put a pillow over his head and struggled to sleep, and Todd sat at the table devouring cookies and chocolate milk and drilling Richard.

The attorney said, "Homer's not only going to live, he should recover enough to participate in court today. He's amazingly resilient."

"Then you need to get some sleep, Richard," I told him. "You look as though you've been rode hard and put away wet."

"Lord knows, that's how I feel. At this point, I can't see straight, much less think." Richard set off to bed.

Todd took a last swig of milk, slung his backpack over his shoulder, and gave Fran a peck on the cheek. She looked at the clock. "It's too early for you to leave for school, young man. And you haven't brushed your teeth."

"Uh, I have a midterm. Thought I'd study in the library. And I'll chew some gum." The teenager winked at me and we charged out the door.

We arrived at the jail by six-thirty. I presented the note Deputy Martin had given me to the blond woman deputy on duty. She looked at it and waved us through. "Homer's been sedated, so he's not gonna be real talkative."

"Thanks, I'll take my chances," I said, dreading longer silences and more awkward conversation than usual. "See you back at the inn," I said to Todd as he headed down the hall in the opposite direction.

Homer lay in the white painted steel infirmary bed, his well-muscled chest bandaged up to his nipples, a tube protruded from his chest, and gauze wrapped around his head. The blood on the bandages had dried to brown, the color of his skin.

"Homer?" I touched his arm.

Grunting with pain and effort, he flailed his arm. I stepped back. He struggled to open his eyes, but quieted when he saw me.

"What're you doing here?" His words were slurred and thick.

"Checking up on you."

"It happened again."

"So I see." I pulled up the metal chair and sat on the cold blue seat. "Looks as though they were more serious this time."

"Fucking skinheads. This time they punctured my lung."

"What did they want?" I asked the question in the same monotone I might use to comment on the insipid room decor.

Homer opened his left eye and rolled his head to look at me. His right eye was too swollen to see. "What d'ya think? They wanted to shut me up. They want me to take the heat for what happened to Anerd."

"Really?" I reached for his water bottle and adjusted the straw so he could take a drink. "It seems to be working."

He took a sip of water and with great effort said, "Fuck you, too. You think I wanted this?"

"There's no need for vulgarity with me, Homer." I set the bottle on the bedside table. "Looks like you didn't eat all your breakfast. Those cinnamon rolls are pretty good."

He stared at his toes.

I took a breath. "I know how you must miss your father, Homer. I haven't seen my mother or sister in ten years."

He looked up at me with suspicion.

I blundered on. "My friend Tony's father was shot and killed when Tony was five. He still grieves for his dad. I don't think you ever got a chance to grieve for your mother. I mean, you were away when she died, and you didn't understand the traditional Modoc Indian ways of expressing grief, and maybe you were so angry but didn't know how to talk about it . . ."

He stared away and was silent.

"Todd—the boy who works at the pizza place—his father died in a fire when he was six. His aunt brought him up because his mother abandoned him. Todd's two years younger than you but I think he might be someone you could talk with."

Just as I was beginning to feel like a complete fool, Homer reached up to wipe tears from his eyes. He shifted his weight to face me and the room filled with the sound of his labored breathing. "Sorry, Dr. Ringwald. You've been real nice to me and I don't have any right to be a shithead to you."

I was quiet, contemplative, while I watched him look at me. Finally I said, "There's one thing that really baffles me, Homer."

"What's that?"

"On the night Anerd was kidnapped the first time, why on earth didn't you run away as soon as you knew what the plan was? You could have said Verlan stole your car. Why did you stay to be implicated by Anerd?"

He tried in vain to lift his head from the pillow. Defeated, he said, "I thought she'd come back. I thought Sally'd get scared and convince Verlan to leave the old man alone."

"You wanted to protect her?"

"I wanted to save her." He choked on the words and began to cough.

I helped him to a sitting position and handed him the water bottle. "Why did you drop the gloves and stand there?"

When he could speak he said, "We were all in my truck. I thought we were going to Anerd's house to get some things for Mavis. She told us she was leaving Anerd because he was mean to Sally and she needed us to get her things. I thought we were doing her and Sally a favor. I had no idea Anerd would be there.

"When we drove past the baseball field across the street, Verlan handed me the gloves and said to put them on. I said, 'Why?' and he told me, 'Just in case.' I said, 'In case of what?' and he said, 'Just put them on.' By then we were in the yard and I could see Anerd inside. I had a funny feeling, and when I got out I stood there looking at him. I don't remember dropping the gloves. I guess I froze."

"What happened then?"

"I saw Anerd staring at me through the front window. Verlan went to the back and I could hear him kicking in the door. I saw Anerd running down the hall and Verlan after him. I knew what was happening, but I couldn't stop it. Sally was crying and telling me to help her dad but I couldn't move."

"I thought Sally was in on it."

"She was at first. But she changed her mind before we got to his house."

"How did they get him from the house to the dump?"

"Verlan backed the pickup into the porch, lowered the tailgate, and rolled Anerd off the porch into the truck bed."

"And Sally went with him to the dump?"

"I think she was pissed at me for not stopping it, and

thought if she went with Verlan, she could keep him from killing Anerd."

"She told me that she and Verlan went to the shop and made out, then he left her there before going to the dump."

"For all I know they did."

"So why didn't you tell that to the police?"

He gasped in pain and sank into the bed. "Don't you understand?"

"You're in love with her, aren't you?"

He looked away. "All the guys treat her like used parts. But she's been so nice to me and . . ."

I touched him gently on the shoulder. "Do you feel up to going to court today?"

He nodded. "I want to get it over with."

"I can understand that, Homer."

His eyes were moist. "I'm afraid. I need to get out of here. The next time, I won't be able to defend myself."

"You'll be okay in the infirmary. None of the other prisoners can get in here."

"Don't count on it. It's not just the inmates—"

He was interrupted by a skinny, bow-legged orderly with a shaved head and a silver stud in his right earlobe. He carried a tray of medicines. "Time for your meds, Homer." He handed him a small paper cup and his plastic container of water. "Bottoms up."

Homer's eyes hardened. He tilted the pills into his mouth.

The orderly looked over his shoulder at me. "Gotta change the bandages before he goes to court, so if you'll wait outside."

I peered around him and said to Homer, "I'll let Mr. Peck know how you feel."

He smiled weakly and winced as the orderly began pulling off gauze.

Richard was sitting at the kitchen table watching Fran pour him another cup of coffee when Todd and I returned to the Yellow Inn. "Any luck?" he asked.

Todd had been chattering ever since we left the jail. "Sorry, Aunt Fran. I didn't go to the library," he said in response to the look of death she gave him. "I went to the jail to talk with Sally. You're not gonna believe this. Sally spilled the beans. Anerd was a real ass. He beat her and her mother up. She wanted to get them away from him so that's why she went along with the kidnapping plot. It was Mavis's idea—she set Sally up."

Richard asked, "How did Homer get involved?"

"He was there all right. But Sally didn't think he really had a clue about what was happening."

"Better take a thermos of coffee, Richard," I said. "It's going to be a long day." I interrupted Todd to talk about my visit with Homer. "The good news is that he was talkative. Maybe we should have put him on pain meds two weeks ago."

Richard didn't laugh at my attempt at humor.

I continued, "The bad news is that I don't think his safety can be assured because I don't think it's only Verlan or Freddy who hurt him. He's afraid to tell because he doesn't know if a trustee or orderly might overhear him."

Richard cradled his head in his hands. He looked as though he'd slept fifteen minutes. "Maybe I'll ask for a change of venue."

"By the time you get it, he could be dead. Deputy Martin was right. We need to finish the trial and get him out of there, whatever the outcome. Besides, Homer wants to continue."

Richard massaged the crease in his forehead. "Why don't we just bring in the vigilantes?"

Todd sat down at the table with a jumbo bowl of oatmeal. "That's what I always say about Trinity County. One hundred years of history unmarred by progress."

Richard managed a feeble smile. "If I knew when I took this case what I know now . . . Oh well, all I can do is my best and motion for an appeal later if I have to." He took a sip of coffee. "Are you ready to testify, Cassie?"

"As ready as I'm going to be . . ."

"Mavis will be on this morning, then Sally. You and Homer are my only witnesses today, so plan on being in the courtroom at ten-thirty." Richard gathered up his notes and rose from the table while Fran shooed Todd off to school.

I put my cup in the sink and went into the parlor. Tony lay on the sofa with a pillow over his head. I sat next to him and poked his ribs until he groaned. "It's almost eight. Time to get up."

He ignored me. I tickled him under his arms. He grabbed my hand and pulled it firmly to his chest. "You're pushing your luck," he grumbled.

I used my free hand to pull the pillow off his head. He kept his eyes closed and grabbed my other hand. Richard walked in to find me squealing and squirming to prevent Tony from pulling me in a prone position on top of him. He walked past us to his room without saying a word.

I bit Tony's forearm to force him to free me. He let go, then sat up against the pillows and yawned. "So I'm not doing much to help you with this case."

"You've saved my life once or twice so far."

He flashed a two-dimple grin. "Besides that."

"To repay you, I'll get your coffee." I jumped up and went into the kitchen.

Fran had already poured his cup. "That young fellow needs you to need him."

I spooned sugar and cream into the mug and stirred. "I'm beginning to realize that. The trick is figuring out how much I want to need him."

Fran chuckled and shook her head. "I'm glad it wasn't all that complicated in my day."

When I handed Tony his cup, he said, "Your suit's hanging in your closet. Maria took it to the dry cleaner's before I brought it up."

"She didn't have to do that."

"There are times I can't do it all for you."

I gave him an appreciative smile.

The phone rang and Fran called to me from the kitchen. "Cassie, it sounds important."

I walked back to the phone and identified myself to the caller.

"This is Janet from the women's shelter. We have a client here who wants to talk to you immediately."

"Who is it?"

"She asked only to be identified as Connie."

"Oh no. How long has she been there?"

"She came in last night. I think you might want to get down here as soon as possible. She said she really wants to talk to you about the trial."

"I'll be there in ten minutes."

I jotted down the directions, and asked Tony for the keys to his truck.

"Give me five minutes. I'll go with you."

"I don't have time."

"It may be a way to get you alone. I don't want you getting kidnapped again."

"Then hurry."

Tony took a swig of coffee and ran down the hall. He came out of his room, shirt open, buttoning his jeans and chewing on a toothbrush. He disappeared into the bathroom and in a few seconds ran into the parlor. "Let's go," he said as he tucked his shirt into his pants with one hand and grabbed his jacket from the hall tree with the other.

We drove up to the Trinity County Women's Shelter in the allotted ten minutes. The building sits in back of the county offices and isn't much more than a cabin. There is no way its whereabouts could be kept secret.

I told Tony to wait in the car. "No sense in escalating the situation," I told him, but he wasn't happy about it.

I knocked on the door. A big-busted woman with gray dreadlocks, rose-tinted Granny glasses, and ruddy cheeks opened the door.

"I'm Dr. Ringwald. Someone called for me to come and talk to Connie."

"Hi, I'm Janet." When she smiled, the woman was bookishly attractive. She led me down a hall decorated only with a black and white pencil sketch of an androgynous-looking adult holding a small child.

She showed me into a small bedroom with a low ceiling and one tiny window. The walls were the color of coffee with too much cream. Connie Troutman sat in the only chair, an overstuffed forties-era armchair upholstered with a rust and avocado pattern from the sixties.

She had been beaten again. The purple bruise on her cheek was obscured by two new red ones, and her right eye was crimson with broken blood vessels. Her left hand was in a sling.

"I'm glad you came," she said in her soft East Coast inflection.

"I was glad to do it."

"Well, you'll be especially glad when you hear what I have to say." She motioned for me to sit on the bed, which was covered with a gray wool blanket that scratched me through my jeans.

"Looks as though he did it worse this time." I tried to sound casual, as though I'd seen this a thousand times before.

"He did it worse all right. This time I'm leaving for

good." She crossed her legs at the ankle and smoothed a nonexistent wrinkle out of her nylons. I wondered if she'd stopped to change into the outdated suit she wore after Laurence had beaten her.

"What happened?"

"I think that's fairly obvious. But what you should know is that Max Valentine has refused to prosecute my husband twice before for spousal battery, and I don't expect that this time will be any different."

"Do you have an attorney?"

She laughed softly. "Do you mean besides my husband and District Attorney Maxwell Valentine? Whom do you suggest?"

The woman had perfected the knack of making me feel like an idiot. I chastised myself for wondering if she drove Laurence to it.

"What do you plan to do?" I didn't ask how I could help her.

"The first thing I plan to do is let you in on a little secret." She smiled smugly. "Would you like to know the reason Max Valentine hasn't pressed charges against my husband?"

"Of course," I said. At last, her agenda was becoming clear.

"Well, you might say Max Valentine has good use for my husband. The first time I went to the police—not the first time Laurence did this mind you—but when I finally got up the courage to ask for help, Laurence told Max he learned his lesson and would never hurt me again. Max believed him and he convinced me to drop the charges with the promise that he would protect me." She laughed bitterly. "That was my first mistake."

Janet knocked at the door. "I hate to interrupt, but your husband is on the phone. He says he's coming to see you. It's prohibited, you know, without a counselor present."

Connie snorted. "Tell him I'm talking to my psychologist, and I'll speak with him when I'm done with my session." She turned back to me. "This is confidential, of course?"

"Of course."

She continued. "Laurence didn't hit me again for months. He was contrite, almost loving. Roses, chocolates, the works." She caught a glimpse of herself in the dresser mirror and gently touched her eye. "But then the frustrations began to build again. He wanted to be greater than he was, more important, more intelligent."

"I married him straight out of law school. It was a second-rate school and not the Ivy League one to which he aspired." She laughed derisively. "That statement alone would probably cost me a broken rib. You see, he wanted to go into a lucrative private practice. Can you imagine that sniveling little bastard attracting, much less keeping, a clientele better than scumbags?"

"Why did you marry him?"

"I suppose I loved him." Self-consciously, she placed her hand over the swelling on her cheek. "I don't know why. He was a bully even before we married." She reached into her purse for a package of cigarettes, then looked at me. "What am I thinking? We wouldn't want another allergy attack."

"We could go outside."

"I have no doubt that Laurence will be here any minute. He'll either fall all over himself in shame, or blow another fuse when he sees me talking with you. I don't understand the reason he dislikes you so much, but he can't say anything good about you." She smiled. "Perhaps that's the reason I wanted to speak with you." I raised my eyebrows in query.

She snapped her purse closed. "I suppose I was too embarrassed not to go through with it."

"Pardon me?"

"The wedding. I didn't want to admit that I had made a

mistake. You know, the usual, I thought if I loved him enough he'd change."

"Many women get caught in the same trap."

"I'm aware of that. I've read all the self-help books on the subject of co-dependency."

If she gave me that superior smile one more time, I was afraid I'd hit her myself. "So the reason that Max didn't prosecute Laurence the next time he hit you?" I prodded.

"Now what do you imagine is the reason that Laurence does so poorly when he defends a case that Max Valentine is trying?"

"Because he's not a very competent attorney?"

"You're guessing." She clicked her chipped acrylic thumbnail against her three-carat wedding ring. "The fact is, he's not competent. But there's another reason." She covered her smile with the tips of her fingers.

"I have no idea." I wondered if her diamond was real.

"To be blunt about it, I guess the fight is fixed."

"Fixed?"

She spoke to me as if I was a schoolgirl. "Max wants to be a big judge and then an even bigger senator. Maybe even governor, or perhaps all the way to the Oval Office. In order to do that, he has to get attention, and in order to do that, he has to win cases. So if my husband loses, Max wins." She held out the palms of her hands toward me. "See, simple."

"You mean that Max is blackmailing Laurence to lose cases?"

"Did I say that?" She laughed merrily.

"So if Sally and Verlan are acquitted, Max blows the whistle about your personal life, prosecutes your husband, and Laurence loses his career."

"Perhaps."

"That's the reason he was so angry when I talked to Sally and Verlan. Laurence was afraid I'd discover something that would help." My brain felt like a rat running in a maze. "I bet your husband can't wait until Max leaves town."

She smiled. "And I'm counting the days myself."

I wasn't going to go anywhere near that one. "Why are you telling me about this?"

"I have no other means of getting revenge. Now that you know, maybe the bastard will leave me alone for a while."

A car door slammed and as if on cue Janet cried out, "You can't come in here, Laurence. Leave her alone." I heard Tony shout at Troutman to calm down. The front door of the shelter banged open.

Connie plumped up the pillows and sat back, the registered Siamese that swallowed the canary.

I made it out the door in time to dodge Laurence Troutman barrelling into Connie's room. When he saw me, he snarled. He flew into the room and I heard him fall on the bed. Sobbing noises echoed down the hall.

Tony walked in after him and peered around the corner. "Looks like he's okay for now." He turned to Janet. "If he gets nasty, call the sheriff."

"That woman is the most annoying person I've ever met," I grumbled.

"What happened in there?" Tony opened the truck door for me.

"I think I was set up. But I'm not sure why."

He glanced at his watch. "Figure it out later. You're gonna be late for court."

Thirty-two

Back at the Yellow Inn, Tony waited in the truck, his effort to encourage me to change into my suit quickly. We made it to the courtroom by quarter after ten, and he dropped me off at the curb promising to be back by noon.

Mavis was still on the stand, weeping over the loss of Anerd, sniffing bravely at the jury, and whimpering to the judge she was strong enough to finish her testimony.

Homer sat at the defense table, tethered to an IV on a metal rack that dripped fluids into him. I noted several jurors staring at him with expressionless faces, and wondered if the sight of his injuries would work for or against him.

With a knot in my stomach, I went into the foyer and paced.

The wind was splattering muddy slush against the glass doors, the only pay phone was half a block away, and I'd left without a raincoat. I peeked back into the courtroom to see Mavis's outpouring of spurious tears prompting the judge to hand her a box of tissues. He would probably call for a break after her testimony.

I leaned on the door with my shoulder to open it against the wind. Tiny grenades of frozen mud exploded against my legs, making me wish I'd worn boots instead of panty hose and heels.

The number I needed was in the half of the phone book that was missing. I called directory assistance and then dialed the shelter.

Janet answered and I introduced myself. "Is Laurence still there?"

"From the looks of it, he's going to be here a while. I think Connie is standing up to him and setting him straight. After all the work we've done to help her—"

"Thanks, Janet. I have to go." I hung up and raced two blocks past the courthouse to the jail.

The tall woman deputy with the bobbed blond hair was still on duty. She buzzed me through but stopped me when I told her who I wanted to see. "I'm not sure if you're authorized to see Sally Woods."

"By the time you check it out, I'll be late for court. Mr. Peck is expecting me to testify shortly."

Her eyes twinkled. "Hey, it's not a problem to me. But make it quick."

For once, Sally was brought down to me before I chewed my fingers down to the knuckles. I got right to the point. "Sally, Todd has told me about your conversations. There's a few more things I need to know."

Her pudgy face screwed up into a ball. She wrinkled her nose. "I'm scared."

"You should be. Are you aware of what's happened to Homer?"

Two tears squeezed out were her eyes. "They beat him up."

"Who could have done it?"

"I don't know."

"Sally, the only chance we have to stop this is for you to tell me. Remaining quiet hasn't helped. You must have an idea who would want to hurt him. This jail's not that big."

Her chin quivered.

"I think Homer won't tell us who hurt him because he's protecting you."

She burst into sobs. Her chunky shoulders shook and she looked at me pitifully.

"Okay, I guess we're done." I pushed back my chair and stood up.

"No, wait." She looked around the cubicle for a tissue and wiped her nose on her sleeve. "I don't know who beat him, but I'll tell you the rest of it." She pressed her quaking lips together and sniffed deeply. "Did Todd tell you my daddy was real mean?"

I nodded, and regretted I hadn't brought a notepad.

"My mom and I have talked for years about getting away from him. But Mommy wouldn't leave until she found out about us."

"Us?"

"Well not exactly my daddy and me. What my daddy wanted me to do."

"What was that?"

"I would have told Todd, but I was too embarrassed."

"You can tell me." I reached over and patted her thick hand.

"You see, all the boys have always made fun of me. Even Verlan. But not Homer. I mean, I know he could get a real pretty girl, but he acted like he thought I was pretty ever since I met him. And I don't think it was phony, because he never tried to do what the other boys did. He was always a gentleman." When she smiled, her face and eyes softened, a winsome look that made me believe Homer could fall in love with her. "Yes, that's it, a real gentleman."

"What did the other boys do?"

"That's the story all around school. They all wanted to have sex with me. I mean, it wasn't make love or anything like that. They just wanted to have a good time."

"It sounds humiliating."

Her eyes teared up again. "It was. I wouldn't have done it except for . . ."

"What happened?"

"The first time it was the entire football team." She bit her lip and looked at the table.

"A gang rape?"

"I was drunk, of course, and high on pills. But I guess it wasn't technically a rape."

"You *wanted* to have sex with eleven men at once?" My words came out too much like an accusation.

She looked up at me through her eyelashes. "My daddy was the one who gave me the pills and got me drunk."

She could have punched me in the stomach to get the same effect. Anerd's behavior was more disgusting than I'd thought.

She twisted her hair with a forefinger. "The second time it was with a few of the men that he worked with at the shop. He watched us. Me and those men. When we were having sex." She pulled on a strand of hair with such force that a few strands snapped off in her fingers. "Sometimes he took pictures."

I could think of nothing helpful to say. "When did this happen?"

"The first time was when I was fourteen." Her voice had taken on a flat, automatic quality. "It mostly happened in our house." She smiled wistfully. "You see, that's why I went with Verlan. Him and my daddy got along and then I didn't have to have sex with other guys anymore."

"What did your mother do about this?"

"What could she do? We couldn't leave until she got the money."

"Sally, you know that you father is dead?"

She nodded.

"I heard from a deputy that they found his head at the

dump." She stared off into space. "I don't know what to feel right now. It seems so unreal. I was angry at him but I never wanted him to die." A tiny sob escaped her lips. "I don't want him to be dead. I just wanted him to be nice to me."

I squeezed her hand and pushed on.

"I know this is difficult, but I need to know. Did you plan to kidnap your father to get his money?"

"We talked about it. I didn't ever think it would really happen. I never thought he'd get hurt." She sighed. "I wanted to teach him a lesson. I wanted him to know how bad he hurt me."

"Who came up with the idea?"

"My mom. Mommy and Verlan."

"Your mother is saying on the stand that she only went along with it to entrap Verlan and Homer."

"I didn't know that. I thought she meant it for real."

"She says she is heartbroken that your father is dead."

"I suppose she is. I really don't know. We didn't talk too much about it."

"What about Homer? Are you going to testify against him?"

"I don't want to. I don't know what I will say. Mr. Troutman said I have to say Homer did it."

"What did he mean by that?"

"He doesn't want me to go to trial. He wants me to plea . . ."

"Plea bargain?"

"Yes, so I don't have to go to trial."

"Plea bargain to what?"

"Just kidnapping and not attempted murder. So it will be a lot better for me."

"Sally, kidnapping is a life term. Why won't he take you to trial? With what you told me he could do much better than that for you." I knew perfectly well the reason Laurence Troutman wouldn't take her to trial. He might accidentally win, and then Max Valentine would expose his sordid wife-beating.

"I don't know why. He said this would be better."

"For him, maybe. Certainly not for you." I lowered my voice. "Mr. Troutman is not a nice man, Sally. I may be able to get his wife to say that he's not doing a good job."

"But my mom said that it was the best he could do."

"Why doesn't your mother get you a decent attorney? An attorney who will defend you?"

"She said that Mr. Troutman was the best and we couldn't afford anyone else anyway."

"I don't know what I can do, Sally, but I'm certainly going to try to help you out."

"What about Homer?"

"I'm trying to help him, too."

The blond deputy buzzed me out at eleven. I ran across the parking lot, and nearly ran into an older model Chevy sedan. I made eye contact with Laurence Troutman through the windshield. I overcame my impulse to turn away and stayed on my course. Before I passed his car, he opened his door and blocked me. I backed up but didn't turn around.

"You better not be visiting the jail to talk to one of my clients."

Connie Troutman sat in the passenger seat, watching.

"As a matter of fact, I just spoke to Sally," I said. "She told me the whole story about Anerd's kidnapping."

"So?"

"Mavis and Verlan were behind it."

"What does that have to do with my client?"

"I think Sally could do better than pleading out to kidnapping."

"I wasn't aware that you received your law degree, Ms. Ringwald." He emphasized the word *Ms.*

"At least give her a chance. What harm would it do?"

"What good would it do? Unless you have some scheme to help Homer."

"Her testimony could help both of them. Homer had no clear understanding of the kidnapping plot, and from talking to Sally I don't believe she did either." I regretted the words as soon as I saw the sly grin on his face.

"In that case, I will certainly have to discuss my client's testimony with her." He didn't say it, but I had the awful feeling that unless Sally testified against Homer, she wouldn't be testifying at all.

"Laurence—Mr. Troutman—it's up to Max Valentine to decide if Sally testifies, and furthermore, it's not ethical for you to attempt to prevent her."

He laughed. "And talking to my client behind my back is ethical?" His eyes narrowed. "I'm getting tired of your interference, Ms. Ringwald. I told you before, stay out of it. Stay away from my clients. Stay away from my wife. Stay away from me." His face twisted into a hideous purple mask, the blood vessels in his temples pulsated, and his eyes projected rancor. He raised his fist and shook it an inch from my nose.

I could see he had not reformed.

He reached for me, and I stepped back to get away from him. I slipped. On my way down to the icy pavement I caught a glimpse of Connie, smug in the passenger seat.

She was smiling.

"You sanctimonious bitch," I said as I hit the ice.

Thirty-three

Laurence slammed the car door shut, revved the engine, and popped the clutch into reverse. The front tire bushed my calf, leaving a black streak on my leg and spraying my freshly dry-cleaned suit with a coating of freezing mud.

Connie waved to me as they sped out of the parking lot.

"You deserve whatever he gives you," I hollered into the Chevy's exhaust.

I picked myself up and assessed the damage. One of my heels was broken off, and my suit looked as though it had been trampled by water buffalo.

I stood in the jail parking lot trying to decide whether to hobble to the courthouse and scare the jurors, go back into the jail and ask for asylum, or call Fran and go back to the Yellow Inn. Or I could hitch a ride to the coast with the leering Deadhead in the passing psychedelic van and complete the increasingly rapid suicide of my career.

I didn't hear the truck drive up behind me.

"Cassie?"

I turned. "Hi, Tony. You're a little late. I already got beat up this time."

"I thought you were supposed to be giving your testimony." He opened his door and climbed out.

"Yeah, well. The universe had other plans for me."

"Get in." He slung his arm around me and led me to the passenger side. "You're shivering."

"Oh." I grunted as he helped me into the truck.

He closed the door and got into the driver's seat. "Have I ever told you that you're more maintenance than this truck?"

"No, but I bet I get better mileage, and I don't backfire quite as often."

Tony drove me back to the courthouse. "Someone has to tell Richard to ask for a recess."

"I can't go in like this," I said.

As Tony opened the door, Richard walked out of the courtroom. He looked at me and shook his head. "Are you all right?"

I nodded and filled him in on my altercation with Troutman's car.

"Do you want to press charges?" he asked.

"As though Max Valentine would prosecute? And besides, Laurence would say he tried to keep me from falling."

"You have an excellent point. But aside from what you might otherwise think, today's your lucky day. The judge called a recess until after lunch. I'm still not finished with Mavis."

"Good. I want to hear the rest of her testimony."

"We reconvene at one-thirty. Think you can get cleaned up?"

Tony hopped back into his truck. "She cleans up good, but she makes a mess even quicker."

Over the lunch break, I returned to the inn. After I showered, I filled Richard and Tony in on the interviews with Connie Troutman and Sally over take-out deli sandwiches Richard had brought to Fran's.

"This is probably not very empathic," I told them, "but Anerd deserved to die."

"Convince the jury of that." Richard bit into his roast beef sandwich.

"Maybe Sally can convince the jury." I picked at a piece of processed turkey.

"From what you say, I doubt Max will allow her to testify for the prosecution."

"What about for us?"

"Sounds like a plan. That is if they don't terrorize her first. Remember what they did to Homer?"

"Do you think someone would hurt Sally? She's only a young woman."

"And this is Trinity County. And the district attorney is Max Valentine." Richard put the sandwich wrapper in Fran's trash can. "I need to go. But promise me you won't go anywhere but the courthouse this afternoon."

"Don't worry," Tony said. "I won't let her out of my sight."

"Ouch!" I flinched and grabbed my waist.

"Sorry, it's the final stitch." Aunt Fran was finishing the last minute alterations on the suit she found for me at the local thrift store. "It's a little out of style but the color's good on you." She cut the thread and stuck the needle into the pincushion. "Just don't stretch too much until I get a chance to machine stitch it."

"How do I look?" I spun for Tony.

He whistled. "Like you mean business."

"Do you think it's too much for court?"

"Maybe. But it will get the judge's attention."

I looked in the mirror. "If I had silk stockings and spiked heels, I could charge admission." I turned and looked back at my image. "Fran, could you sew up the back vent a few inches?"

"If I do, you won't be able to walk in it."

"We gotta go." Tony picked up my briefcase. "Just keep your back to the jury."

Thirty-four

"It's raining harder than a cow pissing on a flat rock." Tony peered through the windshield wipers.

Mavis was on the stand by the time Tony dropped me off at the courthouse. Max Valentine was still questioning her. "And tell us what happened the night Anerd disappeared."

"Homer had gotten out on bail. His grandmother had come up with the money. He showed up at our house before Anerd got home from work. He—he tried to seduce me . . ."

Homer gasped, and Richard jumped up to object.

". . . but of course I refused." Mavis turned to the jury and raised her voice.

"Overruled," the judge said.

"What happened then?" Max Valentine asked as though the information was new to him.

"Anerd walked in and rescued me. He threw Homer out. I think Homer was so angry—and maybe even jealous—that he murdered my husband."

"No further questions for now, Your Honor." Max brushed past the jury close enough for them to smell his confidence.

Richard stood for the cross-examination. "Mrs. Woods, did Homer Johnson ever threaten the life of you or your husband or daughter?"

"Yes, now that you mention it, yes. Several times. We all heard him."

"And your daughter will back you up in her testimony?"

"Of course she will. Sally doesn't lie."

Not like you, I thought.

"Tell the jury about the White People's Brigade."

"I've heard of it, but I don't know too much about it."

"Was your husband a member of the White People's Brigade?"

Mavis jaw slackened enough to add ten years to her face. "I . . . I think he knew some people that belonged to it."

"Did you belong to the White People's Brigade?"

"No," she answered too quickly.

"Are you sure, Mrs. Woods? Do you have a position of influence with the WPB such that you could get support to frame Homer for the crimes of kidnapping and murder?"

Max raised his index finger. "Objection, Your Honor. Argumentative and no foundation."

"Sustained."

Homer scribbled on a legal pad then dropped it on the defense table. Richard walked over to look at the note. He turned back to Mavis.

"Mrs. Woods, did you offer money to Homer Johnson to kill your husband?"

"I should say not!"

"Did you tell your daughter, Sally, that the only way she could be free of her father's sexual abuse was to kill him?"

Mavis shrieked. "How could you say that about my husband? He never laid a hand—or anything else—on our daughter."

"Did you hire Verlan Crumm to kidnap your husband?"

Mavis burst into tears.

I looked at Max Valentine. He was sitting with his arms folded and a smug look on his face. Any intervention by him would hinder Richard's alienation of the jury for attacking this vulnerable widow.

"Mrs. Woods," Richard continued, "what is your relationship with Freddy Steele?"

"Who?"

"Objection, Your Honor." Max leaned back in his chair and lifted a pencil and lazily waved it. "I'd like to know the foundation for Mr. Peck's line of questioning." He dropped the pencil onto the table with a *rat-a-tat-tat.*

"Sustained." The judge leaned toward Richard. "Mr. Peck, can you explain where you're going with this?"

"One more question, Your Honor."

The judge waved his fingers and looked at Mavis.

Richard asked her, "Did you bail Mr. Steele out of jail?"

Mavis's face grew red with fury. "Why would I bail a scumbag out of jail and not my own daughter?"

"That's a good question, Mrs. Woods. Why would you bail a scumbag you didn't know out of jail?" He looked at the judge and then at Max. "No more questions for now but I reserve the right to recall this witness."

Max stood confidently. "Redirect, Your Honor?"

The judge nodded.

"Mrs. Woods, do you know anything about this White People's Brigade?"

"Certainly not."

"Have you ever heard of this Freddy Steele?"

"Never."

"Thank you, Mrs. Woods. You have been most helpful and I hope your ordeal ends soon so you can get back to a normal life."

"Thank you, Mr. Valentine." She wiped a tear from her eye.

The judge looked at Richard. "Recross, Mr. Peck."

Richard ground a pencil eraser into his temple. He stood.

"Mrs. Woods, why would you call a man you don't know a scumbag?" Before she could respond he said, "Never mind, Your Honor." He sat down. "No further questions at this time."

Max stood and smiled. "The prosecution rests, Your Honor."

Troutman had gotten to him. Sally was not to be called as a witness. Richard turned and looked at me, shaking his head.

The judge called a ten-minute recess. I pushed my way through the crowd to the defense table.

"Richard, I have to talk to Homer, right now."

"Cassie, you don't have much time."

I leaned over Homer and lowered my voice. "Sally told me about her father. She told me all of it."

Homer jerked his eyes away from mine and looked at the ceiling. "She didn't have to."

"Homer, I need to know right now, before I take the stand, what happened. I am not going to have egg on my face trying to help in your defense, and I absolutely refuse to be involved in a lie. If you want me to testify for you, you'd better tell me. Now." I glanced at Richard's watch. "You have eight minutes."

Homer drew his finger through a teardrop that had splashed on the table. "I didn't kidnap Anerd and I didn't kill him."

"Convince me, Homer. Did you go to Mavis's house after you were released on bail?"

"I did go there. But not to hurt anyone."

"Seven minutes, Homer."

He took a heavy breath and the words tumbled out in an avalanche of emotion. "Mavis called me after Bruno and my grandmother bailed me out. She said she still needed my help to leave Anerd. At first I told her no but she begged and said it was the only way to protect Sally."

Max Valentine walked backed into the courtroom and Homer followed him with his eyes.

"Go on," I urged him.

"I went over to their house and she said she needed help to get her stuff out."

"Was Anerd there?"

"Not at first. She took me back into their bedroom. There was stuff all over the place like she was packing. She started to undress and I wanted to leave."

Mavis walked into the courtroom from outside. She walked to the prosecution table and spoke to Max before she sat down in the observer seats. Homer avoided her eyes.

"What was she doing taking her clothes off?" I nudged him. "Two minutes, Homer."

His black eyes looked deep into mine. "At first I thought she was getting changed to help me move her stuff." He swallowed. "She wanted to have sex."

"Mavis?" I looked at the mousy brown woman with the saggy figure, sallow skin, and bags under her eyes. "Mavis wanted to have sex with you?"

"She said that if I wanted her daughter, that she had to try me out first and that was the way their family always did it."

"So did you? Have sex with her?"

Homer nodded.

I wanted to ask him if he was as dumb as a rock or just acted like it. I looked at Richard, who had been leaning over my shoulder to hear our conversation. His jaw hung open.

"I wanted Sally." Homer was defensive. "Except that I wouldn't have had sex with Sally. I respect her too much."

"What happened then?"

"We had our clothes off, and then Anerd was there in the room."

I squeezed my eyes shut. That was not what I wanted to hear. "What happened?"

Homer was distracted by the jury entering through the door to the jury room. "He was watching us. I don't know for how long."

"That's all he did was watch?"

Homer shook his head. "He took a picture and told me to fuck her. Then he laughed at me because after I saw him, I couldn't—you know. That's never happened to me before."

The bailiff announced, "Court is now in session. Remain seated."

"Then what?" I stood and leaned over to him.

"I ran away."

The judge sat behind his bench and looked down his nose at me. "Is counsel for the defense ready to continue?"

I scooted back behind the railing.

Richard stood. "Your Honor, I'd like to ask for a continuance. I've just received new evidence in this case."

The judge sighed. "Mr. Peck, I have a full calendar next week and I'd like to get the show on the road here and finish by Monday at latest. Otherwise we'll have to continue until next month." He looked at Homer's bruised face and battered body then at Richard. "And from what I've heard, I'm not sure you want to wait that long." He glanced at the wall clock behind me. "I believe that your expert was about to testify. Are you ready, Dr. Ringwald?"

I stood. "I believe I can get started, Your Honor."

"Can you get your new evidence in order before Monday, Mr. Peck?"

"Yes, Your Honor."

The bailiff opened the gate for me, and I walked toward the witness box. I smiled at the judge, and he nodded back. So far, so good, I thought. I raised my right hand and the perky red-haired court clerk swore me in.

"State your full name," she said.

"Cassandra Elizabeth Ringwald, Ph.D."

"Please be seated."

I climbed into the witness box steadying myself on the two-inch heels Fran had found for me in her closet and praying I wouldn't trip on the stairs. One of the hand stitches Fran had put in the waist gave way with a pop. I held in my stomach to keep the suit from exploding off me.

Richard approached me. "Dr. Ringwald, did you evaluate Homer Johnson?"

"Excuse me, Your Honor." Max was on his feet. "Is Dr. Ringwald testifying as a precipiant witness? I don't recall that she had been qualified as an expert witness."

Richard rolled his eyes. "Your Honor, both Mr. Valentine and myself are familiar with the doctor's qualifications."

"Nonetheless, I'd like them in the court transcripts." Max sat down.

"I'd like to hear them if you don't mind, Mr. Peck," the judge said.

"Very well." Richard leaned on the witness box. "Dr. Ringwald, tell us about your education."

I cleared my throat. "I have a Ph.D. in psychology and post-doctoral training in the administration and interpretation of psychological tests." Richard asked a few more questions about my degree and experience, then deferred to Max.

Max rose and faced the jury. "How long have you lived in northern California?" he asked me.

"I moved to Cedar Gulch right after I was licensed last year."

"So you're a newcomer?"

"I spent many summers visiting family up here when I was young."

"But you didn't live here, is that correct?"

"That's correct."

"I see." Max smiled at the jury and sat down. "I'll stipulate the witness as an expert, Your Honor," his point made that I was an outsider. He didn't ask if this was the first time I'd ever testified. He probably figured he didn't have to.

Richard began with his direct examination. "Again, Dr. Ringwald, did you evaluate Homer Johnson for the court?"

"Yes, I did." I gave the dates I interviewed him and the names of the tests I administered.

"Could you please tell us the purpose of each of these tests and the results you found."

"The Wechsler Adult Intelligence Scale-Revised is a general measure of intelligence. The Minnesota Multiphasic Personality Inventory-2 is an actuarial test consisting of three validity scales and ten basic clinical scales as well as a number of other subscales. Psychologists use scale elevations and combinations of scales to determine personality traits that are clarified and validated in the clinical interview." I continued and attempted to sound animated enough to keep the jury awake.

"Could you speak a little more slowly," the court reporter asked, "and spell the Wes . . . for me."

Relax, I told myself. I leaned back, trying not to bust a seam, and spelled.

"What were the results of the tests?"

"Homer is of above average intelligence, however, in terms of personality he is ambivalent, naive, and gullible. He doesn't have many friends and the relationships he has are superficial because he becomes conflicted between dependency and fear. He may put on a tough front, but when it comes down to it, his doubts about himself cause him to be afraid of the fight."

"What is the reason that Homer, a Native American, joined a skinhead organization?"

"Homer is caught between two cultures and hasn't found his bearings in either one. He has doubts about his Native

American heritage but doesn't trust the white culture either." I winced as a pin missed by Fran jabbed my thigh.

"Homer's mother was killed by a drunk driver when he was fifteen. The tragedy shattered his budding but tenuous identity, fueled his anger toward society, and kept him from maturing into a self-reliant young man. Paradoxically, as a result of his unmet dependency needs, he emotionally connected with a hate group." I looked at the jury and took a breath.

"Homer's the type of young man who would join a gang to make friends and be accepted, yet have little insight into the consequences. When the White People's Brigade, a fringe organization that also professes mistrust of the establishment, discovered he had money, they befriended him and he accepted their lies as truth."

Richard looked at the jury but addressed me. "Would he join a group like the White People's Brigade to, say in part, meet a girl?"

"Homer has a rich fantasy life, especially about having a girlfriend, perhaps to replace the mother he loved. Although he's attractive, he's never had the self-confidence to go after the more popular girls and settles for the not so pretty ones. If he fell in love, he would very likely join a group to be with a woman." I looked at Homer, hoping he didn't take my words as an insult to Sally. He stared at me intently but didn't appear disturbed.

"Does Homer understand—clearly understand—the motives of other people?"

"I would describe him as eccentric in his thoughts. He mixes his own personal idiosyncratic ideas and fantasies with other material in conversations and comes up with conclusions that may not seem logical to other people."

"Might he be involved in a situation in which he makes a poor decision because he doesn't understand what other people are up to?"

Max Valentine stood up. "Objection, Your Honor. Mr. Peck is leading the witness."

"I'll allow it," said the judge. "She is an expert and can qualify her response."

I looked at the judge who nodded for me to continue. "Yes, he misinterprets others' intentions and actions in ambiguous situations, and he can be excessively generous about the motives of others. He's indecisive, he questions his own judgment, and relies on his friends to make decisions. Even though he perceives himself as a moral person, he's nonassertive and hides true feelings, especially when the emotion is negative. This is all related to being trapped between two cultures, and losing his strong family ties after the death of his mother."

"Finally, does Homer have the mental or emotional ability to plot a kidnapping and murder?"

I swept my eyes over the jury before answering. Each of them was listening, and a few looked to be on the edge of their chairs. "I doubt it," I told them. "Although he is intelligent enough, his personality profile would not predict that he would have the motivation or cunningness to carry out such a plan."

"Mr. Valentine may cross." Richard sat down.

Max Valentine adjusted the lapels of his three-piece tweed suit as he rose from his chair. He walked toward me with flirtation in his eyes. "Dr. Ringwald, do you believe what Homer has told you?"

"Yes, from his perspective, yes." I didn't want to admit that Homer had barely told me anything at all.

"Isn't it true that persons of above average intelligence are capable of horrendous crimes?" He smiled at the jury.

"Yes, of course."

"And isn't it true that naive and gullible persons can act out in a rage?"

"Yes, it's possible."

"And wouldn't it be possible for a man, even a man who is easily led by others, to kill someone if he was sufficiently jealous or threatened?"

"Yes. It would be possible, hypothetically." I looked at Richard, who gave me a twitch of a smile. I felt as though I was getting creamed by Max, but my instincts told me to answer the questions, and not dig a deeper hole.

Max smiled. "No further questions, Your Honor."

Richard rose. "Dr. Ringwald, during the recess you asked Homer some questions. Do you wish to tell the Court what you learned?"

I knew Richard was taking a chance because what Homer had told me could work for or against him. But we didn't have much else and I had a feeling he wanted to keep up the momentum.

I took a breath. "Homer told me that after he was released on bond, he did go to the Woods family home. But it was only to help Mavis Woods move out to safety. He had become aware that Anerd Woods had been abusive to both Mavis and their daughter, Sally. He wanted to protect them as he had not been able to protect his own mother."

"Objection, Your Honor. Hearsay."

"Overruled, Mr. Valentine," the judge said. "She's an expert, and can take hearsay into account when forming her opinions."

Richard continued. "And what else did Homer tell you?"

"He told me that Anerd showed up and confronted him in the presence of Mavis. Homer became frightened and ran away. Anerd was alive when he left the Woods' residence that night."

"And the reason Homer didn't divulge this information before?"

"He was getting beat up in jail. He was afraid." I looked at Homer, and then at the jury. They got my point.

"Do you believe that Homer killed Anerd on that night?"

"No I don't. I believe that he ran away just as he said."

"No further questions, Your Honor."

Max Valentine rose. "I'd like to recross, Your Honor."

The judge nodded.

"So, Dr. Ringwald, you believe that, even though Homer told you that he was confronted by the victim while trying to rape his wife, and while he was removing belongings from the family home, that he had no motive to murder Anerd Woods?"

"First of all, Mr. Valentine, Homer didn't tell me he was confronted by Anerd while trying to rape Mavis. You are misrepresenting my statements. Secondly, I believe Homer was set up to take the fall for Anerd's death." I bit my cheek, leaned back, and tried not to act defensive.

"Nonresponsive, Your Honor. Please direct the witness to answer the question."

The judge nodded to me. "Answer the question, Dr. Ringwald."

"No, Mr. Valentine, I do not believe that Homer Johnson had a motive to kill Anerd Woods."

"Not even in self-defense? Come on now, Dr. Ringwald." He sneered at me, and swaggered toward the jury.

Richard jumped up. "Argumentative, Your Honor. Mr. Valentine is badgering the witness."

But Max had done it. He'd pissed me off. Before the judge could rule, I blurted out, "As a matter of fact, I believe that Homer was caught in the act of being seduced, or more accurately, coerced to have sex with Mavis when Anerd walked in on them and told them to continue so he could observe. If anybody initiated the sex, it was Mavis. I also believe that Homer is so afraid of getting into a fight, and so uncertain about his sexuality that he ran away rather than confront Anerd about being set up."

Mavis jumped up from the back of the courtroom. "That's not true. It's Homer's fault. He wanted sex with me because he thought it would help him get into the White People's Brigade. She said so in her report." She pointed to me and her face paled with the realization of what she'd said. Over the banging of the judge's gavel she yelled, "But I refused so he raped me anyway."

And there it was. Mavis had read the doctored report on diskette I had entrusted to her to give to Richard. It was a prank, inspired by the jesting between me and Todd about sex, but it had been closer to the truth than I could imagine. It had worked to flush her out, and now she had lied about Homer raping her.

Max Valentine maintained control only by pressing his lips together until they turned blue.

The judge hollered, "Order! Bailiff, remove that woman from my courtroom!" The bailiff strong-armed Mavis out the double doors.

Richard looked at me with a furrowed brow, shaking his head with incredulity.

When it was all over, the judge called for a recess until Monday. He pointed his finger at Max and then Richard. "And I want you two to figure out what this is all about and stop giving me surprises. Otherwise I will dismiss this case." He stood up, banged his gavel, and stomped out of the courtroom.

Thirty-five

"I can't figure out whether to fire you or congratulate you." The crease in Richard's brow was softened only by the shadow of a smile.

"I know it was a stupid thing to do. I take full responsibility for it. But the woman annoyed me. The whole town is crazy. No one can keep a secret up here," I said. "The good part is that Homer finally told us the whole story."

"And the jury got to see Mavis in a new light. I think they definitely lost some sympathy for her."

We had returned to the Yellow Inn and I had been forced by circumstances to confess my prank. "In the report I gave Mavis," I told Richard, "I had written that she and Homer were having an affair as his initiation into the WPB. The report I gave you made no mention of it because until right before my testimony, I hadn't guessed that Mavis tried to seduce Homer." I wrinkled my nose. "Anerd was a fat old man who liked to watch his daughter and his wife have sex with other men." I envisioned an orgy with baggy beige Mavis, plump sorrowful, Sally and a dozen men in football jerseys under the red and white flashing Napa Auto Parts sign. "Personally, I think the dump is too nice a resting place for him."

"What do you plan to do now?" Fran asked Richard.

"The case has essentially been presented. I would like to put Homer on the stand Monday and then rest the defense." He stretched out his neck. "Do you think he will make a good witness, Cassie?"

"He'll be believable as long as Max doesn't get him on the defensive."

Tony spoke. "If we can figure out who did kill Anerd, Homer's testimony won't be a problem."

Richard laughed. "Good luck."

I slept with my head on Tony's thigh for most of the trip back to Cedar Gulch. We planned to meet Richard the next morning, but I wanted to see Aunt Liz first, and assuage some of my guilt for leaving her alone all week.

Maria was in the kitchen of Liz's house fixing her supper. "Hey, sis." Tony gave her a brotherly hug.

"I can't even think how to repay you," I told Maria.

"Oh, knock it off, Cassie. It's not like we're just acquaintances." She punched me gently in the arm. "Liz insisted on sleeping in her bed. I have all my stuff in your bedroom so I could keep an eye on her."

Tony followed me upstairs to Liz's room. She stopped snoring as the door creaked open. "Is that you, Cassie?" The beam on her face lit up my heart. "Maria said you'd come back tonight."

I reached for her hand and she squeezed it until my knuckles popped.

I sat on the bed. "It's been an interesting week, but most of the excitement is over. We should be done Monday." I looked around. "Where are all the buckets?"

I heard Tony's steps going back down the hall.

"If you don't snag that young man, you are a fool."

"He fixed the roof, didn't he?"

"It's just a patch job for now. He'll finish it when the weather dries out."

I started to get up, but Aunt Liz pulled me back down.

"You will not be ungrateful to him, young lady. After all he did, I refuse to allow you to hurt his feelings."

"The roof was the entire reason I took this awful case. I don't want to have to rely on other people. Especially friends." I tried to pull away. "Auntie Liz, please let me go."

"I will not let go of your hand until you calm down and think about this."

I took deep breaths and looked around the room. "Did they fix the ceiling, too? And paint?"

"He had the entire police department baseball team over here. I never saw such energy." She chuckled. "His captain told me the criminals have all been in hiding with the weather, and the officers were going stir crazy with little to do."

"That's not new wallpaper?"

"I was tired of the old pattern anyway."

My lip started to tremble and I looked away from Aunt Liz. "This was supposed to be my job." I looked at the newly plastered ceiling to keep the tears from spilling out of my eyes.

"Oh, balderdash. You may not have inherited your Great-uncle Chester's blood, but you sure have his temperament."

"What's that supposed to mean?"

"He was every bit as independent as you are. Refused to rely on anyone. He took responsibility for everything and blamed only himself when anything went wrong." Her grip became even tighter and her voice quivered.

"What's wrong with taking responsibility?"

"Nothing, as long as it's appropriate responsibility and you don't allow it to ruin your life."

"Aunt Liz, I don't feel right that those men took time

away from their families to come over here and do what was my job. Don't you know how little time cops get to spend with their wives and kids? Look at Tony, he's gone all the time on whatever shift he's assigned. I can't condone them coming over here and . . ."

Aunt Liz threw my hand on the bed and fell back on her pillows. "You, young lady, are the most selfish, self-righteous person I ever met."

"Me?"

"Don't you understand?"

"No, I don't. How can you call me selfish for not wanting to take something away from those men and their families?"

"It made them feel good to help an old lady and a good friend of someone they care about."

"Oh." I hadn't thought of it that way. I was so involved with my own pride, I hadn't thought about anyone else's feelings.

"Sometimes I wonder if you think about others at all. Just like Chester." She started to cry.

Guilt for upsetting her stabbed my heart. "You'd better tell me about it."

"He was so proud—too proud to talk to anyone about his feelings. He came back from that terrible war so depressed and changed. He never trusted anyone again. The horrors he'd seen, what he'd been through. And he would never lighten his burden by sharing it." She looked at me with accusation in her eyes. "And you are the same way, Cassie Ringwald. And if you don't do something about it you will end up bitter and lonely."

We were both in tears. "Auntie Liz, maybe he felt too guilty to talk about his feelings."

"Guilty about what? He never hurt a soul."

"Guilty for being afraid," I said, "and for not doing more."

"How would you know that?"

"I understand now why he shut down. I left home because I was afraid of my father. Now I can barely stand to think about my mother and sister without admitting that I didn't do enough to help them."

She gave me a wet smile. "You were too busy surviving. So forgive yourself for being human and get over it. You can start by thanking Tony for what he and his friends did for us."

After giving her a hug, I stopped in her bathroom and splashed cold water on my face. It only made my nose redder.

I heard the kitchen door slam as I reached the bottom stair. Tony stood at the kitchen sink with his back to me. I pulled out a chair and sat at the table. "Where's Maria?"

"She went next door to get something."

"Oh."

Tony laid the carrot peeler on the drainboard but kept his back to me. "So am I in trouble? Or to be more accurate, exactly how much trouble am I in?"

My voice wavered. "You're not in trouble, Tony. I want to tell you how much I appreciate what you've done. And all your friends, too."

He turned around. "So, why are you crying?"

"I'm not crying." I stared at the floor. "Well, not really crying."

He sat next to me and started to put his arm around me, then rested it on the table. "Why is it, that no matter what I do for you, I end up feeling like a jerk?"

I sighed and looked up at him. "Are you going to give me a list of my character defects, too?"

"See what I mean?"

We glared at each other for a second before we burst into laughter. He leaned over and kissed me on the mouth, gently, tenderly, at first and then with increasing hunger. He pulled me from my chair and drew me to him, nudging my legs apart with his knees so that I straddled his thighs and felt his hardness against me. He had unhooked my bra when the kitchen door creaked.

I jumped off his lap and turned in time to see Maria high-tailing it back to her house. Tony pulled me back to him and nuzzled his chin between my breasts. "I'll put clean sheets on my bed tonight," he said, his hot breath against my chest.

"That might be an option." I kissed his forehead. "Let's get Auntie Liz fed first."

He groaned. "If there's one thing I could change about you . . ."

"Is this going to be a character assassination? If so, we could make love right now on the kitchen floor and get it over with."

"No way." He gave me a one-dimple grin and raised an eyebrow. "I have other plans."

I sent Tony over to his house to fetch Maria while I finished making the salad. Auntie Liz felt strong enough to come downstairs for dinner and of course insisted on a glass of sherry with Maria's paella. Tony and I giggled through dinner and even more after a glass of wine. We bundled Liz upstairs to bed at ten after twenty reassurances that we were acting silly only because the trial was nearly over.

"I'll stay here tonight, Cassie. You need your rest." Maria managed to say it with a straight face. "You can sleep in my bedroom or"—she feigned innocence—"wherever you feel comfortable."

We ran to Tony's house in the dark and the rain.

I washed my face in Maria's bathroom and dressed in a flannel robe Tony had lent me. Spanish guitar music filled the house and I walked down the hall to the living room transported by Segovia to an enchanted place. Tony handed me a glass of wine while he unplugged the phone. He was dressed only in his jeans, his olive skin dark in the amber light of the fire. He stood so close to me that I could feel his heat and smell his musk.

He took my glass and set it on the tile table. With one finger, he pulled at the robe belt, loosening it so that it fell on the hot pink Moroccan rug given to his mother by his father. His eyes were the color of the mountains after a thunderstorm.

He slid his hand into the robe and cupped my breast, then with his other hand took mine and slid it inside his jeans to his erection. He moaned and his eyes rolled back.

"God, Cassie. There have been so many times I wanted this."

I unbuttoned his jeans and was sliding them over his hips when a pounding at the door broke the spell.

"Tony," a woman shrieked. "Tony, I know you're in there. Answer the door. Tony, I'm not leaving until you answer the door."

"Shit. I'm sorry, Cassie. I thought I'd taken care of it."

"Do you mean taken care of her? Let me guess. Stephanie?"

"I told her it was over."

"Apparently, she didn't get the hint."

The sobs intensified. "Open the door. I know you're in there. I can see your truck. If you don't open the door, I'm gonna go and talk to that bitch Cassie. I will. I'm gonna go next door right now." More pounding and wailing. "Damnit, Tony, you better not be with her."

"Tony, I think you better get the door before she breaks it down." I bent down and picked up the tie to the robe.

Tony buttoned his jeans and shooed me into the hallway. "Go in my room and be quiet."

"Maybe she should see us together."

"Right. You think she's out of control now? Just imagine if she saw you." He swatted my rear. "Get going."

I couldn't resist peeking around the hall to watch the eruption. When Tony answered the door, Stephanie was in tears.

"What are you doing?" she cried.

"Trying to go to bed. What are you doing?"

She was petite, almost anoretic looking, a good fifteen pounds less than me, and maybe an inch taller. Her dark brown hair fell to her waist and her face was pretty but asymmetrical. She fell into Tony's arms, clutched his waist then slid down to the floor.

"I hate my life without you."

"Jesus, Steph. You're humiliating yourself. Get up."

"I thought you wanted me."

"Stephanie, I'm really not in the mood to discuss this." He pulled her off the floor and steadied her.

"When will you be?" she wailed.

"Stephanie, I am truly sorry, but you have got to leave me alone."

She fell on her knees and wept. "I thought if I gave you what you wanted, you'd be with me. I need you so bad."

"I never said I would make a commitment to you. I'm not ready for a commitment. I don't want a commitment. You have to leave. Now." He held her up by her arms. "Please, Stephanie, don't make us both regret the fun we had."

"Can I come back?"

"I don't want you to."

"Can we be friends?"

"Not right now. Please go." He coaxed her out the door and into her car.

"Looks like you got female troubles," I said when he walked back in the door. "That's what you get for picking the tempestuous type."

"Now I really feel like a jerk. To both of you."

"Well, it's been said if a guy is a jerk only a third of the time, he's a pretty good catch."

"How do I rate?"

"You get about fifty percent for tonight. But I have high standards. I expect no more than ten percent jerk from my men."

"I guess that gives me something to work toward." His body was damp with rain and nervous sweat. He wrapped his arm around me and kissed me on the forehead. "I know the mood's been lost. Think you could just cuddle with me tonight?"

"I can manage that. But you need to get the situation with Stephanie cleared up before we go any further." I didn't ask him about the commitment part, but there was clearly going to have to be more negotiation before I gave my heart to Tony Mesa.

"One more thing," I said as we snuggled like spoons in his bed. "What makes cops macho in uniform but terrified by women when they're not?"

"You tell me," he said as he nuzzled into my hair and slipped his hand over my breast. "I wouldn't have the first clue."

That night I dreamed with such intensity of making love to Tony that I woke in the morning gratified and peaceful with contentment.

Thirty-six

Before dawn, I sat at the kitchen table and sipped hot tea while I scribbled on a legal pad. Tony's snores were a whisper in the background. I briefly contemplated the woodstove, then snuggled into his flannel robe and clean wool socks I'd found in his dresser.

If Homer didn't kill Anerd, who did? And who was Anerd's rival? And who bailed Freddy out of jail? And why did Mavis collaborate with Anerd to abuse their daughter?

Through the living room window I saw Maria fixing breakfast at my house. In the yellow incandescent light, her olive skin and Moorish features made her look even more exotic than her brother. The only physical feature inherited from their blond mother was the blue-green of their eyes.

Maria answered the wall phone and caught my eye across the path between our houses. She pressed the mouthpiece to her chest and waved for to me to come over. "Richard," she mouthed.

I found a pair of red garden clogs on the porch and slipped them on. The air bit through the bathrobe and I was cold by the time I opened my kitchen door.

"It's Richard, for you." Maria was dressed for work in gray wool slacks and a white shirt, her long dark auburn hair pulled up into a bun.

"Thanks." I took the phone. The kitchen was filled with the smell of coffee and freshly baked bread. "Good morning," I said to Richard as I watched Maria pour a mug half full of milk and fill it with coffee strong enough to peel paint.

"I got a call this morning from the jail," Richard said.

"From Sally?"

"No." He paused for drama. "From Verlan Crumm."

"No way. What did he want?"

"I'm not sure. Do you want to drive up to Trinity with me to find out?"

"You don't have to ask twice. When will you be here?"

"When can you be ready?"

"Twenty minutes."

I hopped in the shower, and by the time I was dressed, Richard had pulled into the driveway. "Tell Tony I'll call him later," I called to Maria as I ran out the door to the Mercedes. I noticed the windshield was fixed.

Richard handed me a thermos of Earl Grey, and a bagel with smoked salmon and cream cheese. "I figured you didn't have time to eat. There're oranges in the cooler."

"Thanks." I peeled the plastic wrap off the bagel. "So what do you think Verlan wants?" I asked through a mouthful of food.

"Maybe he wants to hire me." We both snickered.

We drove in silence while I finished my bagel and licked my fingers. I glanced at Richard and assumed he was deep in thought about the case. I wrapped my hands around the plastic cup while I sipped hot tea.

"Cassie," he said at last, "I realize you and Tony have chemistry."

I gulped in surprise. The tea scalded my throat, and prevented me from changing the subject.

"I am also attracted to you," he said.

Oh, God, I thought. Here it comes.

"I know I'm not as handsome as Tony, but I have other attributes."

"Richard, I like you a great deal, but . . ."

"Don't turn me down without thinking about it. I could help you with your practice. We'd make a good professional couple. I can offer you security."

I leaned back against the leather headrest. "Richard, I'm not sure what I want."

"Tony is a nice fellow, but he's young."

"So am I."

"He's also involved with that other woman."

"I'm fully aware of that, Richard."

"Go to dinner with me tonight. I won't pressure you. I just want a chance with you."

I looked at his Saturday sports coat and tie, his nascent over-the-hill body, the remnants of his perfectly gelled hair, his well-manicured hands, and wondered what kind of fun he had in mind. Oh, what the hell. Maybe we could discuss the *Wall Street Journal*. "I'll go to dinner with you, Richard. But I can't promise anything else."

He smiled and reached over to squeeze my hand. His hand trembled, but not from the cold.

We reached the jail as the clock tower struck nine.

Richard went in to talk to Verlan, and I asked to see Homer in the infirmary. He looked stronger and happy to see me.

"Did you know Verlan wanted to talk to Richard?" I asked him.

He shook his head.

"Who was beating you, Homer?"

He glanced around the room and lowered his voice. "Verlan was the first."

"That's not surprising." What was surprising was his candor. I took it as a compliment.

"He stopped when Freddy got in here."

"Then what happened?"

"Freddy did the worst of it. I was glad when he got bailed out."

"Who gave him the bail?"

"I don't know. It wasn't his parents, though."

"Was Freddy the one who punctured your lung?"

Homer nodded.

"Why?"

"They didn't want me in the WPB."

"There's something else, Homer. Who else wants to hurt you?"

He shrugged.

"How is Bruno involved in this?"

Homer twisted the bedsheet in his hands. His voice became softer. "He knew about the money."

"What money?" I whispered back.

"The money that Anerd had taken for the WPB. Except it wasn't really for them. He kept it for himself." The muscles around his eyes twitched. "Freddy gave him a lot of money from drug deals," he continued. "Verlan and Buddy stole it. The other guys who wanted to be in had to give him ten thousand dollars each." He ran his forefinger along the bed sheet. "I gave him the money I took out, of my grandfather's trust fund. My grandmother found out and Bruno went to get the money back. Freddy and Buddy and Verlan followed him. They would have killed him if you hadn't driven up."

"So that's what Bruno didn't want to tell me." My chair creaked as I shifted my weight. "You gave neo-Nazis the money of a Jew. Not to mention a Jew who survived a concentration camp."

He nodded. His eyes lowered to avoid mine.

"Homer, why in heaven's name did you want to join them?"

He sighed in resignation. "I met Verlan at a party. Then I met Sally. I could tell he didn't love her and was making her believe all these horrible things about Jews and blacks. She was special. I got to know her and she told me about her father. I wanted to save her. Verlan knew I wanted her, and he said he would let me have her if I gave money to the WPB and helped them get something that belonged to one of them. I had no idea that Mavis was trying to get away from Anerd. I had no idea they would kidnap him."

"Mavis was wearing a wire. What about the tapes?"

"I didn't know she was making tapes." He looked embarrassed. "They did talk about getting even and making him pay. I thought it was a joke and said some things about how to do it. I even said if they took him to the dump, the bears would eat him before anyone found him."

"They set you up to take the fall."

"I didn't know they were serious."

"And you went back to see Mavis . . . ?"

He looked at me. "I know you think I'm stupid. Mavis called me and said I had to keep up my part of the bargain or she would let Sally go to jail. That's when I went to her house. She told me if I helped her she'd make it worth my while." His lips were dry over his teeth. "I didn't want to have sex with her. She knew Sally told me about Anerd. She said it was the only way she could keep him."

"By allowing him to exploit Sally?"

"She hated Sally for that. Because her husband liked her daughter better."

"How did you know that?"

"She told me she wanted to leave Anerd but had to wait until she found the money. There was a lot of it—maybe almost a million."

"Anerd had a million dollars lying around?"

"He had it all hidden."

"So Mavis decided to steal the money and wanted you to help her."

"Anerd was going to leave her and take Sally with him. I couldn't let him do that. He would do horrible things to her."

"Do you realize that gives you a motive to kill him?"

"I don't know who killed him." His face became impassive and I wondered if he was telling me the truth.

The orderly knocked, then opened the door. "Time for meds, Homer."

Homer leaned closer to me. "The one who helped Freddy beat me . . ."

I leaned into his whisper.

"It was his lawyer. Mr. Troutman."

The orderly took Homer's arm and wrapped a blood pressure cuff around it. He listened through the stethoscope. "Boy, what've you been doing, running a marathon?" He looked closely at Homer's face. "Typical Indian. No matter what's going on inside, he's like granite on the outside."

Homer ignored the slight.

The orderly pumped the cuff up again. "Let's try it again." He glanced at me. "You wanna take a breather and let this man cool down?"

I walked back to the lobby and was handed a note by Deputy Martin. "Mr. Peck said you should come to the interview room. I'll buzz you on in."

An adolescent-looking deputy opened the door to the next interview room. Richard sat across the table from Verlan.

"Mr. Crumm wants me to represent him."

"What about Mr. Troutman?"

"I changed my mind." Verlan hadn't gotten any better-looking in the week since I'd interviewed him. His grin exposed his pointy yellow teeth. "Actually, I just wanna have a good-looking lady shrink get into my head." He winked.

I wasn't flattered. "I don't have the time and you don't have the money, Verlan."

His grin faded. "Well, let's just say I got some information that might help your friend Homer. And I'll give it to you if I get a better attorney. I've been told that Mr. Troutman ain't doing the best job of defending me because of his own reasons. I think Mr. Peck here can get me a better deal than some stupid plea bargain."

"Can he do that?" I asked Richard.

"He hasn't gone to trial yet."

"The deal is this," Verlan said. "You call me in again on Monday, and I'll help Homer out but only if Mr. Peck agrees to defend me for a slightly reduced fee."

"That sounds a little like a bribe to me." Richard put his legal pad into his briefcase and snapped it shut.

"Okay, I'll come up with the bucks somehow. Just agree to be my attorney."

"I have no intention of becoming a party to perjury, Mr. Crumm."

Verlan's face fell. "You gonna put me on the stand again on Monday?"

"If you have additional evidence, you need to discuss it with the district attorney. You are his witness in this trial."

"Well, believe me, when he hears what I have to say, he ain't gonna let me get back on the stand."

"I can't recall you unless I have a good reason to do so," Richard said. "For the final time, can you tell me what your information is?"

"Nope, you'll just have to trust me." Verlan laced his fingers together and bent them back to crack his knuckles. "Just like I have to trust you."

"That guy is one weird dude," I said to Richard as we waited to enter the lobby. "What are you going to do?"

"I don't know." He shook his head. "I just have no idea."

He opened the car door for me. "Let's go home. I'll have the weekend to think about it.

Two miles past the lake, the foothills gave way to the valley floor. A winter haze obscured the land and all but the summit of the eastern mountains, which glistened white against the gray sky.

Richard drove me home to change and then across town to Debo's, the best Italian restaurant in Cedar Gulch. The wine was excellent, the atmosphere romantic, and Richard attentive. And I was bored to tears.

In spite of my efforts to keep the conversation light, he used the ride back to my house to broach the subject again, "I would like to know what you want in a relationship, Cassie."

How could I tell him that he was a kind, caring, intelligent, rich gentleman who made me want to stab myself in the thigh with a fork to stay awake. "I told you, Richard, I'm not sure I'm ready for a relationship."

"I don't understand. You've completed your education, and you're not getting any younger."

Oh please, I prayed, not the dreaded biological clock conversation. "There are some things I need to resolve first."

"Such as?"

"Some things with my family." I'd throw him a bone to keep him quiet. "I haven't seen my mother or my younger sister, Viola, in years and I need to find them."

"I could help you."

"The help I need is in the emotional area. The more I don't do it, the guiltier I feel about it."

"I could help with that, too." He reached over and took my hand.

"I appreciate that, Richard, but it's one of those things I need to do on my own."

"I admire that about you. Your independence. In fact, there are few things I don't admire about you."

We reached my house. He took my hand and walked me to the door.

"I'd ask you in," I lied, "but Auntie Liz is probably asleep."

"I understand," he said, too nicely. "Then I'll say my good-byes here."

Before I could reach the doorknob, he wrapped his arm around me and kissed me. He lingered too long, smothering me under the notion of becoming involved with a man who dearly loved me, but who excited me as much as bologna on Wonder bread.

"Thank you," I said when he released me. "I'll see you Monday morning."

As he walked down the steps to the sidewalk, I caught a glimpse of Tony standing on his porch. From the gravity on his face, I could tell he'd been watching Richard and me. I stared back at him.

The sound of the car door distracted me and I looked at Richard. He got in, waved and smiled, and drove off.

Tony turned away. I jumped off the porch and caught him before he slammed the door in my face.

"Fuck you, Cassie." His eyes were gray and the flesh around them mottled.

"For God's sake, Tony. It meant nothing."

"Oh right. You expect me to believe that when you've been with him all day. Why didn't you call me?"

"Tony, I'm sorry. I just got preoccupied with this case."

He looked at me up and down. "Sexy dress. Perfume and pearls. Must be nice having a rich attorney pamper you." His voice was husky and strained. "So tell me what I'm lacking. Money, brains, an advanced degree?"

"The dress is old, and the pearls are Auntie Liz's."

"Pretty feeble, Cassie. Want to try that again?"

"Tony, Richard bores me to tears."

"Right. Just don't expect me to believe it was a mercy kiss."

"Fine. But I'm not going to apologize to the master of the sport fuck."

"Oh, you *can* pronounce the 'F' word." He looked around the living room as though he wanted to throw furniture. When he spoke, his words were tight and controlled. "Stephanie adores me, and doesn't mess with my head."

"I'm so glad for you." I could have hit him. "Richard adores me, too, and he isn't a control freak."

"Get out of my house."

"No problem." I stormed across the yard and made it into my house before Tony saw me sniveling. I clanged the teapot on the sink, splashed water all over the kitchen floor, and slammed the kettle on the stove. I looked through the window into Tony's living room. His chess set exploded into the wall and the room went dark.

Auntie Liz pattered down the hall in her slippers. "Was the dinner date that bad?" she asked me.

"The dinner date was fine—it's Tony who's the jerk."

She shook her head. "The two of you need to grow up."

"Thanks for the support." I yanked two teacups from the cupboard. "Want some tea?"

"Something stronger, please." She took the brandy I poured her. "Now sit down and talk to me."

In the morning, I looked out the kitchen window. As I expected, Stephanie's black Mustang was parked in front of Tony's house.

Thirty-seven

Monday morning Richard put me back on the stand for some final questions. He called Homer, who limped stoically to the witness box and was sworn in.

Homer's testimony lasted less than an hour. Richard asked him about his life and his relationship with Sally and Verlan. Homer gave details about Anerd wanting him to have sex with Mavis. When he was finished with his story, I couldn't tell if the jury believed him or not.

Max Valentine didn't have much to ask Homer. I had the impression that he didn't want to have any more of his story in front of the jury than possible.

After Homer was seated back at the defense table, Richard addressed the court. "Your Honor, I ask to recall Verlan Crumm."

The judge asked, "Do you have a particular reason, Mr. Peck?"

"Mr. Crumm approached me over the weekend and informed me that he had additional evidence he wished to present to the Court."

Max Valentine sprung up. "Your Honor, this is unusual. Mr. Crumm is my witness, and he has not informed me of this."

The judge said, "I'll allow it. If we get off track, you may object, Mr. Valentine."

The court recessed while Verlan was brought over from the jail. When he was on the stand, Richard began to question him.

"Mr. Crumm, did you contact me over the weekend to tell me you wished to retain me?"

"Yes, I did."

"I want the Court and Mr. Valentine to be very clear about this. Did we make any deals or agreements that I would represent you if you provided the testimony you are about to give to the court."

"Well, it weren't for lack of trying on my part." He snickered and winked at the jury. Several of the women were pressed to the backs of their seats in an effort to be as far away from him as possible.

Great, I thought, they won't believe him.

"Mr. Crumm, what was it that you wanted to tell the Court?"

He looked around the courtroom, the crown to his subjects. "Ain't the press here?"

Looking at Richard from the back, I could see a flux of crimson rise from his neck to the top of his thinning crown. I had an image of mercury blowing out the top of a thermometer.

Max Valentine glowed at the jury.

"Mr. Crumm, do you in fact have additional information to present to the court?"

"I want the press."

A woman no more than twenty raised her hand. "Your Honor, I'm from the *Trinity Times.*"

"I want cameras." Verlan was beginning to pout, and Max Valentine did a poor job of suppressing his glee.

I scribbled a note to Richard and leaned over the rail to

give it to him. The bailiff moved to stop me but the judge motioned him away.

Richard looked at the note and approached Verlan. "Mr. Crumm, the television crew was delayed, but whatever you say will be public record and I'm sure the press will be glad to interview you later."

I was certain Max could have objected to that statement, but he didn't bother. Why mess with success?

Verlan worked his jaw like a rat masticating an unfamiliar bit of food. "Okay." He sat back. "I'll tell you the whole story."

Max rose and in a bemused tone objected. "Foundation, Your Honor?"

"I'll allow, Mr. Valentine. This trial can't get much stranger than it's already been." He nodded at Verlan. "You may proceed."

"That means I can talk? Okay, here goes." He looked around the courtroom, busying his eyes over several of the female jurors. When one of them appeared ready to crawl over the back of her chair, he smiled triumphantly. "Homer didn't do it."

Max Valentine's jaw dropped. He slumped back in his chair.

Richard seemed to grow an inch. "Didn't do what, Mr. Crumm?"

"He didn't do none of it. He didn't kidnap Anerd Woods, and he didn't kill him neither."

"How do you know this?"

"Because I was there. Homer didn't know nothing about the plan and what he did hear, he didn't catch on to. No offense"—he looked at Homer—"the boy ain't too bright."

"You testified before that Homer was a party to the kidnapping. Were you lying then?"

"Yup."

"And you expect us to believe that you're telling the truth now?"

"I don't care if you believe it or not. But Homer didn't have nothing to do with it."

"What made you decide to tell the truth now?"

"Couple a reasons. First of all, I'm a charter member of the White People's Brigade. And that means I don't believe in the American justice system. See this?" He lifted his arm and pulled up his shirt sleeve to expose the red and black tattoo of an A imposed on a circle. "This here means 'Anarchy' and that's want I intend to do. Create anarchy.

"The American legal system is corrupt and dishonest. Niggers get off for slaughtering innocent white women, and Christians go to the chair for exterminating vermin who murder unborn babies." Verlan's eyes rolled back. "And this jury here was about to send Homer to the death house for something he didn't even know about. Now I'm not saying I have a liking for Injuns and Jews . . ."

He pointed at Homer. "Yeah, Homer, I know your grandaddy was a Jew because your second grandaddy told us that when he came to get your money back, and that's why he had to be taught a lesson."

He smiled at the jury. "Like I was saying, I don't like Jews at all because they come from Satan, and they're part of the conspiracy to rob the rightful wealth of the white man, but I don't believe that the United States legal system should unrightfully punish an innocent man. So that's why I'm telling you all this."

He narrowed his eyes at the jury, and pointed out the century-old windows to an unseen foe. "I wanted to show you how easy the American justice system makes it to sentence an innocent man to die."

The only sound in the courtroom was the rattle of the wind against the windowpane.

Richard cleared his throat and avoided looking at the jury. "Is there another reason that you changed your testimony?"

"Yeah." Verlan blinked as though his brain clicked back on.

"Please fill us in."

His lips bared to expose his feral teeth. "Because that piece of shit district attorney is in the rack with my supposed public defender, and I'm gettin' screwed up the ass."

Max Valentine cleared the distance between the table and the witness stand in one step. "Objection, Your Honor," he screamed. "This man has a personal vendetta and he's ruining my case because he wants revenge."

Verlan hollered back, "You're damn right I want vengeance. The Lord sayeth, 'Vengeance is mine,' and I want mine right now."

The judge banged his gavel and screamed for order. He called a recess and cleared the courtroom.

Richard told me later that he and Max Valentine provided summary arguments to a white-faced group of twelve jurors and two alternates.

In his instructions to the jury, the judge told them to ignore the theatrics and focus only on the evidence and credibility of the witnesses.

After the judge expelled the observers, I pushed through the crowd outside and walked over to the jail to see Verlan. The lobby was empty, cleared for the best show in town next door.

Deputy Martin was still on duty. "Two hard winters and three gay rodeos and this town's never seen the likes of this trial."

"It's a sideshow all right."

He gave me a cinnamon roll to eat while I was waiting for Verlan to come back from court.

I watched through the glass while the deputy unlocked Verlan's shackles and handcuffs. He grinned and joked, smug about the ruckus he'd caused.

I sat in the metal chair, and pulled at the hem of my skirt.

"I knew you'd come," he said, winking.

"I didn't come to help you, Verlan. I came to find out the truth."

"What difference is it going to make? Max baby ain't gonna arrest who killed Anerd. He's too deep into it."

"Perhaps not. But I have to know."

He sneered. "For a price."

"Verlan, you obviously have high moral standards." I forced the words out, and pretended I was talking to someone else.

"I do?" he bought it. "I mean, yeah, I do."

"I don't know if I can help you, but the only way I can is to know the truth." I pulled my chair a little closer to the table between us. "Tell me, Verlan. Who killed Anerd?"

He stared at my chest and said nothing.

"Was it Mavis?" I didn't move away.

He blinked. "Boy, you're a smart broad. How'd you figure that?"

"Was she his rival in the White People's Brigade?"

He grinned, and nodded.

"How was Mavis recruiting you?"

"How does a woman ever get a man to do something?" He reached his hand down to scratch his crotch.

"She was having sex with all of you?"

"If that bitch had as many pricks on the outside of her as she'd had on the inside, she'd be a porcupine."

"I mean no offense to Mavis but . . ."

"She's kinda old?"

"Yes."

"You put a bag over her head and she's about the same

as any of them." He twiddled his fingers. "So you and Homer been having sex?"

"No, he's my client. I don't have sex with clients."

"Why not?"

"It's unethical. I'm sure you understand."

"Too bad. But I hear he wants to boink Sally anyway."

"That doesn't bother you?"

"Nah. She was just part of the package Anerd put out to get me in the WPB. Then I kept up with her because Mavis wanted to pin Anerd's kidnapping on her. That way she could'a gotten rid of Anerd and Sally both."

"Why didn't Mavis bail you and Sally out of jail when she bailed Freddy out? It seems to me that she could have blamed Anerd's death on you."

"She wanted Homer to take the fall for Anerd's murder from the beginning. She knew Sally wouldn't've gone along with it once she figured it out. And me? She was pissed off at me for bungling the murder. How'd I know that he'd be found in the dump in one piece the first time?"

"So that's the reason you fell out of favor? She dumped you?"

"Yup. For her new partner. Freddy Steele. I heard you got friendly with him, so why wouldn't Mavis?"

"Nice talking with you, Verlan. I should be getting back to wait for the verdict."

"You gonna come back and see me?"

"We'll see." The second I was buzzed out I ran outside to cleanse myself of him. It was all I could do to keep my breakfast down.

By the time I returned to the courthouse the jury had already reconvened. I found a chair behind Homer and rested my hand on his shoulder. His skin was clammy through his shirt, but he remained impassive except to turn and, with a nod of his head, acknowledge his grandmother and Bruno.

The judge took his seat at the bench and nodded to the bailiff. The jury foreman, a clean-cut thirtyish man attired in a citified Western shirt, khaki Levis, and the halting confidence of a middle manager, handed him the verdict.

Richard and Homer stared straight ahead. I looked around to Winema and Bruno. Both stared at the jury foreman, as though their thoughts could guide his actions.

Several women on the jury stared at Homer. One glanced at me and smiled.

I held my breath.

The bailiff showed the paper to the judge, then handed it back to the jury foreman.

The foreman read, "On the charge of kidnapping, not guilty.

"On the charge of attempted murder, not guilty."

I exhaled partway.

He continued. "On the charge of murder in the first degree, not guilty."

I finished exhaling.

The only expression from Homer was a slight nod of his head. He looked at Richard, then reached to shake his hand.

I stood and walked back to Winema and Bruno, who remained seated. My smile was rewarded by a handshake and a thank you from Bruno. I wanted to ask why no one was cheering or at least jumping up to hug Homer.

Winema seemed to read my mind. "He has been found not guilty of kidnapping and murder, but he is guilty of betraying his people. He must go to the spirit place to atone, and grieve for his mother."

I opened my mouth to explain. "But . . ."

She placed her hand on my cheek. "Homer and I will make our peace later when he comes to live in my home. I thank you for giving him the opportunity to have freedom from the white man's prison."

I followed her eyes to Homer, who walked toward her with shoulders slumped and eyes on the floor. "Grandmother . . ."

She turned and walked solemnly away, leaving behind a scent of wood smoke, and an air of censure.

I stood with my mouth open, tempted to run and shake some sense into her.

Bruno touched my arm. "She forgive him later. She isolates him so he make peace with spirits. He need to become a man and mourn for mother with spirit quest." He followed Winema.

I turned to Homer. His eyes were black and his expression flat as he watched his grandmother walk out the double doors and disappear from his sight. His eyes turned to me. "You were right in your testimony about me being angry, Dr. Ringwald. I've let my mom's death destroy me."

"You can change that, Homer."

"I will. I want to go back to Modoc to do what Grandmother says before I can decide about the rest of my life." He moved close to me and his voice was a whisper. "Dr. Ringwald, I have to find out who I am."

I looked into his eyes. "Call me Cassie," I told him.

After the courtroom emptied, I spoke with Richard. "So when Verlan testified that Homer didn't kill Anerd, he got his revenge on Mavis for choosing Freddy as Anerd's successor."

"I suppose so," he said. "But now it's up to the district attorney to figure out what to do with him. And the rest of them for that matter. As for me, I'm going down the hill immediately. I just want to get out of this town." He packed his papers in his briefcase.

"But I have a feeling that Verlan has another agenda.

Who else would he get revenge on if he helped acquit Homer?"

"I don't care, Cassie. The jury acquitted Homer so my job is done. I'm leaving." He leaned closer and his eyes became soft. "Would you have dinner with me tonight?"

"Sorry, Richard. I have so much catching up to do. Maybe next weekend."

The ride back to Cedar Gulch was long and silent.

Thirty-eight

"I want to see the place that got me into all this trouble," Homer said as we drove out to the dump.

Todd had driven Homer down to Cedar Gulch after the trial ended. The two had spent the night on Tony's living room floor.

For the first time in weeks, Mount Shasta had cast off its shroud and glowed pink above the horizon mist. Homer, Todd, and I sat above the dump and watched the sunrise move shadows and colors across the volcano, giving it an eerie aura of movement and life. A hemispheric cloud curved above it like a hand ready to cup a breast.

"You feeling okay?" I asked Homer.

He looked straight ahead, expressionless. "Yup."

"You don't need to do that stoic Indian routine with me anymore."

He grinned. "I suppose not."

"You don't need to thank me either."

He laughed. "I guess I didn't. Thanks, Cassie."

He opened the car door. "Let's go look at the bottom before they get started."

The sign proclaiming Cedar Gulch Sanitary Landfill was an oxymoron at best. We hiked over disintegrating white plastic bags of moldy potato peels and soured milk cartons, discarded lawn furniture, the detritus of modern life.

The scraper operators were having a cup of coffee in a shack. The one in the red plaid jacket called to us, "You stay out of there. We ain't gonna be able to see you once we're in the cans." He turned his back to us, his duty to warn completed.

"There's probably no chance of finding the rest of Anerd," Homer said.

"I doubt it."

We walked to the area where his head had been found. "If the scrapers didn't cover him, the bears ate him," Todd chattered. "I bet Mavis can't stand to lose Anerd's gold ring. She's probably been out here digging for his finger." The redheaded teenager gave a maniacal giggle, and leaned over the yellow police tape to poke at the dirt with a stick.

Homer and I walked over the knoll to look at the pit.

The two scraper operators climbed into their machines and rumbled off. The first one sped into a pit, dropped its lower blade like a mammoth jaw, and scooped up ten tons of dirt. When it was on the verge of stalling, the second scraper butted into its rear and pushed another couple of tons into its maw. The rear scraper hooked onto the first, lowered its blade and sucked up its own tonnage of dirt.

The monsters disconnected, then raced away from the pit and dumped their load onto the garbage mountain.

"Looks like condominiums fucking," Homer said.

I laughed. "That's the first joke I've ever heard you tell."

"It won't be the last."

We turned to leave the gully and look for Todd. He'd disappeared. The roars of the scrapers drowned out the footsteps behind us.

Mavis and Freddy appeared from behind a knoll. Freddy was wearing the same white chinos, a white T-shirt, and white Nikes with black swastikas that he wore the night he assaulted Bruno. His stainless steel tooth glimmered when he sneered. His shaved head reflected pink smudges of clouds. He held an aluminum baseball bat.

Mavis wore a blue and white hausfrau shirtwaist under a Trinity High letterman's jacket and sensible walking shoes. The lines on her face were softened by the pale light but the expression in her eyes was the same I had witnessed when Homer confessed on the stand that she'd seduced him.

I looked at the scrapers. They raced across the dump oblivious of anything but their task. The spotter and Cat operator were on the other side of the landfill. I couldn't see Todd.

"We're going to have to run," I said.

Freddy smacked the bat into the palm of his hand.

"Cassie, you run to the maintenance garage. I'll hold them off." Homer was panting and sweaty from the exertion of walking down the hill.

"The garage is at least half a mile away. Freddy will catch me before I can get there." I stared at Mavis. "Homer, you run. I'll talk to Mavis."

"Dr. Ringwald, don't be an idiot. Run and get help."

"Mavis." I walked toward her. "Can we talk?"

"What's there to talk about? You just ruined my life."

"I didn't intend to ruin your life. Just save Homer's."

"The same thing." Her eyes narrowed and the corners of her mouth twitched.

Freddy swatted the bat into his palm and leered at me.

I kept him in my peripheral vision, and shouted over the noise of the loaders, "Why did you leave Sally in jail?"

"It was the best place for her." The woman's scowl showed the spiderwebs of wrinkles across her cheeks.

"Meaning what?"

"Her daddy couldn't get to her."

"You mean she couldn't stop you from killing him?"

"What makes you think I killed Anerd?"

"Okay, so you hired it out." I looked at Freddy. "That wood ax come in handy?"

"You just don't understand, do you?" Mavis hollered at me.

"Explain it to me."

"I put up with that old man's shit for years. I had sex with his friends, I took his crap, I didn't fight back when he hit me."

"Why didn't you take Sally and leave him?"

"I couldn't get to the money. He kept it hidden."

"Why didn't you protect her from him and his little sex games?"

"How could I?"

"Oh, I see. He liked her better than you."

Mavis snorted. "Don't let that little slut fool you. She craved it."

"No, Mavis, she didn't. She loved her father and didn't know she had any other options. You gave her to him so he'd lay off you, then you got jealous. Your revenge was subverting his skinhead gang."

"It was him or me, and I was faster. Can you imagine what he would have done with Sally if he got rid of me?"

"Do you care?"

The coldness in her eyes answered my question.

"Mavis, what do you intend to do with us?"

Freddy took a step closer and curled his lip. He looked like he couldn't wait to whack me into bear fodder.

"Mavis, don't let him do it."

"Don't give me any bullshit about the calvary coming to rescue you. We'll be long gone before they find you." Her eyes shifted toward the scrapers to give me a clue to my fate.

Freddy walked over to Homer and swung the bat. It struck Homer's uplifted arm. The cracking sound sickened me. Homer steadied himself and reached for the bat with the arm that wasn't broken. Freddy smiled and swung the bat in the other direction. The impact lifted Homer off the ground and threw him into a pile of oozing brown paper bags.

I ran, slipping on foul earth, guilty for abandoning Homer, ashamed for my fear and desire to get away. I ran past the yellow police tapes and prayed I only imagined whacks of the bat against Homer's flesh.

When I reached the top of the hill I remembered the maintenance garage was between me and Freddy. I could barely breathe for the lump in my throat.

I leaned over to catch my breath and looked at the mountain. The pink had faded to a gray haze. I surveyed the landfill. I would have to double back to the garage or run downhill to the scrapers to get anyone's attention.

A glint in the sun caught my eye. Tinsel stood fifty feet away on the next hill, blocking the way to the garage, the muscles in his chest and shoulders flexing under his T-shirt each time he swatted the bat into his palm. When he laughed, the light off his tooth left a tracer in my sight. The tip of the metal bat was bright red.

Mavis leapt out from behind a battered refrigerator carton and tried to grab me. I charged, pushing her down. I ran past the yellow police tapes without looking behind me.

I tripped on a greasy green carpet remnant and slid down the hill toward the scrapers. The monsters sped back and forth moving earth, moaning, and roaring with single-mindedness. I waved my arms but the men took no notice. Freddy's jeers punctuated the silences when the scrapers changed gears. "I'm gonna get you, bitch." He cackled.

I reached the pit a few yards ahead of Freddy. The scrapers were working behind an unexcavated mound of earth. I ran toward the center of the pit swinging my arms above my head and shouting.

The lead scraper screamed around the corner. A shot of adrenaline propelled me into the pit. I kept running and waving my arms and hollering until I became aware that my own noise was the only sound.

I turned around, running backwards, preparing to dodge Freddy's baseball bat.

The scrapers had stopped and the massive engines turned off. The lead operator had climbed from his second-story cab to the ground. "Damn it." He threw his John Deere hat to the ground and pointed a finger at me. "I told you not to play around this place," he hollered. He hitched up his pants a quarter inch to his beer belly.

"Where's the guy who was chasing me?" I yelled back. I kept my distance, expecting Freddy to jump out from behind a boulder-sized scraper tire.

The scraper operator adjusted his privates and pointed to the scraper's rear tire. "He should be about under that one. What the hell were you doing down here anyway?"

"You just saved my life."

"Well, damn. I hope you're worth it." He climbed back into his cab, his pants at half crack. His radio crackled and squawked as he called the garage.

I labored back up the hill, ignoring the shouts of the scraper operator to stay where he could see me.

My lungs burned with the foul gasses of rotted meat and slimy leftovers. I couldn't find the police barricade. I wandered over several hills but saw no sign of anyone. I choked back the fear that I wouldn't find Homer.

From the bottom of a gully, I saw a fat bear rooting through a mound of fresh garbage. I walked toward her figuring that a human might be nearby. When she saw me, she loped off, her black fur shimmering in the sunlight. A happy bear, I thought.

Homer sat on the shreds of a plastic bag holding his arm

close to his side. Blood had clotted on the side of his head. I walked to him and sank to the ground next to a meat wrapper blackened with solidified juices.

"You okay?"

"Fine. Freddy got me down but didn't do me in like he thought."

"Where's Mavis?"

He pointed down a hill. "She fell. I guess the bear scared her."

I stood and looked. Mavis lay sprawled at an impossible angle, facedown in a pile of soiled baby diapers.

"She's dead. Looks like a broken neck."

"She broke her neck on diapers?"

Homer shrugged and put on a silent face.

Shouts erupted behind us and Tony and Todd ran from the road toward us.

I turned back around to face the dump. At a loss for words, I said, "The mountain's so white. Its majesty made me feel small and unimportant."

"Yeah, the rain washed out all the crap in the air." Homer twiddled with a heavy gold ring.

"Is that Anerd's ring?"

"Yeah. Mavis had it in her pocket. I think she was gonna throw it back in the dump so she wouldn't have it if the police searched her house."

"You found it in her pocket?"

He looked at the mountain. "I thought I should give it back to Sally."

"I see." I flicked a piece of Styrofoam from my sleeve. "I wonder why Mavis didn't just throw the ring in the river?"

"I think there was something else she was trying to find that she left behind." He pulled a piece of muddy silk from under a rock. It was the red scarf Mavis had worn over her hair the first day I met her. "Probably wouldn't mean much to anyone."

"Probably no one would have worried about it if you'd been convicted."

He smiled. "Thanks again."

He avoided my stare. Finally I said, "Some people might say that you're the one who should be thanked."

He blinked rapidly. "She wouldn't have quit. She would have taken everything from Sally and abandoned her. I couldn't stand watching that anymore."

"So you wanted to save her?"

He didn't answer.

"I guess Sally's going to be a wealthy young woman now," I ventured.

"That doesn't matter to me. I'd love her anyway."

I couldn't argue with that.

Tony reached us first, his brow furrowed and his eyes intense with worry.

"Late again," I told him. "You're falling down on the rescue job lately."

"Todd saw Mavis and Freddy and ran for help. Dispatch said the scraper ran over Freddy. Jesus, Cassie." He squatted and hugged me from behind, his face nestled in my hair. He pulled back and coughed. "Sorry love, but you reek."

Todd ran up to us and looked down the hill. "See, I told you about the dump. Did you see those scrapers? Boy are they cool—they could squash a rhinocerous."

Tony looked at the teenager and shook his head. "Knowing you has been a real education, kid." He noticed Mavis's body. "Shit, we've been standing here gabbing and we got another casualty?"

He pulled his handheld radio out of his pocket, called dispatch and ran to her. He reached to take her pulse then dropped her wrist with the futility of it. "She has bear claw scratches all over her," he hollered. "What the hell happened?"

Homer grunted as he stood. "I'm not sure. I was knocked out for a while. Maybe the bear got her."

I looked at him, standing wounded but proud against the backdrop of Mount Shasta, the home of his ancestors, and decided that he'd had enough of white man's justice.